my people, myself

my people, myself

MARY LAWRENCE

CAITLIN
PRESS

Caitlin Press Inc.
P.O. Box 2387, Stn. B
Prince George, BC V2N 2S6

Caitlin Press gratefully acknowledges the financial support of the Canada Council and the British Columbia Cultural Services Branch, Ministry of Tourism, Small Business and Culture.

Printed in Canada.

Canadian Cataloguing in Publication Data
Lawrence, Mary, 1950-
    My People, myself

    ISBN 0-920576-59-1

    1. Lawrence, Mary, 1950- 2. Poets, Canadian (English)--20th century--Biography. * 3. Indians of North America--Canada--Residential schools--Biography. * I.Title.
PS8573.A9114Z53 1996   C811'.54   C96-910230-5
PR9199.3.L3385Z47 1996

DEDICATION

To those who read "Torn Roots" in my first poetry novel, *In Spirit and Song*, and asked, "What ever happened to your mom?";

To all the survivors of the residential schools and in respect to those who didn't make it;

To my daughters, Michelle and Jaclyn for being patient since "God hasn't finished with me yet";

To my Aunt Yvonne who never lets me down;

To Shirley Sterling, author of *My Name is Seepeetza*, whose story inspired me to write my own;

To Beatrice Culleton, author of *In Search of April Raintree*, for giving me the courage and determination to give an account of my life after reading her story;

And, to Celia Haig-Brown, author of *Resistance and Renewal*, for her book which stirred my memories of the happenings at Kamloops Indian Residential School as depicted by interviews with the survivors;

Especially to those who sometimes feel in a hopeless state of mind and body—*never* give up!

ACKNOWLEDGEMENTS

A special thanks to the dedicated team at Caitlin Press for the endless hours of diligent preparations to make this possible

Thank you to the Canada Council for the Arts Grant "B" Non-fiction allowance in March, 1994 which allowed me to take time off working to complete the novel.

FOREWORD

My People, Myself is the story of a tormented child who leaves the Reserve at age eight to begin an eventful journey through residential schools and foster homes.

During her late teenage years, she finds herself drifting, drinking and using drugs among the street people on Skid Row. Fleeing the country to avoid prosecution on drug charges, she is accompanied by a ruthless street dealer who brutally tortures her, mentally and physically.

Plunging into a world of alcohol and drug abuse and eventually locked away in California in a women's correctional facility, the young woman goes through withdrawal "cold-turkey" because of a heavy heroin habit. Many other obstacles must be overcome in the aftermath. Then, a light at the end of the road glimmers. Life then takes on a new meaning.

Today, I feel sentiment for the lost "pudgy little girl" and want to nurture her. For the troubled young woman who drifted into places that left her depressed and suicidal, I honour her. She knew no other way to cope. As I tell my story, I acknowledge her stuggles, her pain, the courage to change and together we heal.

Mary Lawrence, 1996

CONTENTS

1

WHERE AM I GOING?

At the turn-off from Highway 97, about eighteen miles north of the small BC Interior town of Vernon, lies the beginning of the sprawling countryside of the Okanagan Indian Reserve. The main settlement is on hills above the rich fields leased to industrious Chinese market gardeners. Shortly after you drive onto the Reserve is an area called Head of the Lake, where Okanagan Lake begins. Beach resorts are strung along the placid lake that winds its way southward along the valley floor bypassing Kelowna and Westbank before ending a 100 miles or so south at Penticton. Famous for the home of the Ogopogo, a mythical creature that lurks beneath the lake of many colours, this valley also has had many unusual sightings of the Sasquatch, an imaginary manlike creature that supposedly roams the hillsides. About ten miles from the turn-off, still on Reserve lands, is Six Mile Creek.

This is where I once called home. I was the third youngest of six kids—a bashful, pudgy fair-skinned little girl with long, tangled, reddish-brown hair that fell down my back.

I'm part this and a half that—Irish and Indian from my grandmother's side as her mother, Mary Ann Alexandria was a full-blooded Okanagan Indian and Grandma's father John Maloney was Irish. When Grandma grew up, she married William Lawrence, an Englishman. Then, my mother Hazel Lawrence was born.

So, I get to be Indian and Irish from my mother's side and Jewish from my natural father's side. I've been told since childhood that my father, Meyer Prince, was a jovial, big man of Jewish background who lived in Oroville, Washington. His family owned Prince's in Oroville, a spacious American discount variety store still under family ownership.

Many people from our Reserve relocated to Oroville every fall to pick apples. Some unmarried women had sexual liaisons with the men working in the various orchards or with business owners such as my father. I've been told by my Aunt Yvonne, who lived at home with Grandma in those early days, that my father always came to the Reserve after apple season to take Mom out.

In our family of six children, my oldest sister is Marge, dark-haired, with brown eyes and darker skin. She was the most serious of us, although she did romp around with us at times. Even as a child she was more intent, a kind of motherly type. She liked to be in charge of things; at times she was too motherly and I found her bossy. Hugh, the next oldest, on the other hand, was the opposite. He was a roughneck, mischievous and often disobedient toward Mom. He had medium brown hair, was pint-sized, and wore tattered-looking pants that were always too short.

Hugh was untamed and went wherever he wanted to go anytime he felt like going. Although Mom often told him to be home before dark, Hugh always forgot and would come home late. When he came home, Mom would break off a thin stick from a big bush outside and Hugh would get a good licking. Mom would grab his hand and as she swatted him on the legs, across the back or wherever she could, he'd dance around the room. She would firmly clasp his small hand and swat him until she thought he had learned his lesson. I know it hurt him, but neither Marge nor I could say or do anything to get Mom to stop hitting him. We'd stand nearby and stare silently as she hit him repeatedly. I always wanted to grab that stick from her hand but knew she would use it on me if I so much as tried. When the licking was over we all became even more subdued, and if we hadn't eaten yet, we all waited for supper and then quietly went off to bed. Our play time was no longer any fun.

The next day Hugh would do the same and forget to come home. Mom would give him the same good licking. The next oldest is Ben, whose father must have been Japanese or Chinese. Ben was taken away by the social welfare people when he was two months old and placed in foster care. Nobody knew why he had to go except Mom. She must have felt she could not look after him and gave him up. After me is Bill, our baby brother who was cute with dirty-blondish hair. He was special to me and I liked him the best. He was scrawny-looking, having hunched shoulders but was always full of chatter and energy. As he got older, he was always playing in the fields, running on the hillside, catching grasshoppers, riding his stick horse or just playing with our cousins who lived in their hillside home neighbouring us.

Our little sister Harriet, the baby of our family, had large wistful brown eyes and long, long eyelashes. She looked so sweet but was very fragile as a baby. She had cradle-cap so badly that Mom had to scrape it off her scalp as normal washing would not remove it from Harriet's chestnut-brown hair. Cradle-cap is a crusty surface layer of hardened tissue that forms over the soft spot of a baby's skull. It is usually caused by letting the scalp dry out or by not shampooing the baby's fine hair regularly. Harriet had gobs of it, even though Mom took good care of her. We each had different fathers except Marge and Hugh. Their dad's name was Pete Louie who lived on another Reserve and later died of drinking too much alcohol. Although we were all half brothers and sisters we bonded like glue when we were young.

The adults in our young lives were Mom, Grandma, Aunt Yvonne and Uncle James. Mom, stocky with a big tummy, always liked to dress in old Levis jeans. She folded the pant legs up to her calves and wore old baggy shirts that she never tucked in.

I don't remember ever seeing Grandma wearing pants. She always wore old house dresses, sometimes with an apron, black shoes with about two-inch heels and light beige cotton stockings. During the summers, often she'd tie a colourful scarf over her head, neatly covering her short-cropped greyish hair. The scarf protected her from the sun's direct rays which would cause sunstroke. Grandma never allowed her arms or legs to show. The only time I ever saw her bare legs happened when we stayed overnight at her house. Here, we put our blankets on the bare floor in her bedroom. As she got ready for bed she'd remove her stockings and I would peek at her pale legs because they were so seldom exposed. Their extreme paleness made me curious. On the rare occasion, I would catch a glimpse of her arms when she washed her hair in the kitchen sink and took off her sweater. It didn't matter how hot it got, Grandma always wore a sweater.

While we slept on the floor at Grandma's, Marge, Hugh and I would giggle and tug at the covers. We usually played "I spy with my little eye I can see . . ." and somebody would keep guessing at what one could see that the others couldn't.

When we got too noisy, Grandma would come into her room. Looking down at us on the floor she would firmly say, "Sssshh, go to sleep now, you guys . . ." Sometimes she'd talk in Indian and it sounded like, "Nik-a-naw, tulth with kee-kust," meaning "Oh you, you're bad." We surely listened when Grandma got annoyed and scolded us.

During those years, Yvonne, who is still as special to me now as she was then, would sometimes stand out on the steps at Grandma's house and little me, only as tall as her waistline would hug her as she stroked my long hair and patted my head. She liked to wear skin tight pants with fitted blouses or tight pullover sweaters. Sometimes she buttoned a cardigan right up and wore the sweater backwards to make it look like a pullover. It was the fashion in the early '50s. To me, she was so pretty and I admired her every move. I thought she had such a petite waist too. I loved to listen to her sing as she crooned Elvis Presley songs like, "Love Me Tender" or "Hound Dog" or "Blue Suede Shoes." She sang in such a vibrant voice and knew the words to all the songs. I cannot imagine what she would have sounded like if she had a guitar and knew how to play it. Yvonne was always kind to me. She used to tell me that my dad often drove up the dirt road to our house in a big car. As a toddler, I squirmed gleefully in the back seat as he, Mom and I left together. Yvonne also told me that he really wanted to marry Mom but she was nowhere near settling down.

Sometimes I wondered why Grandma kept her money in a small knotted rag tucked inside her house dress. She even slept with her money pinned inside her petticoat. It was a small amount as she lived off Grandpa's pension after he died in 1954 of a heart attack. She had a black purse but never left any money in it. Whenever my Uncle James wanted to borrow money she would reach inside to her petticoat strap, unpin and untie the knotted rag and take out a two-dollar bill to give to him. He was still living with Grandma, although he was in his 30s. James would say thanks and get ready to go into town. He would put on a clean pair of Levis, wash up, comb his wavy, light brown hair, and off he'd go down the road. He'd hitchhike into town to meet with his buddies to drink beer. James always came home full of spirits, having had more than enough to drink, although I'm sure the small amount of money he had never really bought that much booze. I suppose it was all he needed to chip in for a bottle to share with his buddies. He never did repay Grandma any of the money she'd given him almost every Saturday afternoon. I suspect now that he was the reason Grandma kept such close watch on her money.

As a youngster, I was a quiet, calm little girl and as normal as any other kid my age. My earliest recollection takes me back to sitting under the big fir tree a short distance in front of our house playing in the dirt. I remember the blazing sun and the cloudless blue sky on a hot summer day as I lazed in the company of Marge. In my mind, I can still hear the airplane that would fly overhead and sound so far away. I would sometimes look up and watch the long streamers of cloud that formed behind the plane as it crossed the big sky. Things were very peaceful in those days until the Indian agent, a runty little man who was unfriendly would come by to check on us. He always drove up to our house leaving a cloud of dust behind the wheels of his dark blue sedan. When he'd step out of the car he didn't greet anyone. He'd just rush toward our house. If we were outside playing, he'd grunt, "Where's your mom?"

If we answered, "She's in the house," he'd keep walking right past us. His manner compared badly to the Raleigh Man, who would always give us a round pink candy with a hole in the middle when he came to sell his products to Grandma.

The Indian agent's name was Mr. Hett and he was responsible to see that we had food and clothing and that we all went to school regularly. He always dressed in a white shirt, dress pants and wore flat-soled, pull-on polished brown boots. He looked squeaky clean, always.

Originally, the Indians were self-sufficient and independent. Although they did not always have the financial resources, they still managed their own affairs. Then, the federal government created "official" bureaucratic offices across Canada to handle the affairs of families on the Reserves. By creating these Indian Affair offices the government wanted the Indians to be mainstreamed into society with access to proper education, medical care, health and welfare. The results, the government felt, would be beneficial to all, Indian and non-Indian, alike. But the plans backfired. The Indian people were used to doing things a certain way. For example, when someone got sick, the elders would gather and boil leaves and wild plants taken from the land to use as medicine. Most food was grown on the land, except for the staples such as flour and sugar which had to be bought at the grocery stores. The Indian language was used to teach traditional native culture and values.

The Indians on our Reserve were a proud band, rejecting the Eurocentric influence. Finally, in the early '70s the Vernon office of the Department of Indian Affairs, located above the post office in town was occupied by the Reserve people. They had a sit in until the office was shut down permanently. The people wanted to administer their own affairs, including education, health, social assistance, extended care to the elderly, and so on. The bureaucrats were soaking up the money that was supposed to be set aside for the betterment of the lifestyles on the Reserve. Instead it was used to pay big salaries to non-Indian employees of the Department. As a result of the sit in an Indian Band office was formed on the Reserve, and the Ottawa bureaucrats reluctantly began directing funds to the band office. Eventually all the Reserves in BC handled their own affairs. However, before this happened, the Indian agent had total control over everything. To Mom, he was like a spy, always turning up without letting her know when he might arrive. Whenever he came, he was always in such a rush to leave. Behind his back, Mom would call him down and swear at him because he never minded his own business, popping up unexpectedly always.

When Mr. Hett came, Mom complained to him, explaining that we needed one of the new homes being built on the Reserve. Our house didn't have running water, a bathroom or anything modern, for that matter. It consisted of one room, with a wooden floor, a potbelly stove, two beds, a couple of coal oil lamps, and an old kitchen table with a couple of chairs.

Once a month Mom had to make the trip into town to pick up our meagre allowance cheque after the Indian agent had dropped by and acknowledged that we still needed assistance. Then we could get staples like flour, salt, sugar, lard, potatoes, rice, tea and coffee. We didn't have a fridge or even electricity, so when we got groceries they were usually canned foods like salmon, tuna fish or Prem, which is a preserved lunch meat that we thought was delicious between slices of bread with mustard and onion.

In the summer we had fresh vegetables such as cabbage, corn, cucumbers and tomatoes. Occasional evenings were spent raiding large vegetable gardens maintained by the Chinese market gardeners. Usually Mom would call on me to accompany her and together we'd head out in the dark of night with a gunny sack draped over her shoulder. She said we were not stealing because there was more than enough to go around. I liked going with Mom at night. I'd keep up right behind her as she walked swiftly toward the nearest garden patch. We'd crawl under any fences we had to and watch and listen for anything approaching that might cause us to get caught. We'd duck down if there were bright car lights coming down the highway as we left the patch. It never made sense to me.

I wondered how anyone driving a vehicle could see us walking through a vegetable field in the dark of night. Probably Mom felt safer lying down on the ground even though we could not be seen. Mostly, we listened and watched for the Chinese owners while in their patch in case they were lying low waiting to catch us. I'm sure they never missed their vegetables but you never know—farmers are clever and don't miss too much; however, we never got caught. Mom and I would fill the gunny sack with a mixture of some cabbage, cobs of corn, tomatoes and cucumbers. We never went hungry and despite Mom's complaints to the Indian agent, life seemed pretty good to us kids.

Then, late one afternoon on a hot summer day, our log house caught on fire. We were all outside playing and no one knew how the fire started. We suspect that a mouse in the small attic space above the ceiling probably got chewing on a match and caused the match to ignite. (We used those long-sticked wooden Eddy matches to light the lamps and stove because the flame lasted longer than the paper matches). I do remember hearing later that Mom was suspected of having started the fire. I don't think she would have although she was inside the house lying down when the house began to burn. Luckily, she was not asleep and made it out the door before the flames got to her. The house burned like paper as big black billows of smoke reached the height of the telephone wires nearby. We could hear the neighbour lady Agnes standing on her front porch across the field yelling "Fire! Fire!" hysterically. Her words struck me as strange as we already knew there was a fire, and we were standing right out in the open watching. No other house was close enough for anyone to hear Agnes yelling.

In minutes the house burned to the ground. Sadly we gaped at the charred remains of our home. All our possessions had gone up in smoke. They weren't much but they were still everything that we owned. The way Mom talked afterward it sounded as if she was relieved this happened, as now we would get the house the Indian agent promised. Eventually, several piles of lumber were brought out and placed a short distance from where our house once stood. Meanwhile, we found shelter at Grandma's small house behind ours.

I remember seeing an empty bottle of Vanilla extract tucked underneath a pile of the lumber to be used for our new home. I knew it was for baking but somehow it stuck in my mind to see it hidden in such an odd place.

Our house was built that same summer a short distance behind the spot from where our log house had been. Our new home had a white exterior with a lime green front and back door and the same green colour trim on all the windows. There were two bedrooms, a bathroom, kitchen and living room. There was no linoleum or carpeting on the floors, but we had running water, a cupboard and sink in the kitchen, and a bathroom with a toilet that flushed. Mom was pleased.

I used to enjoy watching Grandma and Mom working in the big vegetable garden between our houses. I can remember sitting on the wood steps at Grandma's house and watching them toil nearby. Together, they would hoe and dig up the soil, getting ready to plant the many rows of vegetables.

Both worked hard. Mom always liked to smoke while she worked and usually had a hand-rolled cigarette dangling from the corner of her mouth. She also whistled as she worked. She whistled when she was gardening or when she scrubbed clothes in the washtub or chopped wood. Once I asked her why she always whistled and she explained that she did it because it took her mind off the hard work that she had to do. I used to try to copy her whistling but couldn't carry the tune as she so joyfully could.

When planting the garden, Grandma worked briskly, always wearing a kerchief over her head, alongside Mom. Grandma would lightly bend over the freshly turned sod, scattering seeds into the neat rows that Mom had dug. They would make sure the seeds were all covered and then place a peg into the ground. At the front of each row they would place an empty seed package to show which row went with which vegetable seeds.

Mom, pleasant-looking and motherly, was the perfect cook too, baking loaves of yummy yeast bread or concocting delicious homemade soups when she wasn't working in the garden. She always cooked from scratch and never used cake or pancake mixes. I loved the smell of her pancakes early in the morning. Before I got up I would see her leaning over the wood stove humming to herself. She prepared breakfast, stirring the pot of mush or flipping the pancakes in the cast iron frying pan. Sometimes she'd belt into a song like, "Lazy Mary will you get up? . . . Will you get up . . . Will you get up, so early in the morning . . ." I loved the sound of her singing. Soon I'd get up and join the others for breakfast. We'd devour whatever she had made for breakfast. Grandma and Mom visited each other back and forth regularly and sometimes Mom chopped wood for Grandma.

Another fond recollection I have of when I was very young was playing in the dirt and building roads. We played with homemade cutouts of paper "guys" we made to look like boys, girls, moms and dads. To make these, we'd cut strips of moderately thick paper, about three inches long and an inch wide. We used the cardboard taken from empty boxes of macaroni or spaghetti. For the kids we cut shorter pieces of paper. We'd then cut our four-sided figures halfway up the middle to give them legs. For the girls, we would cut half-circular indents halfway up each side to make it look like they had a waist. Then, we'd fold the figures in half to give them a crease that would become their rear end. In this way they could now sit partially upright. We'd then fold the cardboard again a little ways down further to give our "guys" the shape of having bent knees. For the guys, we left them shaped boxlike with no indents at their waistline. We'd then cut the dark blue paper from inside of empty flour or oatmeal bags. We would place these small strips on our dads and boys as blue jeans. We'd cut the blue strips up the middle to fit snugly around the guys legs.

Tearing pages from the old Sears and Roebuck catalogues, we cut up small pieces and dressed our girls and moms. We'd make tiny pleats in the paper to look like pleated skirts. We used little strips of colourful paper for their blouses. We then used our spit to glue the pieces of garments on. Taking small strips of the printed text from the catalogue, we'd then place it on the bottom of the men and boys pant legs to use as their boots. Finally, with pieces of wood, which we pretended were cars, we drove our families along the neatly-made windy, dirt roads. We'd drive in many different directions underneath the big fir tree. The roots of the tree were close to the ground so we had lots of humps and bumps to go up and around and over. We called this "playing guys" and it became our pastime for hours.

The only time we'd leave our guys happened when we had to go in the house to eat or when it was getting dark outside. When we couldn't play, I always asked Marge, "Do you want to go play guys after?" She always did although she always liked being in charge. She did all the cutting and we younger kids did the spitting to glue on the clothing. We used to play guys with our girl cousins from up the road. I don't think my brothers played; it was mostly the girls' pastime. In those days, we didn't have plastic toy people so we made the most of what we had and it was enjoyable. The most treasured memories I have from childhood are those hours we spent under that big old tree. In the dirt we talked imaginary things to one another through our guys. Our pretend families drove a lot and the blocks of wood were very fancy cars to us. Life was simple by today's standards, but it was good, though it hardly prepared me for what was to come.

The next thing I remember is being in grade two and going off to school. The year was 1957. Our one room classroom, then, was in a modern white-coloured building at the end of the road not far from our house. There were large lilac bushes at the entrance of the building and it had a fenced-in area that contained a playground. There were swings in the back along with some teeter-totters. I liked going to school. I remember how tight Mom used to tug my hair to make one neat braid on the right side of my head. First, she'd braid the long piece, then place a big white bow on the top of the braid. She'd then put an orange in my pocket and say, "Gowan, off to school now."

There was one teacher for the whole school who taught grades one to three, probably about thirty kids altogether. Our teacher's name was Miss Siccouse and she was a poised, stout lady who wore bright lipstick, dressed very nicely and had glistening white teeth. As she spoke quickly, sometimes little squirts of saliva came from her mouth. I liked watching her talk and liked the sound of her voice. It sounded different, almost like she curled words around her tongue. I didn't know then but learned later that she talked like that because she had a French accent. Miss Siccouse was a friendly but firm teacher who kept order in the class. She lived in the school building. Her kitchen and living room were in the adjoining room to the classroom and her bedroom was on the second floor of the school building. She lived alone.

When I returned home after school, I'd find Mom busy in the kitchen making bread or she'd be hanging a load of wash out on the clothes-line. Sometimes she'd just be laying down reading *True Story* magazines. She loved to read.

There was one meanie in grade two, Frankie Louis. One morning before class the boys were rough-housing at the back of the classroom. The dull green linoleum floors had just been polished which left the floor slippery and ideal for the boys to slide around in their stocking feet. Usually, I was shy but could not resist the temptation on this day to get the attention of Frankie Louis. I thought it would be fun to push him and run, like the others were doing.

I snuck up behind, playfully hit him in the back and then ran to my desk. As I sat there pretending I hadn't done anything, he came from behind and suddenly punched me in the face. He hit me so hard everything went black. Boy, that stung! I couldn't open my eyes for a minute. Then, he snapped at me, "Don't you ever hit me again!" I was stunned!

I couldn't think of anything to say, not even "I'm sorry" because I wasn't sorry. I wanted to yell, "You stupid!" but didn't. I waited until I could catch my breath again and sat very still until the teacher came into the classroom. Never again did I tease another boy in school. None of the other kids said anything. No one laughed or really noticed Frankie sliding up to my desk and hitting me. He just went right back and joined the others as they romped around.

I loathed Frankie from that day on and stayed as far away from him as I could. He terrified me! I didn't even tell Mom about him when I went home that day. Maybe I was ashamed of myself for getting in the way and making such a nuisance of myself. I don't know why I didn't tell the teacher either. For such a seemingly trivial experience, it was a very significant act of meanness, although I did not understand this until many years later.

As a little girl, I used to watch and admire Mom as she got herself all dressed up to look pretty. She'd comb out her medium-length, soft brown hair. It became shorter and curly when she untied the pieces of white rags that she used to roll up her hair. They would give her hair the effect of a perm. Each rag was about the size of one ply of tissue paper. To curl her hair she would take a clump of wet hair and twist the rag around the clump. Then, with another piece of rag, like a string, she would tie a knot around the hair on the end. She'd roll the hair up tightly to her scalp using both hands. She'd then tie the ends of the rag again into another little knot. It was done the same as someone would do in rolling the hair with perm rods except that she used rags instead of rods. Then she'd have these tight curled rag knots all over her head. Once she was finished, I thought she looked beautiful. She would dress nicely in jeans, style her hair and then put on bright red lipstick. I admired her as she stood in front of the mirror by the doorway. I had no idea where she was getting ready to go away each time but I suspected something wasn't right. Then she would disappear and not come home. Sometimes she'd come home in a few days acting funny, bringing home a stranger and smelling of what we kids called "bad breath." Sometimes she brought food home and other times she didn't. Most of the time she didn't. I can remember her sleeping a lot after the stranger would leave. I didn't realize she was sleeping off a hangover.

Other times she'd be gone for a long time. Whenever this happened and Grandma's watchful eye noticed we were home alone, she'd come to get us to eat and camp at her house. Usually Grandma would be mad when she came to get us. When we got to her house she would tell us to sit in the kitchen and listen as she preached about being proper when we grew up. As she paced the kitchen floor, her eyes focused straight ahead. With hands folded behind her back she'd lecture us on the evil of liquor and how it would make us bad if we grew up and drank it. When Mom would finally come home, she would be slurring her words and acting clumsier every time. Other times when she wanted to go into town to drink, she'd get us over to Grandma's for some reason or other and sneak away. Sometimes, from Grandma's house I could see her leave, briskly walking down the winding road at dusk toward the highway leading into town. She would be wearing her faded, maroon-coloured overcoat. As she disappeared, I would feel very lonely. I knew she would be gone a long time. Finally, she would return, hugging us and promising never to leave us again. Grandma would be so mad at her when she sent us back to our house after Mom returned.

In those days there was very little tolerance or sentiment for the Indian people. The ones who drank alcohol were portrayed as "drunken Indians" and were banned from drinking in beer parlours. They had not adapted to the standards of the white society. The people from the Reserves couldn't vote either. As Black people in the US South could not congregate in certain places, Indians were treated the same. There might as well have been signs erected that stated: "No Indians Allowed" for the way they were shunned. Treatment was worse by the RCMP and the court system. When I was very young, I can remember how everybody called Frank Smith the "Hanging Judge."

He kept sending Indians to jail for no crime, really, except for having one too many swigs of booze. He would hand down three to six month sentences especially if he saw someone more than once in his court room. The condemned person was immediately sent off to Lower Mainland Correctional Centre in Burnaby next-door to the big city of Vancouver. No one seemed to rebel against this kind of discrimination; it was taken in stride. All that the so-called "drunks" wanted to do was to get together outside the close, intense relationships on the Reserve to enjoy a few laughs and shed a few tears.

They liked to gather in the small memorial park in Vernon to share their bottles of booze. Sitting under the trees they would drink, laugh a bit and tell stories to one another. Mom was no exception; she enjoyed drinking with her friends. People in town would walk by the park and look self-righteous at the drinkers. Aside from the small park, there was nowhere for them to drink except in a hidden-away place at Polson Park, also called the hobo jungle. Most of the time everybody drank up town. Sometimes Mom had too much to drink and ended up staggering, seemingly making a nuisance of herself. So the police patrolling the streets would pick her up and put her in jail. Mom began serving lengthy jail sentences.

Then, one hot humid day late in August a social welfare worker came to Grandma's house. It was nearing the end of summer in 1957. Mom was in jail or drinking with her friends again. The Indian agent and the welfare worker decided to send us to a Catholic boarding school in Cranbrook, many miles away. Lucky Bill got to stay with Grandma. As the stocky, officious welfare woman was putting our boxed clothing into the back seat of her car, I clearly remember seeing her big fat bum. It stuck out, almost like nothing else on her body had shape except her rear end. We stood by as she strode quickly back and forth from Grandma's house. During this time no one said a word. She had on flat loafer shoes and I noticed big growths on each side of her feet protruding through her shoes. I didn't know at that time they were called bunions. To me, they looked like big bumps on each foot. Her tightly permed hair had grey streaks and she wore bright lipstick. She then told us to all get into her car, a white, four-door Valiant. I looked back and remembered Grandma and Yvonne standing on the porch. No one waved goodbye.

We just drove down the road, not knowing where we were going. I do not recall any part of the journey on the Greyhound bus. I do remember arriving at this big building late at night. Someone from the school must have picked us up from the bus station. There was a metal fence around the building and a big gate at the beginning of the long paved driveway. As we got closer, I saw an extensive lawn leading up to the entrance of a large two-storey red brick structure. Inside the big doors Hugh, Marge and I were taken down some stairs by a towering but round reddish-faced nun. She was dressed in a long black frock. Her hair was hidden underneath a thick white band across her forehead and hidden underneath a black veil that reached her waist. Rosary beads dangled around her waist. She wore shiny black shoes. She was not friendly and talked in a rough and harsh manner, huffing as she took quick strides in front of us, hurrying us along. She directed us through the doors and into a big dark room. It had many tables side by side. On a table at the entrance were silverware trays containing shiny knives, forks and spoons. The long tables were spotlessly clean. The back of the room was the kitchen. The nun pointed to a corner table and told us to be seated. I remember feeling lost. It was a strange place. It looked dark and spooky inside; the walls were dark. The hallway to the eating area was dim. We were served left-overs, some kind of tasteless meat left in its own grease with corn kernels mixed in. I'm pretty sure it was a hamburger goulash without any seasonings. Boiled potatoes were served with it. I forced the food down my throat even though it tasted awful compared to Grandma's tasty homemade soup and fried bread.

When we were finished, Hugh was taken to the other side of the building to the boys' dorm. I never saw him in the Cranbrook residential school after that. Marge and I were taken to the girls' dorm. My bed was in the corner at the far end. Then, I didn't see Marge anymore that night, although her bed was only at the other end on the dorm. I felt so alone.

The next morning the girls were up, dressed and gone from their beds. I sat on my bed skimming through a cross-word puzzle book I must have bought at one of the stops along the trip. I looked at my strange new surroundings. There were about a hundred beds all neatly made with a grey folded blanket at the foot of each bed, a scene you would see in army barracks. Along the wall beside my bed was a long row of closets where the girls stored their belongings. Directly behind the wall was the boys' dorm. As I sat there, I thought of Hugh and felt very sad. I wished I could be with him again, like we used to, sleeping on the wood floor in Grandma's bedroom wiggling and giggling, tugging at covers until Grandma would come and tell us to be quiet. Feelings of dread settled heavily upon me. Perhaps it was the fear of this big place and all the little girls who were strangers to me. Or maybe these feelings were compounded by another experience: the feeling of loneliness each time my Mom left home and didn't return for a long time.

We were awakened at 6:30 a.m. each morning to get ready for Mass by the same nun who had checked us in. Mass was held in the chapel on the second floor of a small building, adjoined to the rear of the main residence. The nun came from her bedroom which was located on a landing between the dorm and the second floor of the chapel building. I had learned her name was Sister Lois. She would clap her hands and blow a whistle yelling loudly, "EVERYONE UP!" Jumping out of bed, we splashed cold water on our faces and brushed our teeth. This ritual seemed as sacred to the nun as saying her rosary beads during Mass.

After waking a little, we would get dressed. From our assigned closet space we would take the navy blue tunic, white bobby socks, a pair of black oxfords and clean underwear. Right after school we changed into other clothes given to us, long plain-looking skirts and cotton blouses. For playing outside we had denim jeans with various tops. As the seasons changed, we were handed the clothes we needed such as winter coats and boots.

Following Mass, we would have breakfast precisely at 7:30 a.m. Breakfast was usually half-cooked oatmeal porridge, cold and lumpy. If we didn't eat it, we went hungry. We had reconstituted powdered milk to pour over the porridge but never got any toast or juice. Most of the time because the porridge was cold, it had a kind of slimy surface on it.

Then, we would go to the second floor of the dorm building to attend school. I can remember sitting in class and gazing to the far pastures and the open fields. There were boys in the class although we were not allowed to have any contact with them—at any time. They were told the same and if caught talking to the girls, they would be punished and have to leave the classroom. I still never saw Hugh.

I spent a lot of time around Marge that year. She would sometimes get annoyed because I clung to her after school. In the basement of the dorm was our recreation room. In here were several fold-up chairs placed against the wall. There was nothing else in the room and the windows were high up. We did not have a TV although black and white TVs were available by this time. We didn't have any games or toys or anything to play with. I can remember spending lots of time here after school while we waited for supper. The only play-time activity I can remember is Marge pretending to be queen and some of us girls being her servants. She would want us to go and bring her items. We'd come back with imaginary things fit for a queen. Holding our hands out like we were carrying a platter, we brought whatever she wished for. Maybe diamonds or maybe it was food. Who knows? I surely liked to sit at her feet and then go off and return with her orders which she accepted graciously.

Occasionally on a Friday night we got candy. It was such a treat. In the rec room, the nuns would throw candy and the girls would scramble on their hands and knees trying to gather as much as possible. I loved filling my pockets. Many of us did not receive money from home to buy from the canteen. Some kids were lucky enough to have visits, although the school was located far from any Reserve in an isolated wooded area some distance from Cranbrook.

Before going there, I had never used electric light switches. Although our new home was wired for electricity, it was not hooked up and we still used coal oil lamps. At Grandma's we used coal oil lamps too. I couldn't resist touching the switches every time I passed one in the hallway or in the recreation room. Getting caught playing with the switch cost me the strap. Each time, Sister Lois marched me upstairs to the dorm, ordering me to hold out my hand. I obeyed. Sometimes, just as she was about to drop the belt full force on my hand, I'd pull back and she would hit her leg instead. She would get so mad she would give me an extra belting. I don't recall it stinging.

All I remember is this full-figured nun with fierce, bulging eyes, a red face, panting as she stood in front of me clenching her thick black strap. I don't recall others getting the strap. Later, after we had all grown up, Marge said I got the strap quite often because I was defiant toward the nuns. I never talked back but got revenge by doing things I was not supposed to and getting caught. One of my main defiances was at bedtime. After the lights had been shut off, I'd slide on my back the entire length of the line of beds until I reached Marge's bed. There, I'd lie on the floor and giggle with her and the other girls in their beds nearby. We'd all be whispering and chatting away. I'd tell Marge I came so that we could all kiss good night, although at Grandma's or with Mom, we never kissed goodnight ever. Marge would tell me to get back to bed and no sooner had I arrived under my own bed when Sister Lois would appear. Turning the lights on in the dorm, she'd yell, "Mary Lou, get over here!" While she stood erect at the entrance to the dorm, I would hesitate before doing as I was told. Slowly, I'd crawl out from underneath the bed and go toward Sister Lois. As she stood tall and annoyed, I'd have to hold out my hands again to get the strap. She'd hit me over and over and tell me to get back to bed and stay put when the lights were out. The other girls never said a word when this happened. There would be total silence. All I had ever wanted to do was have some time to be close to Marge at bedtime and, I didn't understand why I couldn't do this. It never sunk in that I should stay in my bed. I just knew when the lights flooded the dorm that it was strap time again. Before coming here I had never been hit by Mom or Grandma or anyone, except Frankie, of course.

Sometimes in the evening when it was still light out, we got to go outside the compound with a supervisor for a nature walk along the road. I enjoyed these times. The girls walked in groups and one song always comes to mind. We sang it as we made our way back to the school just before dusk. It was a song called "Running Bear," and the lyric went: "Along the river, a running bear . . ." I can remember the tune but not the words. I think that song just came out and was popular in 1958. I loved walking along the road and looking at all the tall trees that lined the road. But looking back, mostly I can see this big recreation room. We must have spent a lot of time in there.

The winter in Cranbrook was freezing cold. Although the town is in southern British Columbia, it was still cold. Some evenings we went out back for exercise. In the field there was a pond which froze into a skating rink where we went skating. The skates were all piled in cardboard boxes and some fit and some didn't. We put on skates that were closest to our sizes. It was fun, though I never learned to skate. A box of apples was placed outside the basement door, and we could snack on all the soft, bruised apples we wanted as we skated around the ice.

Each girl was assigned a weekly chore to do. My job was to clean the parlour room where the girls visited with their families on Sundays. Lucky girls. Marge, Hugh and I never had any visits but often received a one-page letter from Yvonne telling us that Grandma, Bill, James, and she were all fine. She never mentioned Mom but ended her letter with "Write soon, Always, Yvonne."

I never got a letter from Mom.

In the parlour room my duty was to dust the coffee tables and end tables, mop the floor, take out the trash and leave the room spotless. Often while in there I would discover a big wad of bubble gum underneath the coffee table. Because we were not allowed to have gum, it was such a treat to find and chew a wad. While I cleaned, I'd blow big bubbles and pop them. Most of the time the flavour was still in it and it tasted so sweet. When I finished my chores, I would sometimes stick the gum back where I found it. There was always freshly chewed gum stuck underneath the tables following the Sunday visits. I had my job in the parlour room quite awhile, probably the whole year we were there.

School throughout the year was routine. I forget the name of the teachers or any of the of the boys in our class, except one boy. His name was John Sebastian and he sticks out in my mind because he was cocky and a show off. Once in class, he called us girls "Kotex" and laughed about it. We never knew what that meant until years later. I remember him because he was tall and louder than any of the other kids. He was fair-haired and kind of sprinted when he walked.

He also made fun of the girls by teasing us because we had funny haircuts. Our bangs were cut short and straight across. The sides and back were cut the same length parallel to the chin line. It looked like someone put a big bowl over our heads and cut exactly around the bowl. On some girls it looked okay but on others it looked odd shaped. It didn't really bother me because we all looked the same in our weird haircuts.

The letters I received from Yvonne I treasured. I can't recall what they said, probably just that everybody was fine. It wasn't so much what the letter said, it was just that someone had taken time to write. In grade three these letters had quite an impact on me. I had no idea when we would be able to go home. I simply went to school like any ordinary kid, got my strappings, did my chores, enjoyed my bubble gum, loved it when we could scramble for candy and hated the food. I must have daydreamed through every Mass because I recall getting up early but don't recall going to the chapel. Yet, so many memorized prayers come to mind such as the "Act of Contrition," "Hail Mary," "Glory Be To The Father," "Our Father," and many other Latin begats. Some Sunday mornings after Mass, of course, we had cereal but we never did get toast or jam. I cannot recall what was served for lunch. Often when we were outside in the big yard, a snack was served between lunch and supper. I gag as I think of it. We lined up to get our snack which was molasses spread over stale bread.

When the year ended, we went home to Grandma's. Again, the journey is blocked out. It was about three hundred miles by Greyhound bus. I vividly remember arriving home and seeing how happy Grandma looked when she greeted us at the door. It was late at night when we arrived. She lit a soft light in the coal oil lamp and we sat in the kitchen. She was happy to see us and I think she really missed us. That night she didn't lecture us about the evils of drinking. We sat in the kitchen and talked and talked about anything and everything. Yvonne, James and Bill must have been sleeping. Although Mom wasn't there, for the first time in months, I didn't feel lonely. Unfortunately that feeling would be short-lived.

2

CRUEL YEARS

At the end of summer we left again to another boarding school, one much nearer our home. This time it was about ninety miles north of our Reserve on the Kamloops Indian Reserve. We were riding restlessly on the bus in the early afternoon through rolling hills and valleys under hovering fir and pine trees. I felt sudden stabs of anxiety as we neared the smelly, industrial city of Kamloops. It was such a change. Unlike the beautiful wild flowers crowning the trails back home, here were yellow, dry tumbleweeds covering the barren hillsides. I scanned the countryside, squinting and blinking behind the sooty bus window.

We were picked up at the bus station by an aide from the school and were driven to the grounds, about one mile northeast of the city. When we arrived, the first thing that caught my drowsy eyes was the oval swimming pool directly in front of the building. I rubbed my eyes and looked at the sparkling blue water and the large red brick structure. I moved closer to Marge as we stood there mesmerised by our new surroundings. Marge was then about eleven and Hugh a year younger. I would have been turning nine that September.

We stood in front of the large double-doors in the warm afternoon sun waiting to be admitted. A lanky priest opened the door. Wearing dark-rimmed glasses, Father Dunlop was dressed in a long black tunic. He was greying slightly at the temples and had a receding hairline. He gestured us in. Immediately we were separated.

Hugh went to the boys' dormitory, Marge and I were diverted to the girls' large sleeping room containing many army-like beds. Each bed was neatly made in military fashion. The corners of the sheets were tightly tucked in and one grey wool blanket was folded across the bottom of each bed. The sheets looked spotlessly clean and crisp. Again, my memory fails. I can barely recall the torment I must have felt departing from my pint-sized beloved brother Hugh. I recalled that before coming here Marge, Hugh and I all slept in the same bed and rubbed our feet together during the cold months and grasped at covers to keep warm. I missed that closeness very much.

During this year many things happened—some good, some bad. One of the fun things was the occasional sock-hop on Friday nights when we congregated in the gym, behind the main building. There, blaring music came from 45 RPM records played close to a microphone. The girls were shy but not as shy as the boys. The boys stayed on their side of the room until half way though the evening when some would come over to ask certain girls to dance. It was fun. Everybody just sort of shuffled their feet trying to look like they knew how to dance. As soon as the dance was finished, the boys immediately returned to the far side of the room. When it was over, we all went back to our dorms, lights were turned off, and we went to sleep. The dances were only for intermediate girls and boys between grades four and six. The juniors, which were grades one to three, had to be in bed by eight o'clock.

Another fun activity happened when we all got to go to the fairground on Queen Victoria Day. We just called it Mayday and everybody looked forward to this day. Salads, hot dogs, fresh fruit, buns and desserts were neatly laid out on tables. We got to eat as much as we wanted. The boys and girls had three-legged races and sack races. We bobbed for apples from a tub full of water, and just played catch with each other. It was lots of fun. Then, as the afternoon came to an end, we all returned to the school and returned to our separate sides of the school again. These were the only times that I recall when we could associate with the boys.

The girls rebelled out of hunger and a need for retaliation against the strict rules. When we were sent out to play in the yard, some of us would sneak down to a small orchard. It was a short walk from the school within the fenced compound and contained about ten fruit trees. We caused no harm except that we were forbidden to go to there. The grounds were Brother Joseph's responsibility and he prohibited anyone going near his orchard. Mostly his job was taking care of the grounds, cutting grass where it grew around the swimming pool, trimming the hedges, and making sure the trees in the orchard were watered regularly.

There was a statue of the blessed Virgin Mary in the orchard. Here, Brother Joseph had planted red climbing roses around the shrine. He tended his flower garden here. I thought it looked immaculate—the roses climbing around the shrine and the white apple blossoms that were out in late May. I was tempted to go down and steal apples, but I didn't. I think I learned to behave and stay out of mischief during my year at Cranbrook.

Although he didn't dress in a brown robe, Brother Joseph reminded me of a monk. There was something monk-like about him; he walked slowly with his head bowed as though he were in constant prayer. He dressed in ordinary dark clothes, walked with a limp, and was short-sighted although he didn't wear glasses. With a certain sense of ritual, he went over the grounds daily, picking up scraps of paper, attending to the lawns and keeping the place tidy. Always crabby, he was the subject of much teasing whenever we spotted him. Sometimes he used his cane to get around. He didn't talk to us girls unless he felt he had to scold someone. If we were playing out of bounds near his orchard he steered us back. When Brother Joseph was nowhere in sight, a few of us would sneak down to pick some apples. We had another way of re-belling. Along the river bank alongside the path asparagus grew and we picked handfuls of these as well. If caught, it meant a trip to the dorm for the Sister to decide the form of punishment we would receive.

A year went by and I completed grade four. We returned from our Reserve after the summer holidays and began an-other year, in the same building, with the same regulations. I liked grade five—probably because I discovered puppy love. I sat behind a boy named Vonnet Hall who had curly dark brown hair and a shy smile. We liked each other but were too bashful to talk to one another. His delicate smiles aroused me and my heart would go pitter-patter. Several years later, while he was training at the cadet camp in Vernon, we met unexpectedly and started dating. During our teenage years, we strolled to the movies and joked about our feelings we had toward each other in grade five. Our nostalgic dating was brief during those two summer months. I think we both realized puppy love does not endure.

At the school, the Oblates of Mary Immaculate disciplined the Indian kids every day, and drilled us in the Catholic creed. Sister Leonita's thin, small-framed body emerged from her bedroom at the crack of dawn each morning at 6:30 a.m. She would begin the day by ringing a cowbell. Pacing impatiently up and down the dorm, one hand ringing the bell and the other waving in all directions, she would yell, "EVERYONE UP! WAKE UP! EVERYONE UP, NOW!"

We would tumble out of bed, brush our teeth, and quickly put on our navy-blue box-pleated tunics. We would put on our hand-scrubbed white bobby-socks with black oxfords and assemble in the chapel for 7:00 a.m. Mass. After that, we would line up two by two and go to the dining room picking up our trays for breakfast. Once, I remember having rushed so much in the morning that I didn't have enough time to remove the hairpins from my pincurled hair. As I left the dining room, I removed the green tam that we had to wear in church, and with fingers sticky with jam, removed the hairpins. There was no time to use a comb. Instead, I ran my fingers through the hair and attempted to comb it out between leaving the dining room and beginning the morning chores that we had to do next. Everything was done in military fashion and time was everything. We wasted no time and went directly to class at 9 a.m. after we attended Mass, did chores, made our beds and had breakfast.

On Wednesday night we had Benediction. I liked the smell of the smoke that came from the shiny gold metal container that the priest gingerly rocked back and forth as he murmured prayers in Latin. He walked by the pews, up and down the aisle, and in front of the altar. I liked Benediction because it took less time than Mass. We didn't have to sing any songs from the choir books or kneel or stand for long periods of time.

We sat in the pews as the priest chanted. Smoke exuded from the holder. It was a sweet smelling incense and the whole chapel filled with the fragrance. I liked looking at the illustrations of the Stations of the Cross on the plaques that lined the walls of the chapel, too. My imagination would take me to all the pilgrimage places that Jesus Christ had to go before meeting his Crucifixion. I didn't like all the prayers that we had to recite over and over in Latin or the Sunday Masses but I liked looking at Jesus as he carried His cross.

I hated getting up so early and rushing to the chapel every morning. I easily blocked Mass as it was so regular and mundane, but I recall Benediction services and the odd time of going into the confessional to recite imaginary sins to the priest. I disappeared into somewhere else during Mass time— just as I had done in Cranbrook. I must have begun to despise this forced feeding of religion. My Catholic upbringing was becoming a burden. I could almost recite those Latin prayers in my sleep. Judging from my feelings of tremendous guilt in later years, the Father must have preached about souls burning in hell for eternity if they didn't follow Catholic dogma absolutely. Church on the Reserve had never been like this.

The nuns I remember so well are Sister Leonita and the Sister Superior. Both were very strict nuns who ordered us off to church and ranted and raved at us to go here, go there, be on time, and so on. I disliked all the strict rules. Somewhere during this time I became familiar with the meanings of mortal and venial sins. Mortal, in the Catholic creed, meant really big and bad sins like lying, stealing or doing things considered deadly, like drinking alcohol, stabbing or killing. Venial meant sins that are forgivable such as maybe slapping someone, pulling their hair, or saying mean things to them. For a young child, these messages of guilt and evil were confusing. I just knew that I was never to do bad things, especially commit a mortal sin. We were taught repeatedly that we would go straight to hell and burn in the fires for eternity if we committed mortal sins and did not go to confession or repent, although venial sins were not to be ignored, either.

I recall going to confession to tell my sins to the priest but being unable to think of anything really bad that I had done. Instead, I'd make up sins, such as swearing, using God's name in vain, or telling certain lies. I felt awkward going to the priest without having anything to ask forgiveness for. Following confession, the priest would say, "Say ten Hail Mary's, one Our Father, and an Act of Contrition asking God to forgive you for your sins." Then he would say, "Go now and try not to sin again." I would go quietly from the confessional and return to my pew. Kneeling I would recite the prayers the priest assigned and resolve not to sin anymore.

All these new teachings replaced my earlier impressions I had from following Grandma faithfully as she made her way to church when the priest came to the Reserve on Sunday, usually once a month. There, the Indian folks would all sing from the song books as middle-aged and pleasant Murray Alexis, admired by the congregation as a devout man, in his prim and starched clothing, plucked away on his guitar before Father Cane entered the chapel in his long white robe. I liked the sound of the Indians' singing. If it was winter time the old stove at the front of the church crackled as wood burned with bright red cinders glowing from inside the pot-bellied stove. When Father Cane served Mass, it was a celebration of spirit. I liked the warm feeling when we left. I felt a kinship to everyone, especially Grandma.

She was always in a cheerful mood as we walked home, hungry for her bannock that she toasted over the wood stove. Sometimes Father Cane came to Grandma's after church to visit. Often, Marge, Hugh and I went to church with Grandma before we went off to boarding schools. Yvonne sometimes came to church too. She would wrap a tight scarf around her puffed out hair and walk side-by-side with Grandma as us kids paraded behind them on the long dirt trail to Church.

During the second year at the Kamloops school, Bill, now six years old, came with us. Although the boys and girls were kept separated, I still managed to squeeze his hand in the hallway. I always muttered, "Hi Bill," and smiled at him as he passed in single-file headed toward the little boys' cafeteria. He returned his squeeze responding with "Hi Sis," as he hurried past. I could always spot Bill coming from the boys' side once the doors were opened and the boys proceeded. Bill stood out from the other little boys because of his dirty-blond hair. All the other boys had dark hair and dark eyes. These chance meetings made me feel lonely.

I wanted very much to be with my brothers. I never saw Hugh this year except when Mom came to visit one weekend in the late autumn. We walked about a mile into town and spent the afternoon romping in the park, snapping pictures and having fun. Inside Mom's brown shopping bag was her concealed bottle of booze, probably a jug of red. During the afternoon, she sneaked gulps from the bottle without anyone noticing. By the time we had to return to the school, it was dark and Mom, now intoxicated, kept slurring her words. Instead of walking along the highway to the turn-off, we took a shortcut along the river bank. I became fearful, remembering the tall trees, dark woods, and the scary things that I heard at the school about the swamps and quicksand. I carefully watched every step I took in the dark. We arrived safely, yet I felt cheated one more time.

Once again, Mom's good intentions were swallowed up by a despicable bottle of booze. I felt embarrassed returning to school with a staggering mother. Despite my feelings, I cannot recall anything about our return to the school that day. Mom never came to visit again. Her letters came regularly though—from jail, bearing promises that she would quit drinking when she got out. I never showed any emotion reading her letters although they came in yellow-lined stationery with the envelope clearly marked 'Lower Mainland Regional Correctional Centre.' I had mixed feelings about Mom. On one hand, she couldn't even stay sober for the one day she came to visit. On the other, she was my Mom who used to sing to us as she prepared pancakes for our breakfast.

Regularly, during this year at Kamloops, again I received letters from Aunt Yvonne. Once, she tucked something inside her letter. It was a red diamond ring with two tiny white stones on each side. She used to write things on the envelopes too, like: "Postman, Postman, Get on the ball, Deliver this letter to a Kamloops Doll." I proudly wore my favourite ring until the band got all crooked and my finger turned a yellowish green colour. I was torn between Mom and Yvonne. I wanted Mom to be like Yvonne, really there for us, not going off to jail and writing from jail. It bothered me getting such letters in the rec room when mail was handed out. Nobody said anything or even noticed the kind of envelopes Mom's letters came in but I sure knew. I can still see her letters beginning with, "My darling daughter, . . . " It didn't mean that much to me. I read her promises over and over to quit drinking but after a while I stopped believing her. I was confused. I just wished that we could all be home again at Grandma's. Still, I wasn't as hopelessly lonely as I had been at Cranbrook.

My best friend Annie had short brown hair and big bright eyes. We giggled together and shared our secrets and her food-stuffs. Her family was not poor, so whenever Annie received Care packages from home, she would share with me. We were usually in the playground, twirling around on the merry-go-round with our hair blowing in the wind when Annie would be called by the attendant to pick up her package. It would be neatly packed with packages of candy, fresh oranges, apples and marshmallows. We were seldom provided fresh fruit and never any sweets, so when Annie received her goodies, I couldn't wait to get whatever she had to offer. Tearing her package open, she would usually say: "Mary Lou, do you want some?"

"Ooh, yeah," I answered, ready to hold out my hand awaiting her next gesture.

"What do you want first?" She'd ask.

"Whatever you're having," I replied excitedly.

"How about this?" She said as she handed me a bunch of marshmallows. Sometimes if she was feeling really generous, she'd give me more than a handful of marshmallows. I just loved the sweet taste of those coconut-covered marshmallows. I would lick the sweet flavour from my fingers and hope for some more.

Then she would dig into her parcel and pull out some toffee. Opening the small wrapped packages, she would take a couple of squares and hand them to me. I would thank Annie and wait for more. She would smile at me and tell the others that were standing nearby to quit staring. I was the only one she shared her goodies with. Her display of kindness made me feel good. Taste treats, other than Annie's care packages, were few and far between.

All food was prepared in large aluminum pots and pans. After attending church each morning on an empty stomach, we were faced with cold, lumpy oatmeal porridge that was sticky and half cooked. All other meals produced the same squeamish results for me. For supper, usually we were served a syrupy, googly-gunk mixture of meat, along with instant mashed potatoes. The potatoes were not mixed thoroughly and were usually quite lumpy. I collected many slices of brown and white bread to substitute for the suppers that were unbearable to eat. It didn't matter to the staff if we helped ourselves to as many slices of bread as we wanted. As long as the food didn't go back to the dorms, they didn't care. There were limited amounts of butter so it was mostly filling up on plain slices of bread when the suppers were inedible.

We ate a lot of scalloped potatoes, plus macaroni and cheese. I cannot eat these dishes now, even when prepared properly. The scalloped potatoes were soaked in too much milk and looked all curdled in the big pans. They were usually overcooked and crusty around the edges, and looked like slop to me. When we were leaving to go back to the dorms, sometimes we joked about how the food we had just been served should be fed to pigs instead of us. Meanwhile, the nuns and priests and lay-supervisors enjoyed a feast, neatly laid out on white linen tablecloths. We could only linger on the drift of simmering pot roast, freshly baked dinner buns and gravy as we went to our dining room. I remember walking down the hall in the early mornings enjoying the smell of frying bacon and eggs coming from the staff dining room while I could look forward only to lumpy porridge.

The girls were taught Scottish and Irish jigs as well as different types of dances from other countries, including Mexico and Holland. The dance groups won many medals in competitions, achieving recognition in Kamloops and the surrounding areas. This approval from the community gave glory to the nuns who taught dance and the priests and administrators who ran the school. I always wanted to learn to dance and take part in the gala activities, especially since the girls got to go out and perform in the community. I particularly liked the bright costumes they wore. The girls looked pretty. I admired how they looked before boarding the bus and going into town. They wore bright lipstick, had rosy cheeks and glowing eyeshadow above their dark eyes. With bright green pleated kilts and satin blouses worn underneath the black vests, they were most attractive. Some girls looked Irish and some looked Mexican and others looked Scottish. On their feet they wore soft black dance slippers with all the costumes—shoes like the ballerinas wear. On their heads were fancy green hats, like the Irish dancers wear.

Sometimes I caught a glimpse of the girls during practice. I enjoyed watching them dance to the different types of vibrant music. Under the stern eye of the nuns, some would be performing to the bagpipes. Others would be doing Irish jigs. Still others performed the Mexican hat dance where they danced around a large sombrero to the sound of Mexican guitars. At other times, several girls formed a line across the room and practised other traditional dances. I loved the way they pointed and tapped their toes going in a sideways pattern, lifting their knees as high as they could. It kind of looked like cancan girls as they do their performing—everything is done the same. They lift their legs to the same height, make the same body movements with pointed-feet and straight backs. I liked to watch their fancy footwork. I did try out for dance, but the nun thought I was too awkward. Instead I was assigned to darn any holes in the wool blankets that were used on both the boys and girls' sides of the dorm. I learned to darn pretty good that year. I also learned how to chain stitch, but not to dance.

No one ever swam in the swimming pool that I can recall, even though it always looked so tempting with its sparkling clean water. I don't know why we didn't get to swim. Perhaps it was because there were not enough supervisors to be lifeguards for large numbers of girls—or boys. Instead we congregated in the rec room often. Here, we played string games in which one tried to remove the long string from the opponent's two hands without getting the string all tangled up in the process. It had to retain a specified structure around the opponent's fingers and if the string got all messed while being transferred to the other, the person causing the tangles lost the game and had to try again. We played this for hours. We got pretty good at exchanging the different arrangements of the string and replacing it on the opponent's hands. In the rec room, we also wrote letters, sometimes were allowed to watch TV or just sat on the benches in the room and chit-chatted. I recall once when an older girl, an intermediate, put a scare in everybody saying that the end of the world was coming. She warned it would be during Passover, just before Easter. We were all scared and expected the end of the world to come by a big flash of lightning and fire to follow. Easter came and went, but we were still alive. I think the older girls liked to tease the little ones.

Like Cranbrook, severe and cruel punishment was enforced here as well. The Oblates used religion as a force to shape us into model young people. If anyone was caught so much as chewing gum in church or talking when there was supposed to be absolute silence, punishment prevailed. Punishment, such as being exiled to the dorm for hours at a time, being yelled at fiercely by Sister Leonita, or being sent to Father Dunlop for the strap, was inflicted for any trivial infraction of the rules of the school. Luckily I had finally learned my lessons from Cranbrook and never experienced the strap here. I was very obedient and never stepped out of line except when it came to touching and talking to Bill. I was lucky not to get caught as we were supposed to be silent while standing in line or walking toward the dining room.

The punishment often came in different disguises. There were instances such as the problem of head lice in the school. This outbreak happened although the school was free from dirt and was always kept spotlessly clean. A girl named Grace Williams contacted lice and she went untreated for a very long time. Sister Leonita found out after instructing an attendant, using fine tooth combs, to do a random check of the girls. Immediately, Sister Leonita took action. She instructed the attendant to shave Grace's head completely. She was then sent out to the yard with a towel over her head to wear as a turban as punishment for having lice. She looked funny but no one mocked or laughed at her.

She was still considered a disgrace, though. No one wanted to play with her. Along with others, I just looked at Grace from the merry-go-round and felt so sorry for her. It looked like she was really ashamed of herself as she walked around the yard with her head dropped slightly forward and the big white towel bobbing with each step. She was not allowed to take the towel off her head for many days. Another time, there was a really heavy breakout of lice, and I remember how itchy my head became.

At my bedside, was a small black comb I was using to scratch my itchy scalp. When I held the comb up to the light, I could see a tiny bug with legs wiggling in all directions stuck inside the teeth of the comb. It gave me the goosebumps but I didn't report it because I was afraid I would have my head shaved like Grace. Instead, I kept this a secret until we were all de-loused with a lotion that stunk terribly. It sure killed the bugs though. Shortly after getting de-loused, everyone got their hair cut very short again. We all had the same hair-cuts as in Cranbrook—cropped bangs high above the eye-brows, very short around the back and along the chin line on each side of the head. It appeared that Kamloops and Cranbrook had gathered the cruellest nuns and superiors in the order to enforce a rigid lifestyle, but a similar program was probably carried out at every school in the residential system.

After three years of attending the school, coming home only for Christmas and summer holidays, we returned to stay with Grandma. I tucked away my feelings toward the ill-na-tured nuns, the food, and the repetitious prayer. Sometimes I still feel angry and struggle with putting these memories to rest. I still have bitter thoughts about those supposedly saintly servants who carried out God's work within the confines of that red brick building across the river.

Before going there, I had enjoyed living at Grandma's house gathering food and wood or playing on the hillside with my brothers and sisters. Early in the morning, I liked the crackling sound of the kindling in the wood stove as Grandma started the fire. I loved the smell of her first pot of coffee brewing. Grandma's bannock tasted so good. Her sto-ries were even better. She always mused about her difficulties growing up. Grandma always thought we had it good in Kamloops with three square meals a day, a bed to sleep in every night, and a chance to learn and get a good education. We listened when she talked and dared not ask if we would be going to any more boarding schools.

3

ONE LAST TEAR

I'm sure Mom had convinced the welfare worker and Indian agent she could now take care of us and they had seen the last of her drinking. Mom was home, always had the house clean, and we had remained with her during the summer. When early fall rolled around, we did not have to go back to Kamloops. I had always known how much Mom cared for us because every letter I received in Kamloops was full of promises to take good care of us. Now she seemed to be keeping her word.

I could hardly wait to begin grade six on the Reserve. On a clear, bright autumn morning in 1962 at the tender age of 12, I headed down toward the new school. All during the summer I would glance down the road to the white-stucco, two-story structure, just across from the little school house I had attended for primary school. My new teacher lived year round at the school with his mysterious unseen wife, and two young sons, Norbert and Donald.

On the first day of school that bright fall morning I ran down the road making sure not to be late. It had rained the night before and I slipped in a mud puddle down by our gate. I quickly stood up and brushed myself off. As I inspected my clothes, I found mud smeared down the pant leg of my light green stove-pipe peddle-pushers. I did not have time to run home and change. Instead I went onto school, hoping no one would notice the smudges of mud.

The teacher rang the bell and all the kids gathered in front of the building. Mr. Sibbleau emerged at the top of the stairs. He was tall, slim and neatly dressed, wearing a white shirt with grey trousers. Once we were inside, he instructed us to sit in the various desks neatly arranged in rows. We were told to sit in the different rows according to what grades we were going into. Mr. Sibbleau taught grades four, five and six in the middle-sized classroom which was decorated with colourful posters.

Mr. Sibbleau's intelligence and orderly fashion matched his fancy clothing. He had a distinct French accent. To my dismay, Mr. Sibbleau reminded me of the Oblate teachers at Kamloops. Like my grade three teacher, Mr. Sibbleau was a well-bred French Canadian educating the kids in European customs and history. We did not learn about things such as pride, honesty, understanding, truthfulness, or respect for our elders.

We did not discover how the jackpine pitch can be nature's treat as a chewing gum or that the huckleberries can be boiled and canned. We did not learn that certain green leaves are a good medicine for healing infections or that sunflower plants are a good source of natural vitamins. During the year, we did not go on any walks observing the nature of our existence or discuss any of the philosophies of traditional native culture. We were not given the opportunity to study our native language and its history. We learned how to write compositions, to read, to write neatly and do arithmetic. We learned about the early European explorer Columbus "discovering" America, the famous French explorer Jacques Cartier and the queens and kings of England. The Indian way of life was depicted as primitive. In text books we used to look at illustrations of Indians hunched bareback on horses with tomahawks held upright in their hand as if they were ready to scalp someone.

Although I did not feel particularly comfortable in this school, I did not object to it either. By now, I was used to switching schools. It was comforting just to be living at home. Anything would have been better than the previous years spent in Kamloops, including Cranbrook.

At morning recess, Mr. Sibbleau distributed glasses of reconstituted powdered milk and hard biscuits to all the pupils. This was a hearty mid-morning treat compared to the cold, burnt tasting, lumpy oatmeal porridge that we ate in Kamloops. At lunchtime, I would run home. As I hurried up the road, I liked watching the smoke curling lazily from the roof of our modest home. I would rush in and enjoy a hearty dinner with Mom. Usually it would be warm homemade vegetable soup and fried bannock.

Being at home, I loved the closeness of our family. Mom would be busy washing clothes on warm sunny days, making homemade yeast bread or, sometimes, she would be just lying on the couch resting and reading *True Story* magazines. Most days, I would come home after school and do whatever chores Mom asked me to do. Usually I had little jobs like taking the clothes off the line or helping with supper.

Bill attended school in the building where Miss Siccouse taught. Marge was fourteen years old and Hugh was thirteen. They caught the bus into town to attend the public high school. For the first time in four years, our family was living together, pleasantly. Mom stayed home most of that year. The odd time she would go on a binge but always made it home, sometimes drunker than a skunk.

That year Mom got pregnant and had Harriet. She was born a very tiny baby, but she was the sweetest little thing. She always smiled and her big brown eyes watched every move anybody made. When she was old enough to stand in her crib, she'd hold on tightly to the rail. I would go over to her large, old-fashioned brown crib, give her a quick little hug and say, "Hi Harriet." She always giggled.

As the year wore on, though, things changed. On some days Mom would ask me to stay home from school in the afternoon. She'd say that she had to gather firewood from the field and asked if I would watch Harriet. Several hours would pass and she still would not come home. The following day I would have to stay home and look after Harriet, feeling very angry at Mom. Several days would go by but she still hadn't returned. Bill wouldn't go to school and would stay with Grandma when Mom was gone. I wanted to go to school like all the rest of the kids rather than be a mother to Harriet. I was only twelve years old and had to learn how to boil potatoes and cook spaghetti. I also had to prepare Harriet's bottles, using cans of condensed milk.

During the following months, Mom would come and go, usually bringing home a few cardboard boxes of groceries and bottles of cheap red wine. She'd stay home a couple of weeks and sometimes she would take Harriet with her when she left. Occasionally, I attended school but had to repeat grade six.

Periodically during this year, unannounced, the Indian agent would come to visit. One day he came and saw that we had been living alone. Very shortly after that, Miss Oram, the welfare worker, was sent out to remove us from our home and place us in foster care due to Mom's continuous absence from our home. Immediately Miss Oram had us pack our few belongings and pile into her car again. She still drove the same white Valiant.

Marge was transported to a foster home, the Leducs, in town while Hugh and I were placed together in the same foster home on the Reserve. We attended St. James Catholic School that year. Our new foster mom was named Edna and I liked her. She was kind to me, but I disliked our foster father Mike because he was mean looking. He never smiled and he insisted that I make his breakfast every morning because Edna worked the night shift at the hospital. Reluctantly I would make him a pot of oatmeal mush and two slices of toast each morning. He was very stern and never smiled or engaged in small talk. He expected his breakfast every morning before I got ready for school. Then before I boarded the bus, Edna arrived home to take care of their little ones, Byron, Cheryl and Brenda.

Edna was originally from the Barriere Reserve near Kamloops and Mike was from our Reserve. Miss Oram had moved Harriet to the little town of Lavington, which was not far from us, to live with a non-native family. Bill stayed on the Reserve with Grandma. Our family dissolved right before my eyes, again. I felt so empty and numb. I did not know which was worse: our family being separated or living on our own, unattended. Tears swelled up in my eyes each time I thought of Harriet. I missed her so much. My stomach tightened as I held back the anger I felt toward the Indian agent. I pushed all these mixed, hurt feelings deep down inside me hoping that our family would one day be together.

While in the foster home, Hugh and I asked for regular visits to see Grandma, Bill and Yvonne. We were allowed to visit them whenever Edna, Mike and their kids visited Mike's family who lived across the field from Grandma's house. Usually we got to visit every other Sunday. Edna never minded us keeping in touch with our relatives. In fact, she thought it was good that we visited our family often. Yvonne would be happy to see us. Sometimes she would bring out her Brownie camera and snap pictures of everyone together. We were unable to see Harriet as often as we would have liked to. One Sunday while Edna and Mike were on their regular visit, Hugh and I went to visit Grandma. I noticed that Mom was home. Right away, I went over to our house to see her while Hugh stayed at Grandma's.

We sat on the couch together. She was just sitting there and the house looked so abandoned. I didn't like to see Mom this way and it made me sad. She asked how I liked it at the Louis house. I said it was okay. Asking if I had seen Harriet, she wondered how she was doing. I told her I hadn't seen Harriet that often. I consoled myself with thoughts that at least Bill was there and could keep Mom company, although he was always off playing with the cousins up the road. Miss Oram insisted that Bill stay with Grandma permanently. I suppose it was for the best because Mom never stayed at the house very long after we were taken away.

Mom did not admit her drinking problem at the time nor did I shun her for drinking too much. At this point, I blamed the Indian agent and Miss Oram for splitting up our family.

On another Sunday, I visited Mom again. I found her untalkative and lonely. We sat on the couch and she asked me if I was hungry. I answered, "No" but still went to the cupboard. I found it empty, except for a half-full bag of soft oranges. I took an orange and sat on the couch eating it. I did not realize this would be our last visit for a long, long time.

Usually when we came to visit Grandma, Mom was in town drinking with her buddies. She probably got too lonely at home alone. Even though Bill was at Grandma's, Mom didn't stop drinking. In town the police continued to patrol the park regularly, and when they found Mom too tipsy, she had to serve the standard three-to six-month jail sentence.

After we had been living in different foster homes for one year, Miss Oram decided to reunite our family, except for Marge—she stayed at the LeDucs. Miss Oram placed Bill, Harriet, Hugh and me in another foster home, many miles away. We went to live with our aunt and uncle, Bonnie and Jeff, who had five kids of their own ranging in ages from one to seven. I was delighted to be with my brothers and sister again. Harriet, now one-and-a-half years old, still remembered us. She didn't remember our names but her smiles and twinkles in her eyes showed she remembered us. We lived in a small, three-bedroom house in Oliver. We slept in bunk beds, four to each bedroom in the basement of their very small, cramped house.

I fussed over Harriet. I'd comb her hair and dress her everyday. She looked cute in a bright pink outfit or in colourful pop-tops and shorts. I cuddled her all the time. She looked so frail, but was so sweet. At other times, I would find myself hitting her real hard on her tiny arms for no apparent reason. Sometimes I would feel angry because I did not like living with relatives. Bill and Hugh did not seem to mind. It was better than having the authority people shuffling us around to different foster homes.

I entered South Okanagan High School to begin grade eight. I felt awkward and unsure of myself. I couldn't make any friends. I lacked self-confidence. Shortly after we began school, Bill and I got homesick for Grandma and Yvonne. We decided to run away and hitchhike to Vernon. We did not pack any food or clothes. We did steal coins from the mason jar tucked inside a canner in the kitchen, probably about two dollars in quarters. Downtown we slept inside an old van that was abandoned in a parking lot. The van did not have any glass in the windows, so we were quite chilly during the late fall night.

Early the next morning, Bill and I wandered idly around Main Street gazing in store windows. Our new freedom was short-lived by a police officer who was called to locate us. He leaned over and poked his head out of his car window. He lectured us about running away and escorted us back to Jeff and Bonnie's house. When Jeff came home from work, he did not say anything right away to us. He then scolded Bill and strapped him with a belt. He gave me a glassy stare as if to say, "Don't you ever try this again, or else!"

A year went by and things did not work out too well. Hugh was getting into too much trouble and would not listen to Bonnie. I also grew tired but never complained, of washing out dirty diapers because Bonnie could not do it herself. Her hands were always infected and swollen from eczema, so I did a lot of her work like peeling potatoes, washing clothes in the wringer-washer, or scrubbing soiled diapers by hand, in the toilet.

Eventually we moved again because of all the problems we brought to Jeff and Bonnie's household. Besides, their family was large enough and the four of us did not help matters any. Miss Oram returned us to Vernon and placed us in different foster homes. Bill went to Novitskis', a nice home on the far side of town. Harriet went to another foster home, and I was placed in a home, especially for problem kids, a few miles out of town in a rural area. This home must have been the only place available at the time because I am sure I was not a problem child. While I had failed grade eight, I was placed in grade nine at W.L. Seaton Junior High. Hugh went back to the Reserve and stayed wherever he could. Later on, he started breaking and entering into places, and he was in and out of Okalla Prison.

As I settled into my latest foster home, the foster parents Mr. and Mrs. Stone told me that the foster kids all called them "Mom and Dad." Usually they had at least five foster kids in care. They also had three children of their own, Deanna, Joe, and Missy. I disliked their "parents policy" because I already had a Mom. Reluctantly, I started calling them "Mom and Dad" but it sounded very peculiar to me.

Mrs. Stone, a perfectionist, kept the house spotlessly clean. In the morning she would pull out the vacuum cleaner and go from room to room picking up any little particles. She would strip, wash, and wax the kitchen and living room floors every Friday. She diligently cooked and cleaned every day. If she was upset about something, she would relieve her frustrations by vacuuming. In a fury, she would bump the walls and hit the corners of furniture as she cleaned. The shrieking of the vacuum echoed throughout the house.

I witnessed many bizarre things while living at the Stones. One I remember well. A five-year-old boy named Timmy was placed in the Stone residence. Timmy was a victim of physical and sexual abuse before coming to the Stones. He was a hyperactive child, constantly clearing his throat and using his fingers to push his nose upward.

Mrs. Stone started to punish Timmy soon after he arrived. He was always looking for attention, either from being praised or punished. One day, after school I came home and peeked in Timmy's basement room. It was easy to see inside. There was no door, only a rough barrier made of boards nailed halfway up the frame. Timmy was sitting on his bed, soaking wet after being dunked many times in ice-cold water in the laundry tub in the basement. He was being punished for acting up at school that day. This dunking became a daily ritual and it did not surprise me to come home each day to see him sitting in his room, sopping wet, talking to himself with a strange grin on his face.

Mrs. Stone dunked him in cold water because her whippings did not do any good. She never left marks on him. Following these incidents, Timmy's face would be flushed and his bright blue eyes always had a subdued expression at the supper table. Later, while disclosing her ordeals with Timmy, Mrs. Stone would laugh, relaying her problem as though it were a big joke. I did not like participating in such merriment. I felt sorry for Timmy. Sometimes his teeth were still chattering when he came up for supper. Naive as I was, I thought Mrs. Stone's actions were warranted for such a naughty, troubled child and did not question her discipline.

I also thought it was normal to see Mrs. Stone fighting with her own daughter, Deanna. These fights were not that often and usually consisted of pushing and yelling in the doorway of the bathroom. It was upsetting to me. I thought Mrs. Stone was on the verge of a nervous breakdown whenever she had these crazy outbursts. I believe there was conflict because Deanna, now an eighteen-year-old, was too old to be still living at home.

All foster kids were entitled to a monthly family allowance for school clothes and other necessities, but I did not receive this money. Instead at the beginning of each school year, I was provided with a couple of new outfits. Mrs. Stone did the shopping, but she did not shop for style. I had a plain-looking, average wardrobe. While our basic necessities in clothing were taken care of, Mrs. Stone spent money often on new clothes for her youngest child Missy. She always got something new when Mr. and Mrs. Stone went shopping on his weekly day off. Missy's dresser drawers were filled with brand new sweaters. I comforted myself with thoughts that she was just a pug-nosed, buck-toothed, spoiled little brat. Besides, all those new sweaters looked tacky on her, and they were also a reflection of Mrs. Stone's drab taste in clothes. Meanwhile, I had to sneak nylons from Deanna. One time I was at school and looked down to see one stocking was burnt umber and the other was beige. The bright lighting at the school revealed the colours of my "mix and match" stockings. It was embarrassing and I always felt out of sorts because I could not afford the fashionable clothes other students wore.

We had plenty of food, and Mrs. Stone was an extraordinary cook. We could not snack between meals so I usually gorged myself at supper. On Friday nights Mr. Stone always brought home a gallon bucket of ice cream and packages of chocolate *eclairs*. Whoever stayed home indulged in the luxuries of chocolate and ice-cream. Of course, I binged on this junk food. I gained a lot of weight and developed eating disorders. My weight became a problem. I tipped the scale at one hundred forty-five pounds, and being only five feet four inches tall, I felt porky. I began to exercise with a passion. I couldn't lose weight so I tried something else. I would eat a big meal and stuff myself with seconds then go into the bathroom and throw up. Finally after three weeks I was so repulsed by my own vomit that I decided to stop doing this. I had no idea this disorder was called bulimia.

After retching, I would be hungry. In the Stone household foster kids were not allowed to open the fridge between meals, though we were never told in so many words, we knew better than to push our luck. To satisfy my hunger pangs I would go into the kitchen to pack my lunch around eight o'clock in the evening, just before I went for my bath. I would place my nightgown on top of the kitchen counter and make two extra sandwiches. With no one around I would hide the sandwiches underneath my nightgown. Before climbing into the bath tub I would gobble down the sandwiches. This was not the first time I smuggled food, as occasionally, I had done it at Jeff and Bonnie's home whenever I was still hungry after meal time but afraid to ask for a second helping. There, I would help myself while taking the leftovers out to the compost. Besides, Bonnie made such delicious sweet and sour pork that I could not see any going to waste!

Being as weight-conscious as any teenager, I decided to diet. For breakfast at the Stones I would eat two dry pieces of hardtack smothered with raspberry jam. I tried to eat small amounts at regular meal times. Eventually, I grew tired of dieting and decided to accept being pleasantly plump. I wore baggy sweatshirts, loose-fitting pants and colourful tent dresses to hide my supposed weight problem.

Sometime after May 17, 1966, Mr. Stone called me into the master bedroom. I knew it must be something important because we were only summoned in there for serious lectures or reprimands. He turned to me and bluntly said, "Your mother died."

Shocked I responded with, "What?" I could not believe the words that were stinging my ears. I shrieked, "It can't be!" I felt so numb and began to sob, saying over and over again "No! No! No!"

I had just seen Mom walking down the streets a few months before, but she had looked quite different. Her face was quite bloated and she looked much older than her forty-one years. Instead of those fashionable curls she used to have, she had a dreadful, short haircut. It looked like she had tried to cut her own hair with dull scissors. It was ragged and messy-looking.

Mom's wake was held at Grandma's house. Slowly, friends and family members arrived. Everyone was absorbed in hushed conversations. Long-lost relatives greeted each other sombrely but lovingly. My eyes filled with tears. Every now and then I would stand by the cheap grey coffin resting on the floor and stare at Mom's body. She was dressed in a light-purple flowered dress. Her short, uneven hair was stiffly combed in an upward sweep off her forehead. I examined her closely. Her face was swollen and her body was so bloated I hardly recognized her. There were bruises around the left side of her neck.

I was told that she died from alcohol poisoning. Later on, I heard a different story. I heard that Mom was beaten to death and found on Skid Row in Vancouver. The case was never thoroughly investigated by the police. To this day, I still want to know how she really died. Apparently, Mom had given her bus ticket to a friend upon their release from Okalla Prison. She wanted to see her friend return safely to Vernon so she gave her ticket to her friend and stayed behind.

Mom's classical good looks and '60s style were gone. She now looked like a typical skid-row derelict: abandoned, forgotten, and deserted. I looked away. Feeling hollow and lifeless, I searched for the love and devotion I once held for her. It was not there. Instead, I felt more emptiness inside. I cried because everybody else was crying; it was appropriate at the time. What I really felt was a hollow gap of about sixteen lost years. I was torn between the love and memory of a mother who raised us the best way she knew how and feelings of abandonment and anger. I could not understand all the different emotions running through me. I moved to the couch where I had a close view of her coffin. I wanted to tell her so many things. When I remembered her from happy childhood days, tears rolled down my cheeks. A sadness ached inside me. When I remembered all the things that happened as a result of her drinking, I stiffened up. I pushed all those painful memories far, far inside me. I resolved that one day I would understand why things happened the way they did.

Upset about Mom's condition, Grandma went into town and bought a beautiful oak coffin, flat shoes and a white lace dress to put Mom in. She was changed in privacy, then her coffin was placed on a stand and long white candles were lit. The flames of the candles flickered and smoke curled softly as Mom lay peacefully beneath her long white veil. People came carrying bouquets of fresh spring flowers. I brought African violets. We said many prayers during the three-day wake.

We gathered at the Catholic church to have the funeral service. As we sang "Amazing Grace" with Murray Alexis playing the guitar, we slowly left the church. Clusters of people wandered toward the graveyard. Tumbleweeds, dried-up flowers, and thick patches of weeds and brown grass covered the many burial plots. In the quietness of the late afternoon many little sobs were heard. Sadly, I felt the immensity of the day. My mother was no more.

Reluctantly, I returned to the Stones. Mrs. Stone gave me a mild tranquillizer and told me to get some rest. I finally fell asleep. I was exhausted from the three heart-breaking days. When I awoke the next day, Mr. Stone called me into their master bedroom for one of his talks. He did not understand why I was sad. Without feeling he said, "When someone dies, it's just a shell in their coffin!"

I thought to myself, "How could you be so cruel? Mom meant so much to me." Rebellion set in. I found the rules in the Stone household too rigid. When I did something minor like forgetting to turn the bathroom light off, Mrs. Stone would give me the silent treatment for several days. Sometimes three days would pass and I could not stand the silent treatment so I would say, "Sorry Mom, it won't happen again." Meanwhile, the anger swelled inside me as I consoled myself that one day I would leave this unfriendly home. I was now sixteen and wanted more freedom. I wanted to go to parties, drink booze and stay out late. For taking part in such activities, I kept getting grounded, sometimes for weeks at a time. My best friend, Sue, and I would drink almost every weekend. Usually I stayed overnight at her house because her dad was hardly ever home on weekends and her mom was no disciplinarian. We would go on sprees of chasing boys and guzzling booze. I was grounded whenever I came home to the Stones smelling of "spirits."

I went to Sue's house one weekend and told her I wanted to run away. She was having problems with her dad, too. We drank several bottles of beer and staggered up the hill, weaving south toward "The Big City." We wanted to see the bright lights and have a taste of freedom. Hitchhiking along the highway we got picked up by a perverted old man. He was talking vulgar and the only thing on his mind was sex. We stayed in the car and laughed off his dirty comments, hoping our humour would keep him from going any further. The next morning we arrived in Vancouver.

Luckily we were unharmed. We were scared and now wished we were not in this big, unfriendly city. Very shortly after arriving, Sue called her dad and asked him to send her bus fare to come home. He sent extra money so I was able to go home as well. I went back to the Stones and was grounded for one month. I really resented my lengthy punishment and became even more rebellious. Finally, I decided to settle down and to try concentrating on school.

Once again, I complained to Miss Oram, telling her I wanted to move from the Stones. I felt that I was not being treated fairly. All I wanted was a happy home where there was fair treatment for everyone. I did not like the special treatment Mrs. Stone showed toward her own kids, especially Missy. I felt their "love" for the foster kids was insincere.

There were some happy times and I must acknowledge these as well. I really liked their older daughter Deanna, and we became close. During her last year at home, we shared the same bedroom and always got along quite well. She was like a big sister to me. Later I would feel privileged to be one of her bridesmaids when she married.

It would be improper for me not to mention or give credit to the Stones for another happy occasion during those three years. Mr. Stone urged me to compete as a candidate for the Queen Silver Star Pageant. The Homemaker's Club of the Okanagan Indian Band in Vernon had asked me to run as Miss Indian Band. I was thrilled.

I came in as First Princess to Queen Silver Star for 1967/68. The most important highlight of the entire pageant for me was looking down into the dimly-lit, crowded auditorium and seeing Grandma sitting in the front row. Half-way through, I forgot the lines of my speech and felt a big lump in my throat. I swallowed hard, blinked back the tears and finished my speech entitled "The Throbbing Drums of the Indians." I could feel Grandma's pride in me that evening.

While living at the Stones, I would visit Marge, who lived with LeDucs a few miles up the road, toward Silver Star. We would spend time together talking. I would sit and watch her put on make-up or style her pretty, dark brown hair into the then-popular bee-hive hairdo. Sometimes we would just sit on her bed and listen to popular music as she played records. I liked listening to her chattering about all her boyfriends. Whenever I went there I always asked if I could come to live with her. Marge seemed very happy at the LeDucs.

They lived in a large, brown and white stucco house on the hillside. Their home had exquisite furnishings with off-white plush carpeting in the hallway. Gus owned his own paving company and the family was quite wealthy. They had three children Gussy, Greg and Sherri. A close-knit family, the LeDucs really liked Marge. In fact, I thought they loved her.

I completed the ninth and tenth grades but failed grade eleven and had to repeat while living at the Stones. I was finally relieved of the Stones. I convinced Miss Oram that the tension had become extreme, and I was quite unhappy there and I had been for a long, long time. Marge had now left and was on her own. I loved living in my new home. Lil was the mom that every girl dreams of. She was nicknamed "Laughing Lil" by her co-workers in her old job as a nurse. Lil had left nursing to raise her family. She was kind, gentle, and she had a great sense of humour. All settled in, I had my own huge bedroom downstairs with my own bathroom. Lil soon gave me a generous monthly allowance. We talked openly together like mother and daughter. I did much better in school. My marks improved as I repeated the subjects I failed in grade eleven, combined with a couple of grade twelve subjects as well.

While I may have said goodbye to the Stones, their in-fluence on my family was far from over. In 1967, just prior to my move to LeDucs, Harriet was placed with the Stones. I was happy that we were reunited but the animosity I felt toward the Stones was stronger and I did not want to stay a day longer. While Harriet was in their care, she reported to me years later that she was abused by them. Harriet told me she needed a hearing aid very early in school and the Stones never got one for her. As a result, she did not do well in school. In high school she took courses that are structured for slow-learners such as life skills, job orientation and learning technical skills of working in fast food restaurants. This was the extent of her high school education. Harriet also reported to me that Mr. Stone punished her with the belt when she once ran away to find me living in Westbank.

Living at LeDucs, I learned to drive an old Volkswagen around the yard that year and prepared for my driving test. I went to Miss Oram and asked permission to get my driver's licence. She denied my request, saying that I had to wait until I turned eighteen. Although it was only a few months away I was so upset with her I thought, "You fat slob, I'll show you!" I vowed to break all their darn rules and become my own boss. Ironically, it was not until I turned thirty years old that I attempted to drive again, finally passing the drivers test. I managed to finish grade 11/12 that year and summer finally arrived.

One day, for some unknown reason, Lil and I had a rare disagreement. I got mad and wouldn't speak to her. I had learned well from living at the Stones on how to give the silent treatment and I thought Lil deserved it although she hadn't really done anything. I decided to leave this beautiful family and their comfortable house on the hill. I decided to try it on my own. I had just had it with people always telling me what to do. First it was the social workers, then the nuns and then the Stones. Orders, even from someone as wonderful as Lil, were not something I was prepared to live with ever again.

This is how I fondly remember mom with her pin curled hair.
She is holding one of my cousins.

This is how I fondly remember Grandma.

Grandma and I after the first year in Kamloops. I did not like this haircut!

Brothers William (left), Hugh and myself on a winter day in front of Grandma's house.

This is Marge, young and beautiful.

The Kamloops Indian Residential School.

4

TWIN CITIES

Downstairs in my bedroom, I packed my clothes neatly inside my blue vinyl suitcase. It was early July and the year was 1968. Anxiously, I squeezed everything that was hanging in the closet into the suitcase—a purple plaid mini dress, a two-tone green empire waistline dress, a couple pairs of denim jeans and sweat shirts. For such a long time I waited for this day. I took one last look around my master-sized bedroom. I remembered the day Lil and I laid the purple tile in this big room. We got down on our hands and knees and did the entire job ourselves.

I walked into the adjoining bathroom and picked up a few towels lying on the white linoleum floor. I tossed my make-up, hair dryer and other necessities into a black shoulder-strap bag. With suitcase in hand and the bag slung over my shoulder, I walked up the steep stairs into the kitchen. Without a farewell note to my warm-hearted foster parents, who were not home at the time, I left. Feeling heavy-hearted, I closed the kitchen door behind me.

With no real destination in mind, I headed down the long winding paved road. Walking past the trees, I took one last look at the brown and white ranch style house on the hill. Sadly, I thought of Gus sitting at the kitchen table, chain-smoking Du Maurier after supper, sipping on his favourite drink of Scotch on the rocks. I thought of Lil, warm and loveable with her contagious laughter echoing throughout the big house. I thought of their three kids and how special they had become to me. I pulled out my package of No. 7 cigarettes and lit one up. I inhaled the smoke deep into my lungs and slowly breathed out. I felt like an independent young woman, full of freedom yet still afraid.

I shifted around for a few days staying with friends here and there, living out of my suitcase. I then moved in with my school chum, Diane, in her modest downtown basement apartment. She was just freshly out on her own too. I assured Diane that I would have a job very shortly and could pay my own way. I went to Social Services and obtained my first welfare cheque to help pay the rent. All settled in, I phoned Lil and our fight was never mentioned. I told her I just wanted to be on my own. She understood and mentioned that Gus would probably have a part-time flagging job available soon and asked if I would like to work on the highways. Of course I accepted her offer right away.

In August, the job came through. LeDuc Paving won the bid to pave a long stretch of highway outside Salmon Arm and was now under contract with the Department of Highways. Marge, now twenty, had kept close contact with the LeDucs since she moved out on her own. Being their foster kin, we were both offered the jobs as flag girls. Marge rented a two bedroom apartment in Salmon Arm for us. Diane didn't mind that I moved out. Besides, she had many friends around her all the time. Being bright and outgoing, she was a popular seventeen-year-old.

While working in Salmon Arm, I would return the odd weekend to spend time with my old school pals. My good-natured friend Diane, of course, was always fun to be with. Georgette, also about seventeen, was more serious and mature. She was the intelligent one. Colleen was the wittiest in our tight little clique. She wore skin-tight blue jeans, was short and quite plump. She laughed at everything. Noreen was my best friend. I admired her dark brown shoulder-length hair and her pretty features; she was the most attractive of all my friends. Sometimes, we all talked about travelling to Toronto but never made any definite plans.

Every morning at seven-thirty Marge and I stood out on the highway directing traffic. The freshly paved black stretch of highway reflected the hot sun's rays, scorching and baking us every day. Exhausted each night, we would return to our apartment on the second floor of the rooming house.

It was early September and I had just turned 18. We had worked long hours the entire month of August. We worked some weekends as well. With the summer now coming to an end so did our jobs. I decided to move out of the apartment, not quite sure of what I was going to do. I had saved about two hundred dollars. Marge now had her tall, good-looking boyfriend Billy pretty well moved in, and I was feeling much like a fifth-wheel. Independent and adventurous, I was ready to travel, not quite sure of the destination.

I packed my suitcase and headed to Vernon and stayed at Diane's place again. Getting together with my school chums that weekend, we decided to take a journey across Canada to Toronto. We would use Mike's beat-up, brown four-door sedan. Mike, a little older than Georgette, was working as a mechanic and finished school a year earlier than the rest of us. He adored Georgette and jokingly we teased him behind her back saying he was "pussy-whipped." Mike, a gentle young man with light brown hair, was really a ladies' man in our eyes. Even though there were small blemishes over his face, Georgette still found him attractive and loved him dearly. We asked Mike to be our designated driver. The car was in pretty good condition but I wondered if it really would hold up for the three thousand miles across Canada. I phoned Marge and said goodbye. When I asked her what her plans were, she said she and Billy were preparing to move back to the Reserve and live at Billy's house.

We set out for Toronto. We giggled in the back seat of the car and were excited about our journey. Georgette sat close to Mike, and Marie, a cute dark-haired school acquaintance, squeezed in beside them. Marie and Noreen were very close friends and, of course, Noreen invited Marie to tag along. I didn't care that much for Marie. Noreen and I had the back seat and chit-chatted away. Half-way across Canada, Mike and Georgette decided they did not want to go any farther. They wanted to travel into the American Mid-West instead and eventually return to Vernon. So here we were, Noreen, Marie and I in the middle of the night in Winnipeg, stranded. We didn't want to spend our money on bus fare because we knew we'd need it in Toronto, so we started hitchhiking. We caught a ride to Thunder Bay and eventually landed in Toronto two days later. We hitchhiked the entire way, taking turns cat-napping as we drove with strangers in different cars.

Our last ride took us to Yonge Street, the centre of downtown Toronto. Arriving late in the day, we walked from one strange street to the next. Feeling a little uncertain, but curious about our new surroundings, we were not as spirited as when we set out in our journey. We were feeling somewhat weak from the long trip and were quiet. We walked up and down many streets looking for a "Room For Rent" sign in the windows of the big houses. All the houses along every street looked the same. They were fairly old three-storey buildings with little space between each house. Tall elm trees lined the sides of each street. We came to a house that had a "Room For Rent" sign in the window and knocked on the door. A heavy-set Black woman opened the door a crack and asked, "What you want?" She curiously looked us up and down.

Noreen replied, "We're new here and looking for a housekeeping room." The house was dark except for a faint light which looked like the beam of a candle flickering from the bedroom behind the woman. She opened the door and gestured with her hand for us to follow her up the stairs. She led us down a dark corridor and up the stairs. While climbing the long staircase, Noreen whispered that this place gave her the creeps. I agreed it looked spooky, and we concluded witchcraft was probably going on here. The darkness in the house did give us the goosebumps. We examined the room which was clean and cosy. It contained a queen-size bed with a plain comforter, a dresser with a round mirror, a small walk-in closet, a card table and two wooden chairs. We rented it right away and paid the woman our first week's rent of $15. Exhausted, we unpacked and put on our nighties and went right to bed. Marie and Noreen shared the bed. I made a bed in the walk-in closet space on the floor. The very next day Marie decided to return to Vernon, boarded a train and went home.

Over the next few days Noreen and I discussed finding jobs. Our money was running short and we needed to find work soon. I knew I could easily learn waitress work. Noreen preferred an office job because she had done quite well in typing classes at school. Both eager to find work, we walked to the corner store and picked up the *Toronto Star*. Back at our room we spread out the newspaper on the floor and scanned the "help wanted" columns.

Within a week we found jobs. I got a job at the Varsity Cafe and worked the afternoon shift. I quickly learned how to be a waitress. Noreen had found a clerical job. She had never worked in an office before and began on-the-job training. I didn't mind working in the "greasy-spoon" restaurant. In fact, I enjoyed waiting on tables. However, I did not enjoy the sleazy owner's behaviour in the back room on pay days. He'd sit at his desk in the little room with his back to the door preparing our cheques. When I came in and stood there waiting for my cheque, he'd try rubbing his hands on my knees before handing the cheque over. I would recoil from his touch. I wanted to tell this short little fat jerk he was a dirty old man. Instead, I remained quiet because I needed the money.

During that past summer, while we were still living in the BC Interior, Noreen had met a fair-skinned, curly-haired hippie named Kevin. Originally from Toronto, he was roaming the country when he met and eventually started dating Noreen. They became passionately involved with each other. Eventually Kevin returned to Toronto. I found his move unusual as they had been deeply attracted to one another and inseparable the entire time he spent in Vernon. When Kevin moved back to Toronto, Noreen had missed him and talked about him often. He was now living with his parents but had left a forwarding address with Noreen. It was just a few blocks from where we were now staying. While I found it reassuring to know one person in the big city of Toronto, Kevin started spending quite a bit of time with Noreen. I began to feel like an intruder in our own room. He was always there when I came home from work. Finally, I decided to leave the love-birds alone in their nest, quit my job, and go west. I didn't give notice at the Varsity Cafe. I just quit. Noreen had been writing letters home to keep up on everything, so we knew that Marie had gone to be with her Mom in Vernon while Diane and Colleen had settled in Vancouver's West End where they shared an apartment. Mike and Georgette had returned to Vernon shortly after dropping us off in Winnipeg.

It was in the middle of December when I boarded the train and headed west. Leaving a blizzard behind, I looked forward to the little bit of slush that Vancouver might have. Three days later, I arrived in Vancouver. I left the train station and took a bus up Davie Street to find Diane and Colleen's apartment. I went up the two flights of stairs and knocked on the door of their apartment. Colleen answered the door and was happy to see me. She said I could bunk at their place. Both had jobs and were doing okay. Diane worked in a pizza place and I think Colleen was working in a factory at the time. Their one-room apartment was sparsely furnished with a pull-out couch and small kitchen table but it had a wonderful large bathroom. Diane spent all her free time with John, her dark-haired, good-looking boyfriend.

He lived in an apartment just down the street. As they spent most evenings together in his apartment, I had the couch to sleep on. Colleen, like myself, hadn't met "Mr. Right" as yet, nor were we really looking for anyone. We hung out on weekends at three draft-dodgers' attic room just around the corner on Davie Street. We listened to popular records on their stereo and drank beer. The young men were from the States but did not want to fight in the Vietnam War because they did not believe in war. We sympathized with them, not really understanding war.

I found a job at the Sportsman Cafe in a better part of the East End district and worked the graveyard shift. I worked for about two months and was never late or missed a shift. For leisure, on weekends, I began to hang out in Gastown, a small town of its own, with neat little shops and lots of night spots. Hippies were roaming the country. Girls were wearing flowers in their hair and the guys never bothered to cut or comb theirs. The Beatles song, "Give Peace A Chance" was every hippie's catchphrase. Besides, who wanted a war in Vietnam? The young people wore frayed bell-bottom jeans with tie-dyed T-shirts and let their hair grow long, parting it down the middle. They strolled barefoot in the streets and hung out on Granville Street. I was attracted to the hippie movement and tried psychedelic drugs the odd time. I enjoyed the peaceful easy feeling of kicking back and listening to the Beatles, the Rolling Stones, Jimi Hendrix and the Doors. I wanted to remain in the midst of my new liberated friends, living peacefully.

But within three months, I quit my job at the Sportsman Cafe. Instead of joining my flower-power friends, I had decided on the spur of the moment to go back to Toronto. I had about one hundred fifty dollars tucked inside the last little brown pay envelope from work. So off it was again to the train station, destined for Toronto. Eagerly, I entered the train station and bought a ticket. I did enjoy the long trip. Somehow the mountains and all the greenery gave me a lift. As I had very little money left, I splurged only once or twice during those three days to sit in the dining-room on the train and enjoy a hamburger deluxe with a coke.

The train pulled into the huge Toronto central train station. I stepped off the train and walked through hordes of people. It was late afternoon and everyone was rushing around bumping into one another without any "Excuse me" or "Oops, sorry!" I pulled out my little black book and looked up Noreen and Kevin's new address on Howland Avenue. I just wanted to find this street to see if I could stay the night, then find my own place the next day. I wandered around the train station until I found an entrance to the subway station. I put a thirty-cent token into the slot and went to the nearest directory, looking at the maps posted on the concrete walls. After I found Howland Avenue, I looked further to see which subway I needed to board. With a light blue suitcase in one hand and a shopping bag in the other, I pushed my way through the crowds and found a seat on the right car. As soon as it was time to get off, I jerked on the cord and stood by the door feeling very claustrophobic. I dreaded being confined in such a closed space.

Exhausted, I finally found Kevin and Noreen's place. They lived in a small suite on the top floor of a spacious rooming house. No one answered when I knocked, so I turned the knob on the big wooden door and looked inside. A flight of stairs led upward. I climbed the stairs which led into a cramped but bright and clean kitchen. Off to the side were glass doors with lacy white curtains hiding an airy, modern bedroom. I peeked through the window and saw a floor model stereo, a king-size bed and a fireplace. The spick-and-span apartment didn't surprise me. Noreen had always liked her place neat with pretty things.

Both were surprised to find me sitting in the communal kitchen when they returned home later that night. They were still happily in love. They couldn't keep their hands off each other, always hugging or squeezing one another. I disliked the way Kevin was so stricken by Noreen, kissing her every time she was near him. I stayed and visited awhile, then decided to find a place although it was late at night.

I left and walked up the street looking for a "Room For Rent" sign in the windows of the old Victorian-style houses. I spotted a vacancy farther up on Howland Avenue, near the busy downtown intersection with Bloor Avenue. It was about ten short blocks from where Kevin and Noreen lived. I needed a room, so any room would have been sufficient. I knocked on the door and when the woman opened I asked how much the rent was for the room. She responded, "$10 a week." I paid her a week's rent and moved into a room the size of a jail cell. I tumbled into bed right away.

The next morning I tried to make it look like home. I taped my posters of Jimi Hendrix and the Doors on the bare white walls. I brought out the brown transistor radio that I carried since leaving the LeDucs. It had been a Christmas gift and was precious to me. It reminded me of the beloved family I left. I plugged in the radio and lay on the bed. Thinking of the last Christmas I spent with Gus and Lil and their three kids, I became very lonely.

I got even lonelier and stayed in the small room, day after day. I disliked the thought of another search for a waitressing job. I had about $65.00 to my name and that was it. I tucked the money underneath my mattress and listened to the soft rock'n'roll music playing on the radio. One song in particular really caught my attention. As the singer crooned, "....and this will be the day that I die...", it caused distress in me. Never before had I felt this empty.

Occasionally, I would go out and walk down Yonge Street in the evenings. Many couples strolled together and others walked briskly, but all avoided eye contact with anyone passing by. Many people lined up to see the movies every night. I had never seen so many theatres on one street, ever. One evening, I joined the long line of people and bought a ticket to see *Easy Rider*, staring Peter Fonda. In the theatre I remember thinking, "In a city this size how could I be so lonely?" I missed the closeness of Noreen and her bubbly personality. I disliked Kevin and thought he had become too possessive of her, so I stopped spending time with them.

Not really wanting to go back into another restaurant to work, I knew I would still have to find work pretty soon or starve. I walked along Bloor Street and stopped when I came upon a "Help Wanted" sign in the window of a One-Hour Martinizing shop. Luckily, I got the job and started the next morning. The job involved loading dirty socks, underwear and shirts into the big spin washing machines, moving the wash to the dryers and then folding the clean laundry. I would always feel so tired at the end of the day from working around the hot steam cleaners. I disliked this job and it didn't last very long. I didn't know what I wanted to do. I didn't know where to go. I was not happy in Toronto, nor was I happy in Vancouver. The life in both cities left me feeling alienated from my old school friends and feeling alone. Noreen still worked at the same office job and really liked it. She was spending all her extra time with Kevin and this left me feeling like I lost my best friend.

I quit the Martinizing job. With the rent due but with only a few dollars underneath my mattress, I bought the *Toronto Star* and scanned the "Help Wanted" ads again. I decided to check out a dry cleaning job on the outskirts of Toronto. It sounded the most promising of all the places I had called that day.

I left my room and headed to the nearest bus stop. I bought a couple of cream-filled French pastries from the corner store on Howland Avenue and boarded a bus to go to the outskirts of the city. After getting off the first bus, I needed to go farther into another bus zone, but I had become stingy about paying more bus fare. I decided to hitchhike instead. I stood at the bus stop and stuck out my thumb enjoying the warm, sunny afternoon in the early spring. A light blue convertible with its top down pulled up to the bus stop where I was standing.

The driver, a skinny man probably in his early fifties, leaned over and asked me if I wanted a ride. I looked at driver and his passenger wondering if it would be safe to take a ride. The man in the passenger side was quite handsome. He was wearing a blue Wrangler jacket and worn Levis pants, but the driver looked peculiar. I carefully studied his sharp features and smiled at this small, shrivelled-up man with a receding hairline and pointed chin. I found him skinny and unattractive. With some fear, I climbed into the back seat of the car. Once inside the car, I began telling the men of my predicament. The driver told me they owned a jeans factory in downtown Toronto and bragged how successful their business was. He offered me a job in their factory, assuring me I could start right away.

Delighted to have found a job I slid back in the seat and rested my head on the leather upholstery, enjoying the afternoon breeze. We drove to a small delicatessen not far from the spot where they had picked me up. As we entered the unkept deli, the pungent odour of stale salami filled the air. I waited by the door. Inside, the skinny driver told me to follow him to the back room. I obliged. Calmly he told me to lift up my skirt, pull down my panties and bend over.

Shocked, I stood there. I wanted the job and thought that if I did not do as he asked, the job would no longer be available. I did as he requested. He unzipped his pants and forced his hard penis into my anus. I could feel sharp pain as he entered. I begged him to stop.

"Not until I'm finished!" he replied sharply. I couldn't hold back the tears anymore. It hurt and I whimpered as I counted the many times he poked his long hard penis into my rectum.

I wanted to scream, "STOP!" It was frightening and I felt like throwing up. Finally, he finished and I went into the bathroom, gagging. I soaped my bottom until it felt like I was tearing the skin off. When I came out of the bathroom, he simply told me to leave. I made my way out the back door and walked until I reached the highway. I stood at the nearest bus stop, almost parallel to where they had picked me up but on the opposite side of the eight-lane freeway. Dwelling on what just happened, I was humiliated! I wondered where the other man had waited. I suspect he was out in the front of the deli. I hated the creeps and became very angry. I seethed at the thought of their taking advantage of me. I hoped I would never see either of them again. I caught the next bus and returned to my room, still shaken. I checked underneath the mattress to again count the few dollars I had left. My money was stolen! All $65.00. I was now flat broke and immediately suspected the landlady because she was the only one who had a pass-key. Her room was down the dark hall from mine and she stayed in her place all the time. If she had a husband, I never did see him. Her room was always locked and she came out only on rent day. I asked her who used a pass-key, entered my room and stole my money. The overweight, introverted woman denied going into my room and proceeded to ask where the rent money was. I told her I would have it shortly, although how I would get it I didn't know.

"How dare she ask me," I thought, "after stealing my last few dollars. The nerve!" At the same time, I was furious because I knew she was the thief even though she denied entering my room. How I longed to get even—with anyone for the kind of day this had turned out to be. First, I was raped, then robbed. Wasn't there anyone to trust? If only I had just one friend, someone to comfort me or even just listen to me. There was no one! I never felt so rejected and helpless.

The next day, I wandered around the neighbourhood trying to figure out what to do next. I came by a strange looking little fellow, somewhat of a weirdo. He was scrawny, had natural curly hair and wore horn-rimmed glasses. As I approached him, he stared at me with inquiring eyes but continued cleaning the windows of the house. I walked up to him and asked him if he knew of any place I could stay. I told him I had no money and was desperate. I assured him that I could get jobs, but I was in a bind right now. He introduced himself as Waldo and said he could help. He mentioned that he was the landlord and could put me up for a couple of days. I was so relieved. I thanked him and said I would be back in a very short while. I returned to my former room and quickly packed my few belongings and snuck out before the landlady appeared. I went right back to Waldo's place.

Waldo showed me to a bedroom with two rickety old mattresses on the floor. I unpacked and rested on a mattress thinking about the many moves I had made in the past year. It did not please me. Sometimes I'd just sit on the mattress and watch Waldo run up and down the stairs to all the different rooms with a bunch of keys jangling in his pocket. There was always a flurry of activity in his two-storey house. Scruffy-looking bikers lived in the basement and were always coming in and out. They scared me. Waldo was constantly talking on the phone. Once, I asked him who he was always talking to. He said he just knew a lot of people. He was a "square john" but informed me his tenants in the basement were druggies. He claimed he had no part in their drug activities. He told me they were selling speed and sold their drugs right from their basement home. I thought this pretty risky but didn't question it further.

Although I found Waldo rather dull-witted, he still had normal sexual urges. I was not attracted to him in anyway. However, since he had normal sexual desires, I had to let him fondle me; otherwise I would have had to live in the streets. He fondled me a few times until I persuaded him we could be friends without touching. He repulsed me sexually but was kind in every other way. When Waldo approached me, it turned me off even more as I had the feeling that I was prostituting myself for a place to stay. I was also affected by the earlier experience as well. The rape in the deli was very fresh in my mind. All men were repulsive to me now. But I needed someone. Waldo would go to the corner store and bring something home for supper every night. Usually it was just a sandwich or sweet rolls with some Cokes.

At first, I stayed in my room and hardly went out. I found this too tiresome so I started going downtown to the Village where all the hippies hung out. Gradually, I made a few friends and joined them injecting speed or dropping LSD. This was ideal. I didn't have to work because Waldo provided a place to stay. With my new-found friends, it became routine to rush on speed all night. Other times we would drop hits of purple micro-dot acid and wait for the hallucinations to begin. I dove right into the drug scene.

I wanted to fit in and be a part of the crowd so much that I would do anything anybody asked me. I had a few bad trips of acid so I decided to stick to injecting or swallowing small crystals of speed. I would ask Waldo for money whenever I couldn't get drugs freely. At first, he would give me a little money but soon he refused. Within a short time of using drugs, I started to become paranoid. I became depressed and withdrawn. I stopped going downtown and stayed in my room, seldom letting anyone in. I contemplated ending my life. I wanted to die.

One afternoon while sitting on the mattress on the floor in Waldo's room, I spotted a bottle of turpentine in the corner of his room. Quite depressed, I decided to poison myself. Eyeing the bottle, I thought I would wait until he went out for supper that night and steal it. Returning to my room, I closed the door and waited for him to leave. Finally, I could hear the jingling of keys in his pocket. When I heard him dash down the stairs, I walked down the hallway and into his room. I took the bottle of turpentine and hid it in the bathroom. I decided that I would drink it later, not really having the courage at the time. However, life in the spirit world seemed my only escape. I did not care for—nor understand—this futile existence of depression and loneliness which tugged at me daily.

When Waldo returned he carried a medium-sized pizza. He tapped on my door and asked me to join him in his room for supper. I came over and nibbled on a piece of pizza, but then told him I was tired and wanted to go back to bed. I walked down the hallway and into the bathroom and opened the bottle of turpentine that I had concealed underneath the bathroom sink. I was ready now.

I poured out a capful and drank it quickly. It tasted dreadful. I felt like throwing up, but knew I would have to drink much more for it to be fatal. I found the taste so dreadful I could not drink anymore. I put the cap back on. Feeling very sick to my stomach I spent the rest of the night burping up the after-taste of turpentine flavoured with pepperoni pizza.

I never did tell Waldo what happened that night, nor did he miss the bottle of turpentine. There were times, though, when he did mention the drop-in clinic and suggest I go there. The clinic was on the same street as we lived on, Madison Avenue. He had become concerned because I stayed in my room and was unusually afraid of everyone, even him, at times. Several days later, he went to the clinic without telling me. That afternoon, I heard a tapping on my bedroom door. When I peeked out Waldo and a well-dressed young woman stood outside the door. Waldo stepped back and leaned over the railing. The woman smiled. She introduced herself as an alcohol and drug counsellor. I gave Waldo a questioning look and he began explaining why he brought her here.

She and Waldo coaxed me into checking into the Clarke Institute to get help for my drug problems. They both assured me the paranoia I was experiencing could be treated. Finally I replied, "Let me think about it." A couple of days later I asked Waldo to walk to the institution with me. It was at the corner of College and Spadina, some distance from where we lived. When Waldo checked me into the psychiatric ward on the twelfth floor, I actually did feel relief. I would now be getting help. Waldo left assuring me he'd come by for a visit after I got settled in. We had become pretty good friends, and he did come to visit once.

The first few days on the psych ward were frightening. I needed to let someone in my family know what was happening to me so far from home. I dialled the operator and asked her to place a collect call to my Uncle Jeff, who lived in a small community on the outskirts of Vancouver. When Uncle Jeff's soft voice came on the phone, he asked what I was doing in an institution. I didn't tell him the truth. I did not want my family to get wind of any drug dependency. Instead, I said I just needed a good rest and some help to sort out my problems. We talked briefly. Upon hanging up the phone, I returned to my room and cried. I was feeling lonely and so confused. I had just wanted to hear my uncle say, "We love you, Mary, and care what happens to you." But he hadn't.

The nurses at the institute were supportive and watched every move the patients made, especially at meal times. There was one friendly Black nurse who sat beside me at meal times. She observed everything I put on my plate. The food was superb, and I enjoyed sampling almost everything on display in the self-serve cafeteria. I loaded my tray with fresh fruit, tossed green salad, the main meat dish and a dessert. I loved the creamy Boston-cream pies but usually had only room for Jell-O. Food was consoling and my appetite really improved. I started to feel comfortable but still isolated myself in my room a fair amount of the time. On some days I'd feel so homesick for my hometown, friends and family. A lump in my throat would form as I'd stand by the locked window, gazing down at the tiny figures hustling and bustling in the streets below.

Each day I compared myself to the other patients but felt that I was not mentally ill like them. One lady talked continuously about the shock treatments she underwent for a nervous breakdown. Others wandered around the day-room idly with no real connection to anything. Some were in pretty bad shape and talked to themselves. Others, heavily sedated, would just sit and stare at everybody. Some fell asleep shortly after their meal. The doctors were more attentive to the severely disturbed patients. For me it was a time to dry out and deal with drug addiction so that I could return back to some sort of normalcy.

Becoming a patient after leaving the house on Madison with all the bikers was a relief to me. However, I did not anticipate bringing along little crotch critters when I entered Clarke Institute. We all shared a communal bathroom over at Waldo's place and the house was infested with crawly crabs. When admitted to the clinic, I didn't feel too itchy so I didn't say anything. A few patients started scratching soon after I came. I dared not confess that I was the culprit but looked on as the entire floor was fumigated. We were all told to shower and rub a white lotion all over our bodies to kill the little pests. I found it amusing when one of the patients, a mentally ill young man, about six feet tall came bouncing into the recreation room with a large towel over his head, laughing loudly and still scratching his crotch.

I stayed at Clarke Institute for a month. Now in a clearer state of mind and much healthier, I considered finding a new place to stay. The Black nurse at the institution referred me to the Sancta Maria house, a government-sponsored half-way home for discharged female patients. I was now prepared to start living a better life rather than continuing to induce drugs and making me mentally and physically lethargic.

It was a bright warm afternoon. I enjoyed the long walk to Bernard Avenue, carrying my light blue suitcase. Beautiful elm trees lined both sides of the street. The Sancta Maria house, situated at l04 Bernard Avenue was a homey, older style three-storey house. I reached into my pocket and pulled out the piece of paper to double-check the address. Nervous and uncertain, I walked up the few steps and knocked on the door. A woman opened the door and smiled widely. She was very gentle and kind. She had long grey hair pulled back in a ponytail and was in her early fifties. She stood quite tall. With enthusiasm she said, "Hi, come on in." She introduced herself as Betty and added that she was expecting me. Right away I noticed her harelip and thought what a good job had been done to correct it. Her face radiated genuine tenderness.

Betty led me upstairs to a cute, country-style corner bedroom. Bright pink bedspreads were on each of the two single beds. There were frilly curtains on both windows. Every room in the house was spotless and contained modern furnishings. The home accommodated about ten girls. A place for parolees and pregnant young girls, it also served as a drop-in centre for those who had resided here before. Betty lived in during the week and had a supervisor replace her on the weekends. My next impression was that Betty loved the girls and mothered us as though each girl was her own.

At supper time, it was a family-get-together in the big dining room. Betty would sit at the head of the long antique dining room table and banter with everyone. She was genuinely concerned for our well-being. I felt shy and awkward in this halfway home. I felt like a drop-out. At first, I remained quiet and ate supper with my head down. I was always the first to leave after the meal. I never added to the conversations but merely answered if Betty asked how I was doing. Paranoia still plagued me.

As the months slowly passed, I became more relaxed. I enjoyed lazing around in the early summer afternoons in the back yard. Betty wanted us to all get back on our feet and become self-sufficient as soon as we could. We were allowed to live here for six months.

Eventually, I found a job, within walking distance, at the Snow White Laundry. I worked in the reception area waiting on customers who came to pick up their dry cleaning or laundry. I enjoyed my work here. It only paid the minimum wage which at that time was $2.50 an hour, but it did feel good to be working and away from the rooming house on Madison. I contributed some of my earnings toward room and board at Sancta Maria house. We were lucky—a cook came in everyday to prepare nutritious meals. I enjoyed coming home from work to tasty, hot suppers. I opened up and was much more comfortable with the girls there.

Having ballooned out to about 155 pounds during my stay at Clarke Institute and living at Sancta Maria house, I did not like feeling so chubby. I visited the neighbourhood doctor and requested a prescription for diet pills. It cost only ten dollars for 30 Preludin pills. I did not realize these enormous pills were amphetamines. The pills were very potent. I wondered why I couldn't stop talking and why I became so energetic each time I took a whole pill. I would feel high from the pills and stay up all night, grinding my teeth to jibber-jabber to anyone who would listen. I needed to keep my hands busy, as I could not stay still. One evening, I stayed up all night and made a beautiful silk caftan for Betty. She was very pleased with her long pink flowered gown and paid me $20 for sewing so energetically. I did not tell her I was high from the diet pills and was rather surprised she never noticed my erratic behaviour. The pounds gradually dropped off and I started taking half of a pill. Still, my heart fluttered and I always had a nervous twitch around my eye when I took even half a pill.

I didn't like working in the laundry anymore because I was having paranoia attacks again. I was paranoid of people who were in authority. Their voices were enough to make me shaky. While I had felt quite secure when I left the institution, the use of prescription drugs took me right back to the same crazy thinking and fear I remembered so well from Madison Avenue.

During the fifth month of my stay at Sancta Maria house, I contacted Noreen and asked her to come for a visit. Within a few days of the call, she did come. It was a cold winter evening in December, and she was wearing a long black maxi coat. It looked like her secretary job had changed her social status because she acted like we were strangers. She didn't stay too long. We found very little in common and hardly talked while sitting together on the living room sofa. I suspected she now shunned me because I was a drug addict.

I was finding the winter too cold in Toronto and debated whether to move again. This time, I didn't know where to go. I did not want to wander around the streets of any big city anymore and had certainly grown tired of Toronto. Coming to this city had left me scarred. Toronto had seen me raped, robbed of my last dollar and finally confined to a mental institution. When I talked about leaving, Betty advised me of a half-way home in Vancouver that housed native women. She suggested I find the place, try to get settled, maybe stay in one place and do something with my life. I left, saying goodbye to Betty. I loved her and knew I would miss her and all the other girls. Once again I found myself leaving people I'd grown to like and almost trust.

It was shortly after Christmas when I left. I was back at the Canadian National Railway train station boarding another train. I slumped in a seat on the train, staring emptily at people walking in the aisles. The conductor, a jovial Black man recognized me from the many train trips and said, "You look like you have stars in your eyes." Of course, I had concealed some speed in my purse before boarding the train and injected some in the bathroom on the train before it started moving. I still found the high helped to relieve some of the fears I was feeling. When I came down it was worse. I wanted to hide from people and, although this temporary escape from reality took the edge off, I knew its after-effects. I didn't really care too much about my mental health at this point.

A very distraught twenty-year-old, I arrived on the front steps of a large, three-storey colonial house at 666 West 12th in Vancouver. A native lady opened the door and asked me to come in. I asked her if this was the place native women could stay. She replied, "Yes" and asked where I was from. I told her I was in between cities and needed a place to call home. The short native lady with a shy smile and a limp introduced herself as Florence.

"Welcome," she said softly. "Come on in. I'll introduce you to the other girls." I was happy to find a place and live with people of my own kind. I thought of Betty and was very thankful she told me about this place. I just knew this would be the end of all the tiresome train trips back and forth across Canada. The one thing I really did enjoy on my cross-country train trips was the beautiful scenery. I would sit up in dome car and watch the bright lights of the train blazing through the dark night leaving a parade of trees behind.

I just knew this place would be the ideal home. A week or so later, after getting all settled in, I talked to Florence briefly about getting some professional help for the barrage of mental inconsistencies I had been experiencing. She said she would talk to Bea, the house counsellor, within the next few days.

Bea arrived at work on Monday morning and my first impression of her was that she sure had pretty long blond hair. Having a sunny disposition, she laughed loudly at anything. Sometimes she roared with laughter even though the joke wasn't particularly funny. She understood the girls and had an answer to any problem. I took a shine to her right away.

Her office, tucked away in a far corner of the basement, was always busy with young women coming in and out. Mostly, they were getting some kind of help, usually counselling or some type of career direction. Bea and I talked in her office for quite some time. I explained the things that had happened since leaving Vernon. She explained to me that I was in dire need of seeing a psychiatrist and immediately set me up to see a prominent analyst who treated all the wayward Indian girls who landed on the doorstep of Nasaika Lodge.

Bea spent a lot of time with a young, Chinese-looking native girl Jo-Anne who continually slashed her wrists or arms. This behaviour happened almost every weekend after Jo-Anne inhaled nail polish remover. She would pour the polish remover into a plastic bag and sniff it until she was dazed and staggering around in oblivion. After almost every weekend, Jo-Anne would come home with bandages on her arms. Her arms were scarred from wrist to elbows with old and fresh razor blade marks. Sometimes she would break a glass and use the sharp edge to cut herself. Compared to her, I didn't think I had any real problems. Sometimes she lay on the highway after getting high and wait to get run over. Someone would always spot her and call the police. I could never figure out why Bea did not commit her to an institution where she could get professional help to stop sniffing and stop carving herself up. I have often wondered whatever happened to Jo-Anne. I don't expect her to be alive now if she didn't get straightened out. In the meantime, my "straightening out" began.

On the third floor of a downtown, high-rise, Ben, a short Oriental psychiatrist, emerged from his plush office. He stuck out his hand and squeezed my hand firmly as Bea introduced us. He escorted us past the reception area and into his office. He was quite jovial, smiling constantly as he peered through his dark-rimmed glasses. I studied him closely and hoped he would have the answers to all my problems. He listened attentively when I told him I was fearful and depressed. I told him I always felt I was on the brink of suicide. He prescribed antidepressants and we agreed to meet for one hour each week to discuss my progress. Each time I went to Ben, I told him I needed more tranquillizers. He kept prescribing more pills. Before long, I was swallowing up to six pills a day including three antidepressants during the day, 2 five-milligram yellow tablets of Valium to balance everything out and a sleeping pill at night. I imagined I was taking so many tiny yellow pills the whole room started to look yellow. I was so sedated

I could not identify with any feelings, but this was better than the anguish of before.

Bea suggested I attend the day classes held at the Vancouver Community College which was on the same street we lived but several blocks away. The school, located right next to Vancouver General Hospital, was an old run-down building with furniture that seemed to have been discarded by the regular schools. The teachers looked as ancient as the dimly-coloured school itself. Bea encouraged me to attend the adult basic education classes to upgrade and complete grade twelve. I went for about two weeks but was so foggy-minded from the pills that I almost fell asleep everyday. I decided school was not for me and dropped out.

Lounging around one day, I got a phone call from my long lost cousin Janice. I was surprised to hear from her. She asked if I would be home for the rest of the day. I replied that I would, and she said she would be over promptly. Within the hour she was ringing the doorbell. I couldn't figure out why would she wanted to see me so urgently. We greeted each other amicably and I asked her to join me for a cup of tea in the kitchen. After I poured the tea, she asked me to sit down. She said she was sorry, but she had to bring me bad news. I still didn't understand. Sitting down, she said, "Your brother Hugh died."

I couldn't believe it. My brother? He was perfectly fine the last time I had seen him while I was living at the LeDucs. With great emotion, Janice told me he had been in a car accident. He had been hitchhiking home after getting out of Okalla Prison and caught a ride with a drunk driver. Just outside of Vernon the car rolled and hit a telephone pole. Hugh went through the windshield. I took the cup of tea, smashed it on the floor and began to sob. Florence came right away and comforted me.

The next day I went to Vernon to attend Hugh's funeral. It was a closed coffin and the whole family was at Grandma's. It was a very sad time. It was good to see Marge again, but she was crying the whole three days and for a long, long time after the funeral. I left right after the funeral. I went back to Vancouver and numbed the loss by taking more tranquillizers. The drunk driver served three years in prison for criminal negligence.

I joined some of the other Indian girls, started to drink alcohol and frequent the bars on Hastings and Main Streets. I didn't want to work at any low paying jobs anymore. I didn't have to pay rent at Nasaika, so there was no real pressure to get a job. Most of the other girls hung out on Skid Row and invited me to join them. I accepted their invitation.

Sitting in the Rainier Hotel one Friday night, I experienced my first taste of saki, the Japanese liquor. A good-looking non-native man had ordered it for me and then introduced me to the delicate saki-drinking ceremony. We sipped it and later spent the night together in alcoholic oblivion. The prescription drugs mixed with the alcohol would make me black out any evening I drank. I didn't realize the effects the drugs were having but found I suffered more depression when I drank while taking antidepressants.

On my next visit to Ben's office, he realized the pills were not helping so he decided to wean me off them. I turned to heavier drinking. I began to feel like I was falling apart. I couldn't cope with anything anymore. I continued to drink heavily.

While still fairly new at Nasaika, early one morning around seven o'clock, I noticed a native fellow standing in the dining room. Busy in the large kitchen, I could feel him watching me as I made a cup of tea and some toast. Just standing there, he made me nervous. He introduced himself as

Tom and we started talking. He said he had just been re-leased from Okalla Prison. I asked what he was doing time for and he replied, "Assault causing bodily harm." He men-tioned that he hung out partying all night with the other girls from the house. Even though we were not supposed to have anyone at the house after curfew, Tom still made his way into the house. We talked easily and, as I looked at him, I was attracted to his good looks.

I had never seen such a handsome full-blooded Indian in all my travelling around the country. He was only twenty-four years old but very mature. Admiringly, I would glance at him then look away nervously. His wide shoulders fit snugly into his olive green shirt. I liked his dark complexion and shoulder-length hair, which he parted it down the centre.

I asked Tom where he was from. He smiled and replied, "Sechelt."

Of course, I had to ask where the heck was Sechelt. We talked quite awhile and he asked if I would be around later that day. I said, "Sure."

We started seeing each other and I felt like the happiest girl at Nasaika Lodge. I couldn't have asked for more. He wasn't interested in any of the other girls and I was pleased. Besides, I thought they all drank too much for him. We started going together right away and it wasn't long before I was hid-ing Tom upstairs on the third floor in my bedroom as he had no place to stay. Sometimes during the day, other girls would sneak their boyfriends up to our rooms and we'd keep them all harboured quietly. If we wanted to go out, Tom would climb down the fire escape and I'd meet him outside. We'd go up town and hang out in the streets or go to the parks. After supper each night, I would sneak food up to him. It wasn't long before one of the other girls squealed on us to

Florence. We knew we'd be getting kicked out, so we decided to leave Nasaika and find our own place.

Tom became the most beautiful person in my life. I never realized how much I had been searching for love until I met him. We were so happy together. In a room on East 12th, we set up housekeeping. We both filed for welfare and lived off our small income of $300.00 per month. Tom and I found happiness and a place to call home. Our home. I wanted this ecstasy to live forever.

I continued taking tranquillizers but not as many and was now seeing a different psychiatrist. Ben stopped prescribing pills so I found another psychiatrist, a few blocks from the Vancouver General Hospital. The doctor prescribed Librium and I was being treated for manic-depression. I sneaked the pills behind Tom's back. I dared not tell him I had severe emotional problems. I just knew each night as I lay in his arms that he would make everything perfect. Tom was there for me and I was there for him, or so I thought!

5

THE STREETS OF VANCOUVER

Living on social assistance, we decided to move downtown because where we were on East 12th was too far from the action. We rented a cheap room on the second floor of the Ford Hotel on Granville Street. We had to share the bathroom, and there was nothing in the room except a double bed and dresser.

Frequently, during our year together, Tom and I went to the bars on Granville Street where the Indians hung out. Every few days, we'd walk the streets and Tom would bum money from Indian brothers or sisters who would "lay" a couple of bucks on him. With an entrance fee of two dollars, I would sit alone in a bar. I'd eye some old man until he joined me and had drunk enough beers to become drunk and generous. Later on, Tom would slip in. By then, the tipsy old man didn't mind Tom joining us.

One afternoon, I was sitting in the Royal Hotel, a popular "Indian bar" on Granville, with enough money to buy a beer or two. We didn't have any more money for drinking, so Tom was out scavenging around for booze money. As I sat there, a transvestite befriended me. We talked for awhile until "she" urged me to follow her into the bathroom. Inside the bathroom she mixed a capful of heroin and injected the needle into her vein. She cleaned the syringe and offered me her "washing," or resin left over in the spoon with a little bit of water added. I couldn't resist and for the first time experienced the effects of heroin.

There was no real euphoria but it did set off a chemical reaction in my brain. I became obsessed with experiencing the real stuff; washings simply would not do. When Tom returned I told him what happened in the bathroom. He wasn't surprised as he had already experimented with heroin. Without any money, we returned to our hotel room but planned to get a cap as soon as possible. A few days later Tom made a good score and returned to the hotel room with a bundle of bills. I never asked how Tom got the money but was pretty sure he rolled somebody. We left for the Royal Hotel and started to drink. He left the bar and returned shortly with a cap of heroin. We quickly went back to our room and fixed. From that moment I wanted to "use" any chance we could get. Back then a cap of heroin cost $14.00 and it was usually cut, or watered down considerably, with other white powder granules. Lactose was commonly used to replace a good portion of heroin. Ether was added too. When heated to its boiling point the ether would give that breath-taking big rush when the heroin is injected into the vein or main-lined into the main artery. This mixture of China White was then sold on the street in small clear jell capsules or caps.

We planned to "put out" or sell heroin in the street so we could use everyday. Tom knew a dealer who could front us our first few caps until we made enough to pay the money back and score again. We sold what he gave us and kept selling more until we saved enough from the profits to buy our first "bundle" which was twenty-five caps at a cost of two hundred dollars. Within a month we were up to fixing about four times a day, doing half a cap each. We sold merely to support our habits and were not too concerned with making a big profit. We were able to move out of the small and cheap hotel room into a modest and bright one-bedroom apartment on the corner of Fraser and Eleventh Avenue.

Since leaving Okalla Prison, Tom had not reported once to his parole officer. He had a year of parole to complete and was now wanted on a parole violation. Regardless, we strolled the streets and continued to sell. Sitting in the Columbia Hotel on Skid Row one muggy summer afternoon, Tom got busted by the police and was taken to the city jail for a routine check. This wasn't unusual because a lot of the Indians were often taken into custody to cross-check to see if they were suspects on any recent robberies or crimes in the city. The police didn't do a fingerprint check on Tom. Consequently, he was released the same day under his alias, Doug Norris. Nevertheless, he went into hiding. He knew the cops would pick him up sooner or later on the bench warrant and correctly identify him.

In order to support our habits, I had to sell in the streets alone. I dreaded this. Dealers were being held at knife-point by thugs. Dealers handed over their bundles of dope or suffered the consequences. Stabbings were an everyday occurrence. One hot afternoon, Tom and I with other native friends lazed in the park just up from Pigeon Square on Hastings Street. We saw a man running to the water fountain to wash off the blood which was squirting from his face. He had received a long knife slash along his cheek. Word got around later this man was supposed to smuggle two caps of heroin to someone in Okalla but used them for himself instead. So every time he looked in the mirror now he had a reminder:

do not rip people off. This happened in broad daylight yet nobody saw anything!

A code of silence existed; otherwise any snitch could easily get bumped off. Another incident happened when I was sitting in the bar selling dope. A petite, good-looking Indian woman named Harriet went into the washroom and never came out alive. Some guy wearing a woman's wig walked in behind her and slashed her throat before she could lock the bathroom door. She was stabbed before sitting on the toilet and died instantly after her jugular vein was cut. Apparently it was over a deal that went unpaid when Jake, her husband, got busted and landed in jail. Word soon got around that Jake owed money and the supplier used Harriet as collateral. Few people stood around and watched as the ambulance arrived and she was taken away on the stretcher. The paramedics hauled her into the alleyway and into the ambulance with a blanket covering her entire body. The knife and wig were retrieved and it became another unsolved crime involving an Indian.

Jake ended up serving a lengthy time in Okalla Prison for trafficking heroin, but business carried on as usual in the Broadway Hotel after Harriet's murder. There was really nothing that shocked us that happened on Skid Row. It was the way of life on the streets. Even though Harriet and Jake were a young couple with two little children, no one on the streets cared. While I really didn't feel any fear despite everything that was happening around us everyday, Tom wanted someone to work with me since it had become too risky to walk the streets alone. We asked our friend Jim if he wanted a job. He was agreeable and it didn't cost us too much because he liked to "chippy," meaning that he was not hooked yet and could get by with fixing very little in a day. We could afford him because he was content with fixing one cap a day, which cost us only $8.00. He didn't draw heat from the narcs because he looked like any working man. Jim didn't dress in grubby street clothes. He always wore a nice pair of dress pants and a clean shirt. He kept his hair cropped and neatly combed, unlike most of the long-haired brothers.

Every morning Jim would stop by our one-room apartment over on Fraser and Eleventh Street. We'd all fix for breakfast and catch the bus downtown to do our business. Tom would sit in the Palace Hotel or the Grand Union Hotel, both out-of-the-way bars farther up Hastings Street. These places were seldom patrolled by the narcs or police on the beat looking for drug dealers or wanted individuals. I strolled beside Jim everyday. Underneath my tongue, I carried a balloon filled with the gel caps rolled in baby powder to keep them from sticking together. A maximum of 25 caps could fit in the balloon and by keeping it in my mouth it was easy to swallow if I had to.

Around eight or nine o'clock every night I would come and join Tom for a quick fix. We would take turns in the bathroom mixing and cooking up a cap of heroin in the teaspoon. Quickly, I'd crank up, injecting a cap of diluted heroin into my main artery to feel "well" again. Already we were hooked. We'd fix again when we went home. Then, off I'd go back into the streets with Jim to sell the rest of the bundle. Usually by about eleven o'clock each night I would have sold the rest.

We couldn't get another bundle until the first bundle was sold as we needed $200.00 to cop our next bundle from the middle man. For each bundle sold, there was a profit of $150.00 but we didn't make this much because we were fixing up and giving one away to Jim.

Narcs were popping up everywhere. We never sat in bars very long, as it was too obvious if there was steady traffic around the table as people came to score. A narc sitting nearby could spot us easily and once the heat was on, selling downtown was pretty well over. Police were always walking through the bars looking for the regular dealers. Snitches were common too and worked with the narcs to set up dealers or lead narcs to the middlemen.

I sold only to people I knew well. Word got out pretty quickly if someone was a snitch. While I ducked into alleys to sell, Jim kept watch on the street. We briefly sat in bars and exchanged money and caps underneath the table. We sold in small cafes. We did our business right on the corner in front of the Broadway Hotel at Broadway and Main Street. We sold when and wherever we could. Tom and I opened a bank account at the Royal Bank on Broadway and Main Street. It grew gradually. In about four months we saved almost two thousand dollars. But that dwindled within a couple of weeks when there was a gigantic round-up on the streets. We stopped selling with all the heat around.

Drug dealers were busted everywhere. Luckily, I did not land in jail. I had always sold to people who I knew weren't snitches. But now the streets were dry and scarcely anyone was putting out or selling. Most of the connections were sitting in jail, trying to get bail. The cost of a cap went up to $20.00 so Tom and I were taking out $150.00 a day to feed our habits. We were up to three caps each a day. It was hard to get our own supply, but we managed to score. It was eerie—the streets were deserted! A few weeks later and nearly broke, we began selling again. Most of the middlemen had been able to raise bail and were back in business. Others faced sentences for long, long periods of time. It didn't matter, though, because when one middleman left the streets there was another to quickly take his place. The price dropped to $14.00 a cap, as there was plenty again.

Back in business and for about three months, we continued selling on the streets. One day the police were doing a routine check and arrested Tom at the Grand Union Hotel while he was playing pool. He was taken in, fingerprinted and charged with parole violation. He was not released on his own recognisance and remained in Okalla Prison waiting trial. I was now on my own. Jim and I worked the streets until it become virtually impossible to do business anymore.

One warm summer afternoon, while walking down a side street I was eating cherries. I popped a few in my mouth and spit out the seeds. As I was digging in the bag for more, I spotted two straight-looking men just ahead. One man was standing inside the doorway of a side entrance to a bar. The other was standing a few feet away, directly across from him. I suspected these men were narcs. Sure enough they were! I nudged Jim and said, "Just keep walking." I sensed danger and became nervous. Instead of eating more cherries I popped the baby-powdered balloon of dope into my mouth and swallowed it.

As I came up to them, one man leaped at me. I got choked right on the spot. My knees buckled as I dropped to the ground. I could hardly breathe, and as I went down, I wet my pants. The narc held me by the throat until my tongue hung out and I started to black out. Jim stood by, shocked. He didn't say a word. Finally, the narc released his big hands from my throat and seeing I didn't spit anything out, he gloated, "We'll get you, sooner or later." He got off me and stood up and brushed himself off. They took me to the police station and I was searched. I had almost $200.00 stuffed in different pants pockets.

Receiving $14.00 for each cap, I was paid mostly with 10's and 2's folded together, crumpled in my pockets. The narcs couldn't charge me because they were unable to prove where the money came from. They asked where I got it from. I told them someone had borrowed money and paid me back. Sarcastically, they said it was ironic all the ten and two-dollar bills were folded together. I continued to deny selling. It was a comforting thought to know the bundle was safe in my stomach with the chewed up cherries. I was released without any charges and warned to quit selling on the streets.

When I went back downtown Jim was nowhere in sight. I caught the bus and went to our apartment and stuck my hand down my throat and threw up. The bundle came up easily, all mixed with semi-digested cherries. I washed the balloon off and fixed. The next morning Jim came to the apartment and told me he did not want to put out anymore. He said it was too risky. I agreed. Our partnership came to an abrupt end. However, I continued to sell but moved from Skid Row to the streets in Gastown, a short distance away. I thought it would be safer because the cops and narcs in that section of town didn't know me. I still had a habit and didn't know how long I would last putting out alone.

Early one morning, after a quick visit to Okalla to see Tom, I went to the Gastown Inn. Since restoration by the city took place, this area, although still in the Skid Row district, had a better image than around Columbia and Hastings Street. Therefore, it was not patrolled as often. I was less conspicuous here. The street had nick-named the resident RCMP officers the "Bobsie twins." They "knew" that everybody in drugs spent most of their time over on Hastings, not in Gastown.

With a bundle of heroin inside a balloon tucked under my tongue, I sat in the bar in my new location. The regulars came in and out looking to score. Others were selling their own caps. In the bar, a thin, ordinary-looking bartender would often come by with his tray of beer. I hardly drank. I sipped slowly on a beer for long periods of time. The bartender looked curiously at me. Each time he came by, he'd raise his eyebrows to see if I wanted to buy another beer. I'd shake my head. Periodically someone would come to the table and buy from me. Usually, the people from Skid Row came to Gastown Inn to score if they couldn't find it on the streets. I also had my regular clientele. They all said I sold quality dope. Feeling uncomfortable with the bartender, I thought of how to pacify him. Whenever he came by, I'd order a beer, although it sat and went stale. I'd lay extra coins on his tray. Pleased with his tips, he looked the other way when I was busy selling.

I came regularly to the Gastown Inn. Most afternoons I sat inconspicuously amongst the regulars. I kept my distance from the bikers. I did not want to interfere in their business and went pretty well unnoticed by them. Without too much trouble, I sold under the table to the sniffling druggies. I felt safer selling in the bar but constantly watched the front door for police and narcs. The bartender introduced himself as John and we became friends. He was not the type of person I had expected to co-operate. John had warned me of the usual times the "heat" came in so I would make myself scarce. The crowds hanging around Gastown Inn were mainly hookers, pimps, and so-called "rounders." Rounders was a fashionable street name to describe those who were regulars on the streets and had been around a long time. These were the ones dealers turned to in order to find out who was selling good dope, who were good middlemen, who was selling bad stuff, who the snitches were and so on. They were the most well informed of all the street people. Rounders were respected and were usually older males who fit in at the top end of the street hierarchy.

I was nearing my twenty-first birthday and not proud of what I did in order to survive. I didn't like putting out in the streets but with a full-blown habit of about six caps a day, I had no choice. I didn't feel the loss of Tom too much because I was always "fixed" and unconnected to any real feelings. I visited him a couple of times but soon stopped phoning or going to see him. Our relationship ended, and I never did find out how long he was sentenced for, but somehow I suspect it was for another year.

At the Gastown Inn, John became more friendly. He was curious about my small operation. He seemed to tire of tips on his tray and wanted more. Late one afternoon, he asked me to join him in his hotel room upstairs after work to discuss business. I agreed. His shift ended and we went to his hotel room on the second floor. Once inside the dingy room, he explained his background a little. He told me he travelled quite a bit, was from the States and picked up odd jobs in big cities. I wasn't concerned about his past; I wanted to find out what his business proposition was. As we sat and talked longer I found him quite boring. He didn't rush to explain the purpose of our meeting. I thought he dressed fashionably but looked old for his thirty-five years. He didn't seem the type to settle with working in bars; he appeared more like a businessman.

He asked me if I was making a profit in my operation. I replied, "Business as usual. Supports my habit." I also told him I was being watched by the narcs over on Hastings, and my time was very short before they'd catch on to my new spot. He listened while I told of the situation involving Tom as well. Soon after, our meeting took a different twist.

John asked if I would like to get off the streets and let him handle my business. I hesitated and asked what was in it for me. He assured me I could live in the nicest apartment, have all the drugs I needed, and be safe from the narcs. In return, he wanted to know who my connections were and asked that I turn him onto them. I hesitated because there is a loyalty amongst the dealers and middlemen on the streets. Their identities are always kept highly secret. I didn't know John well enough to take him on my next pick-up and had to give his proposal some thought. He told me to think about it and asked me where I lived. I told him I was living on Eleventh and Fraser. I felt a trust as our talk continued.

The thought of getting off the streets was too good an offer to resist, so I agreed to take him on the next pick-up. The next day, I phoned the middleman. John met the first middleman, and I introduced him to a second. In return he handed me a bundle of heroin, and in a very short time I moved in with him into a modern one bedroom high rise apartment in the West End. The apartment had plush green shag carpeting and modern furniture. The view of English Bay was spectacular. I thought the blue waters were magnificent. I'd sit in the easy chair, fix and stay high. John would come home at the end of the day only to shower, get dressed in trendy clothes and go out again. He wasn't very interested in me. I'd watch him bring out his wads of money and count the $100-bills in the bedroom and put them back into a shoe box. I asked how he could make so much money when I couldn't and he'd simply answer that it was because I was a junky and he wasn't. I settled for that and didn't bother asking any more questions. Whenever my supply got low, he'd replace it with another bundle of twenty-five caps. I could fix at any time of the day. All I did was sit in the apartment, stare at the blue waters, close my eyes and nod.

Not only was John selling heroin, but also he was getting to know the speed dealers. Often he would bring home crystal methadrine. I didn't like speed because of what it had done to me in Toronto but thought I would try some anyhow. Already, within probably a month, I was up to using about fifteen caps of heroin a day. I started cranking speed too. When I'd be on a four-or five-day run and needed to come down, I'd pop the big blue barbiturates that John provided. I became oblivious to the day or the month. My mind was so fogged up from the drugs I became a vegetable. I just lay in the bed or sit in the easy chair and stared out into space. My mind was like a vacuum. I had lost the desire to eat or sleep or do anything. I'd just sit and vegetate.

Sometimes at night I would scream at the ugly hallucinations which formed regularly on the wall. Mostly, they were big ugly faces that sneered at me. When I'd close my eyes I could see them. They were, of course, caused by lack of sleep, as well as by my dropping the barbs, inducing heroin and cranking speed. I was a zombie, yet John didn't object to how much I used. He was only concerned about making big bucks and thriving in a very lucrative business. I imagined things and became very paranoid. I lived in a locked apartment and what little was left of my mind whirled with crazy thoughts everyday. I imagined fires in the apartment, but they were really only the heat coming from the heat register. I constantly watched the "armies of soldiers" protecting me while I lay on the bed in the bedroom. They were really the many tucks or pleats in the drapes, but which I hallucinated then as armies of little men. Anytime I tried to nibble on food, it transformed in front of my eyes into decayed little worms, some of which were live and crawling. Once John left behind on the coffee table a Mars bar, and I went to nibble on a piece of it. When I opened it, it turned into a chunk of faeces, and I became repulsed and dropped it on the coffee table. I couldn't look at any food without its changing shape.

Once, I spotted myself in the mirror after a bath and was freaked out by the ribs that stuck out. I hardly recognized myself. I knew it wasn't a hallucination because I could feel and plainly see the bones that stuck out. I hardly had a bath after that and never looked in the mirror anymore. I was down to about ninety pounds, and being five foot four, looked like a severely under-nourished, hunched-over and pathetic dope-user. It did not occur to me to seek help; I just got weaker and weaker. During this ordeal, the odd time John would try to interest me in sex, but I was a basket case. I was incapable of doing anything, let alone having sex. I regressed to lying in bed most of the time, never changing clothes, and getting up only to go to the bathroom to urinate. I did remember to sit on the bed and fix. I was not conscious of how much heroin I was putting into the teaspoon anymore nor did I know if I was really getting high. I could no longer distinguish reality from hallucination. I suffered no aches from withdrawal, so even in such an idiotic state of mind, I must have held some very regular sessions of cooking up to keep withdrawal at bay.

At nights, sometimes John left the FM radio on before going out again. He liked the soul music by Black singers and by flute-player Herbie Mann featured on this station. Listening to the sound of the flute made me feel lonely. The music on the radio was soothing, and it was the only thing that didn't change; the sounds remained normal and did not become imaginary voices in my head. I lay in bed, day after day, like this. No longer having any desire to eat now produced no need to use the bathroom to relieve myself anymore.

I felt like I was going crazy. One day, while sitting in the easy chair I started to hallucinate again. I looked out at the blue sky and across the bay to the top of a mountain. On top of the mountain I imagined three crosses. Two of the crosses were standing. The third cross was upside down, the cross-bar close to the ground. I had a startling revelation that the third cross was for me and soon I'd be six feet under, going to hell. I realized my self-destruction, but it seemed too late. The drugs didn't make me feel good anymore. I became fearful at the least little sound. The paranoia was getting too much.

One day I decided to leave the city and go to Jeff and Bonnie's place in Surrey. I wanted to get off the drugs and get help but didn't know what to do. That morning, I mixed up the usual, probably two caps, as that's what I usually put in a spoon, although I was brain dead and not all together sure of what I was doing. Sitting at the kitchen table I contemplated how to get to Jeff and Bonnie's. I hardly knew my way around the apartment but somehow I figured I could find a way to get out to Surrey. Taking the balloon from a corner spot where the carpet had been lifted, I tucked it in my pocket and headed out into the streets. It was an early fall afternoon, so it was a bit chilly out. I had some money because I took a cab from Vancouver but got out long before arriving in Surrey. The next place that I remember was a large parking area in a mall somewhere between Vancouver and New Westminster.

The cab driver must have let me off in the parking lot, as I told him I didn't have much money. While wandering around the parking lot, I looked at this large building. On the far side of it was a mural painting of a beautiful girl with a big hairdo. Right away I thought it was a painting of Marge and wondered why someone would have her picture on the building. I must have been homesick as I imagined this. What I distinctly remember is standing inside a fast food restaurant waiting to be served something to drink—probably coffee. As it turned out, I leaned my arm up on the counter and nodded off standing at the counter. Someone there called the police. They couldn't believe that I could just fall asleep standing up. It was easy—I just closed my eyes and dozed off. Soon the police car arrived and I could feel someone tugging at the sleeve of my jacket. "Excuse me, Miss" I heard the officer say.

"Yes," I answered sleepily.

"You'll have to come with me," he said arousing me from my nod. "These people say you have fallen asleep while waiting for your order," the officer continued.

Not at all surprised by the commotion, I just stood there, unresponsive. The officer led me to his car outside. He could see I was harmless and offered me a seat in the front. By now I had become fully aware of what was happening but was still pretty tired.

I asked him where he was taking me and he replied, "Down to the station, to do a check on you." I didn't mind. I told the officer I was planning to go to my aunt and uncle's place in Surrey. I stated that I just wanted to get out of Vancouver. When we arrived at the police station, the officer came around and opened the door and escorted me in. The first thing they did was search my pockets. In the pocket of my jacket was a bundle of heroin—probably close to 20 caps. I was busted! Immediately booked on a possession of heroin charge, I was placed in a holding cell. When the officer was driving me to the station, I knew the balloon was in my pocket, and there was an opportunity to swallow it when the officer got out and came around to open the door. I just didn't think rationally anymore. I was not in reality. Everything was meaningless until the cell door slammed shut and I was locked inside.

Being allowed to make one call, I called Uncle Jeff and asked him to come and get me. He sounded disgusted but didn't refuse. He came and picked me up the same day. I was let out on my own recognizance and a court date was set for the near future. Conviction on a possession of heroin of this large an amount would warrant two to ten years in prison. I was not aware of this at the time. All I wanted to do was get out. When Jeff arrived, he shook his head at me in disgust. During the ride back to our apartment I hit him up for $20.00 to score as I had nothing at home and was needing to fix again. Even as spaced as I was, I sure knew the price dope was now selling for.

He refused and dropped me off in front of the building, warning I should get my life together. While driving with him, I recall the World Series being forecast on the radio, so it must have been late October. Whenever the World Series is on now, I think of Jeff. During his ride home across the Port Mann bridge, he collided with someone. It was his son's birthday and he was rushing home for this occasion. I suspect his anger with me was partly to blame as well.

When I got home, I waited for John to return and told him what happened. He slapped me around that night for going out, but I was given another supply of twenty-five caps and the merry-go-round continued. I deteriorated more and more. Finally, John had enough. He couldn't make any sense of what was happening. He decided to take action. One afternoon, he entered our apartment. Behind him were two paramedics.

He told me to get changed and said I would be going to the hospital before it was too late. I refused to go and assured him that I would stop using so much. I promised to start eating. The paramedics took one look and shook their heads. They tried to get me on the stretcher, but I refused so they left. They told me I was going to die if I didn't go to the hospital and get help. It wasn't long after this incident that I stopped mixing the large amount of drugs. We stopped taking speed and barbiturates, and I cut back in the amount of fixes.

In due time the hallucinations became less frequent and deranged thoughts were fewer. John threatened to cut my supply off completely if I didn't start eating. So, I forced myself to eat. The only thing that tasted half-way okay was corn flakes with whipped cream with lots of sugar and milk. I ate a large bowl of this every morning as my appetite slowly returned. Still, when I tried to sleep on the couch again, there were visions of those big ugly faces on the living room wall that leered at me with awful smirks on their dark faces. I couldn't stand to see the monstrous creatures. No wonder I fell asleep at the fast food restaurant: the only time I felt safe was out of that apartment! When I think of this behaviour now, I realize these are the mental disorders linked to schizophrenia, although, at the time, this bizarre behaviour was attributed to the overuse of drugs. During this year of abyss, we moved several times, but always in the West End. John worried about the narcs so we moved often. His business was becoming much more prosperous than I realized. I hardly saw him. Pretty soon we were living in the ritzy high-rise hotels with big king-size beds and very expensive furniture. We were wealthy. It didn't matter to me where we moved, how we lived or what happened for that matter. I followed John like a little lost child.

As I became more dependent on him, he treated me more like a helpless little girl. I would put my hand out as he passed me the small balloon of capsules. Then he would disappear from our apartment. He'd return a couple of days later and replace the empty balloon with another. Some days, I would think that if I ever got my mind completely back, I would get out of Vancouver. I was unhappy, lonely and distraught. My thoughts were jumbled and distorted. I still had imaginings of streaks of fire crossing the living room. Once I ran into the hallway to escape. Banging on the neighbours' door, I warned them a fire was in my apartment. Coming in, they'd check the apartment and assure me there was no fire. Of course, it was only the heat register again. I would wrap a towel around my head and sit for hours at a time. The towel must have reminded me of the way Grandma used to wear her scarves over her head. It gave me some security.

John got more paranoid of the narcs, and we kept moving from one high-rise hotel to another. We never stayed more than a week in one place. Pretty soon were moving to different parts of the city, living in expensive motels. I packed and followed, never asking any questions. John's behaviour changed drastically. He didn't go out in the streets as often, and we started doing speed again. He became affectionate and very chatty. We became increasingly active with each other sexually. He insisted on perverted sex and was turned on with bananas or anything that was hard and caused pain, like the long neck of a pop bottle being shoved in his rectum. I thought it was disgusting but this was his fantasy, and I knew if I didn't do what he wanted, he'd stop my supply of drugs. As the speed wore off, he became paranoid and wouldn't leave our apartment for days. He imagined things as well. He accused me of working for the narcs and setting him up. I assured him this was not true but he suspected more. He started to beat me.

The beatings were severe but I didn't feel too much pain because I was too sedated from the drugs. Usually after John would accuse me of spying, he would tell me what happened to spies. He'd start punching my face and body until I was dizzy from the blows. Other times, he'd bounce me off the living room floor, lifting me up and flopping me on the floor and I'd fall flat on my back. Once in the small kitchen area, he lifted me off my feet with his hands tightly around my throat. With my feet dangling, he held me there until I passed out. I later came to on the living room floor. For no apparent reason, he'd beat me and after each beating, he'd baby me like a little hurt creature. I'd beg him to stop hitting but once he started, he wouldn't stop. His scariest threat came when he took me in his rented car, and we drove toward Stanley Park. On the way, he promised to kill and then bury me in the park. He said that I deserved to die because I was no longer any good for him. I assured him I was not an informer and that the speed was getting to him. I was very frightened for my life and tried to figure out a way to be free from him. Luckily, along the way he changed his mind, and we returned to the apartment. The thought of leaving and moving out of the city began to dominate my thinking, but in the end I was more consumed with where my next fix would come from.

Somehow I coped with the physical pain from the many beatings. The most distressing experience was the time he took all my family photos. I had carried these everywhere since leaving Vernon. He shoved all the photos inside a big green garbage bag and put them down the garbage chute. Inside that bag was an enlarged coloured photo of my deceased mom, my favourite photo. Oh, how I now despised him! I wanted to seek revenge in the worst way for all the horrible things he did on a daily basis. I thought of ways to destroy him and hoped I could get up the courage to do so. But then, if I did leave him, where would my next fix come from? Once while in the bedroom, he was jumping up and down in a rage. I was lying on the bed, made up of two single beds pulled together. For protection, I suppose, he had placed a butcher's knife in the crease between the mattresses earlier. As he was jumping up and down getting ready to beat me, I reached inside the crease and pulled out the butcher's knife.

I wanted to stick it in him if he lunged upon me one more time. The knife came up in my hand, but I threw it onto the floor in the corner of the bedroom instead. He proceeded to beat me. He saw the knife go flying but didn't pick it up from where it landed.

Following the beatings he would go out and always return with something for me. Usually it was expensive clothes. One time I got a whole new wardrobe, only to face the beatings again and again. In my tortured mind and body, I knew I had to get away from him before he killed me. His rage was more violent each time. On one occasion I followed him in the West End to his mother's apartment. She was not home, so he used his key and we went inside. He sat on the couch across from me as the apartment was ground level, I sat and watched people walking in the streets outside the big living-room window. He bolted across the room and whacked me in the face, with a closed fisted. He punched me so hard he broke my nose. Blood oozed from my nose. I ran into the bathroom and placed a wet face cloth on my nose to stop the bleeding, but I didn't go to the hospital.

When the bleeding stopped we returned to our own apartment. I sat in the living room. Both my eyes were getting blacker and blacker. Meanwhile, he was in the other room, relieved as though he had a sexual climax. I thought he was crazy. All that kept going through my mind was how I hated him and how I wanted to get away from him before it was too late. Meanwhile the beatings continued. Eventually we stopped doing speed, as he became too much of a maniac.

Again, it was another move to a motel on the far side of town, no different than the rest. I unpacked the many suitcases which contained mostly John's fine apparel of dress pants, silk shirts and soft leather shoes. He had hordes of cosmetics and I wondered if he wasn't a little gay the way he groomed himself. Sometimes he looked so feminine. The silk shirts he wore were of soft pastel colours. After showering he let his hair fall into natural, soft little curls. In addition he preferred to have oral sex rather than regular sex, something I found odd.

I believed he learned all his destructive behaviour from being locked up so much and the violence directed at me was really meant for the penal system. He had a history of incarcerations during the last eleven years of his life. There were very brief periods of being out of the federal penitentiary—or as John always called it—"the joint."

Tired and exhausted from all the "tweeking" (a drug term used to describe the imaginings brought on by using speed) the prolonged insomnia, the crazy outbursts by John followed by vicious beatings, the paranoia, and the total insanity of everything caused me to stop "goofballing," or mixing speed, heroin and barbiturates. Instead, I stuck to using heroin only and John went completely off everything. He was restless and got mean again. I urged him to try heroin. He did and liked it a lot. He became peaceful and all warm and glowing. I actually saw a side to him that was likeable.

There wasn't any meanness in him and the beatings subsided. I also told him I was not going to put up with any more meanness. I assured him I would leave the first chance I got if he continued to beat me. Before, he had beaten me for even threatening to leave, but now that he started using, he was as meek as a church mouse when high. We stayed in the apartment and used daily. The only time he went out was to replenish our supply. By now, he had stopped his drug dealing and we dipped into the profits he had acquired. There was plenty of money to buy plenty of China White when our supply dwindled.

A few months later, in December, late one night, we packed our clothes again. We loaded everything up in the rented car and drove. I expected we were going to another motel. We drove to an area on the outskirts of Vancouver and John pulled over. He got out of the car and returned shortly, carrying a brown paper bag. He told me to open up the tightly taped bag. I did and could not believe my eyes.

Inside, were hundreds and hundreds of bills, all 50's and 100's, held together with a big brown elastic band. He snickered, telling me to start counting and I began. There were so many 100's, I'd get so far and forget where I left off and have to start counting over again. John was elated! I had never seen such an excited look in his eyes. He turned and examined the bills while driving and mentioned that it looked like all the money was there. I asked where he got it from, and he told me to mind my own business. He then said to put it back in the bag and get ready because we were going south. I didn't ask any questions; I remained silent along the drive. I now had an enormous heroin habit of about twenty caps a day, putting two caps in the spoon at every fix. John was using just as much. I didn't care as long as he supported my habit. I had succeeded in seeking revenge because he was now as hooked as I was!

6

SAN FRANCISCO, HERE WE COME

John drove all night. It was around five o'clock in the morning when we entered Seattle's freeway system. My memory of driving all night is distinct. I recall drinking sodas, eating cookies and an occasional retreat off the highway to fix at a rest stop. Our bag of dope, a half-ounce of China White was concealed in a long condom, tucked under the seat of the car.

Tired and tranquillized, John would nod off at the wheel and cross the white lines on the freeway. Whenever the tire hit one of the reflectors along the dotted lines of the highway, he would open his eyes and steer the car back in its own lane. Luckily, in the wee hours of the morning there was very little traffic.

Even so, a patrol officer behind us turned on his siren. We sat up, wide awake and alert. John pulled off to the side of the highway. The officer walked up to our car. Sternly, he told John to pull the car off the highway and get some sleep; otherwise we'd end up in a serious accident. John explained we had been driving all night and assured the cop we would pull over at the nearest motel. We were relieved the cop didn't search the car. Soon, John made an exit off the freeway and drove to the airport in Seattle. We abandoned the rented car in the airport parking lot. There he told me we would be going south to California. I had never been farther south than Spokane in my life. Still, I did not feel thrilled to be flying to the fabled California. John bought tickets for San Francisco and we boarded a 747 jet. We must have fixed before the trip because I cannot recall sitting on the plane, eating anything, or the trip itself. I do recall getting off the plane hours later and walking down the ramp at the San Francisco air terminal. The climate was much different than Vancouver; the air was much heavier, more humid. With all the pollution, I wheezed during the cab ride downtown.

Once downtown San Francisco, we checked into the Hilton Hotel. It was Christmas Day. I can be so definite about the date because John ordered two turkey dinners with all the trimmings. We ate, unpacked and fixed. The luxury room cost a hundred dollars a day, and we lived like movie stars for the next week. I asked John again where he got all the money and the answer was, "None of your business!" I suspected he made quite a big sale of heroin in Vancouver. All his business was done in secrecy, even though I turned him onto his first connections. I did not ask again. I merely went along with whatever he said; I enjoyed the luxury. Everyday we had room service. Sometimes we would go downstairs into the lavish dining room and have ice cream with chocolate syrup. I enjoyed it. We ate fillet mignon every night and I even acquired the proper pronunciation for such an elegant slice of beef.

Our relationship turned into a partnership in San Francisco. Being so far from home, I depended upon him for everything. I felt a sense of loyalty now, rather than revenge. I still didn't want any intimacy with him, but felt I could now tolerate him. He hadn't beaten me for a few months and he started talking to me as if I was an adult rather than a little lost child. Since he had stopped doing speed, he was not so violent. Money was no longer a worry as it was when I was selling drugs in the streets before meeting him. Since being with John, I usually had five hundred dollars tucked in my wallet stuck in my jacket pocket. It was "mad money" and I used it to buy little trinkets such as address books or cosmetics or scented toiletries. In the drugstores I always looked at cards and thought of sending some home because no one in my family knew where I was. In restaurants, I also liked tipping the waiters or waitresses generously. Soon after we arrived, John began making phone calls. First, he contacted his brother Art a short, energetic man with curly brown hair who lived with his small family in Milpitas, about fifty miles from San Francisco.

Before the week was up John had made contact with some drug dealers in the area. Art smoked pot and had a lot of friends in Daly City, the drug centre of the San Francisco Bay area. He let John know who might be able to supply Mexican Brown heroin. When John scored, we tried the brown dope at the Hilton. I sat in the bathroom and came very close to an overdose. I did not realize how potent the stuff was and, being greedy, put too much in the spoon. I sat in the bathroom and slumped forward, trying to breathe regularly. I should have had the ambulance come but managed somehow to come out of it a little. My heart started to beat normally again. John paid little attention to the near overdose. He checked on me but was too busy in the other room talking on the phone with Art, who said he was coming over.

When Art arrived, he was impressed with our lavish lifestyle and John's carefree spending. He did not like seeing his brother hooked, though. John bragged about everything. He played the big-shot role and teased Art about his small-time job as a TV repairman. Art assured him he would one day have his own TV business and added that at least it was a legitimate way of making a living.

Following the near overdose, I was more careful about the quantity that went into the spoon whenever I fixed. We stayed at the Hilton one week. John had purchased a big green Cadillac before we checked out. More stingy about our living expenses, we moved into somewhat less expensive motels around San Francisco, staying at Ramada Inns or Holiday Inns during the next few weeks. Our address never stayed the same. We used up most of the money buying Mexican Brown. Regularly, we met with John's friend George in Daly City. Upon one meet he jokingly commented to us saying, we had "Cadillacs in our arms." Within the month we were flat broke. It was the beginning of a bad dream where I wished I could wake up and be back in Vancouver.

Although we had exhausted our money supply, we both had massive habits to support. John came up with a plan to support ourselves using the large chain stores. He would purchase items of clothing or merchandise by writing a NSF (Not Sufficient Funds) cheque. We would then drive to the next county and find the same chain store and return the merchandise for cash. With that we would buy our supply for that day and the next morning. On a good day we would make around two hundred dollars. A quarter spoon of Mexican Brown cost twenty dollars, but we needed many fixes during the day. We'd then rent a cheap room, have one meal a day, usually a cheap breakfast of pancakes or a burger deluxe, and buy our cigarettes. Most of our clothing and the nice luggage and shoes and cosmetics had been left behind in the different places we stayed. We left a few things at Art's place. We ended up selling the car for very little.

Destitute and homeless, we wandered around the Tenderloin District in San Francisco. We walked the streets with nothing but the clothes on our backs. The sole on my shoe had opened up and flapped when I walked. I used an elastic band to secure the sole to the upper of the shoe. We found it more important to get money for drugs than worry about a new pair of shoes. Eventually while I waited outside a store, John picked up a cheap pair of shoes amongst other items which he paid for with a bad cheque.

One night after fixing a spoon between us, we took the bus to go to Art's house. We were waiting to transfer to another bus at the Redwood City Mall when John decided to shop in a small clothing store. It was almost closing time, around nine o'clock. Inside, he proceeded to pile pants and sweaters on the counter. The cashier rang up the items which exceeded two hundred dollars and John paid with a cheque. We were not aware that the stores called in credit checks on purchases this high. The manager must have done the check in the back room. Just as we were about to leave, a security man approached us. John was immediately taken to jail, a short distance away. The police informed John he was being booked on suspicion of fraud. I am sure all the department stores he ripped off had filed complaints.

I wasn't arrested or questioned. I was left standing in the store with no money, no place to stay and no idea where the police station was. The only thing I could do was hitchhike to Art's house. By the time I got to the freeway, it was getting quite late. I stuck out my thumb and hitched a ride to Milpitas. It was around eleven o'clock when I finally made it to Art's. I was relieved that his wife Sharon was in bed when I got there. She had never liked John. She had no use for hard drug users, although I had heard from John that she enjoyed toking on marijuana and sipping white wine at every opportune moment. To her, John was sleazy and she tolerated him because, as brothers, he and Art were close. I suspected she would not like me.

When I arrived at their house, Art opened the door and invited me in. When I told him of our ordeal he called the police station and confirmed that John was charged with forgery and would be kept in custody awaiting bail. Art asked how much bail would cost and found out it would be $200. Art said he would bail John out the next day as soon as he got off work. As we talked late into the night, I contemplated how I would get twenty dollars for my morning fix. I thought about how sick I would be in the morning if I did not get it. Early the next morning, I left making sure I was out of the house before Sharon was up. I hadn't met her yet and didn't want to either.

I hitchhiked back to Redwood City and caught a ride to a huge shopping mall there. When the doors opened at nine o'clock I went right to a big department store in the mall. Even without a cheque book or any ID, I still had a plan. I headed right to the linen section. I found a big soft blanket and pulled off the twenty-dollar price tag and opened the wrapper. I walked down the wide aisle and found the cashier counter. I told the cashier I was returning the blanket because it was unsuitable and I would like a cash refund. The cashier asked for a receipt and I told her I had lost it. She nodded and asked me to wait a few minutes, as she would be right back. She returned with a strange man in a business suit. The man told me I would have to come with him. Inside his office, he dialled the police station and asked for an officer to come to the store. Within the hour, I was taken to the police station and booked on my first charge: illegally returning merchandise for a cash settlement. I had been observed from the moment I walked into the store—an obvious, dope-sniffing, sick junkie. I was unaware of any security watches except that I was getting sick and needed a fix as soon as possible. I had planned to get the cash, go into Daly City and be well by noon.

Later that morning, in the holding cell two police officers came to my cell and told me to stand outside while they did a room check. They pulled up the mattress and one of the officers returned to where I was standing. He was holding a syringe and dirty spoon in his hand. The officer informed me I was being additionally charged with concealing paraphernalia. I declared that I had no such thing in my possession and had no idea how the dirty spoon and used needle got under the mattress. Nevertheless, I was charged with smuggling in the paraphernalia. That afternoon, I was transferred to the women's prison in Redwood City, next to the men's quarters where John was. I was fingerprinted, booked on the two charges and advised that I would be eligible for a public defender at the expense of the county. I was also told that a public defender would visit me on the morning of the court day.

As the night progressed, I started going into what I feared the most: heroin withdrawal. Crouched on the mattress on the floor, I sat in despair. My ears hurt from the sound of the cell door as it was slammed shut and locked. My body began to ache. I couldn't stop sniffling. My mind was consumed with the thoughts of cooking up a fix, smelling the sulphur of the match as I watched the liquid come to a boil. I craved a fix. The cramps in my stomach spread to my legs and to every joint in my body. I ached.

Asking to see a doctor, I was told I had to wait until Monday morning. It was Friday night and I didn't think I could make it two days. As the night progressed, the cramps got worse. My knees felt like rubber and excruciating pain wracked my body. Every nerve twitched and it felt like little bugs were crawling on my skin. Uncontrollably, my eyes watered and my nose dripped. I began to dry-heave. I yelled at the sergeant and deputies for help. My body was wrenched in pain I had never experienced before. I yelled and yelled, pounding my fists on the rubber mattress until I was exhausted. I wrapped the thin wool blanket around me and stood behind the bars begging for something to ease the pain. I screamed for a doctor, but no one paid any attention. As far as the officers were concerned, I was a measly and sickly heroin addict.

In their eyes I was the scum of the earth. Who cared about any medical attention? I deserved every ounce of pain. Whenever the officers came to the cell they told me to be quiet, or I would go to the padded cell which was at the end of the short cement hallway. I continued to beg for something to stop the pain. My memory recalls vividly what happened.

Each hour became more panic—and pain-filled. I writhed on the mattress and screamed. Stabs of pain darted throughout my body. I tugged at the mattress and bit on it to muffle my screams. Somehow with an unknown strength, I managed to tear the blanket in half. I held the blanket in my arms. I started hallucinating. After tearing the blanket in half, I tucked it in my arms and began to yell louder. It looked like I was holding a dead baby. I called it my "blue baby" because its face was blue and there was no life to the body form. I didn't want it dead. When two officers came by, I told them they must call a doctor to examine the baby. They smirked and raised their eyebrows at one another and laughed. I rocked the baby in my arms until the officers unlocked the cell and one of them pulled the blanket from me. They grasped my arms firmly and led me down the short hallway. I was placed in the grey, padded cell and the last thing I heard was the clink of the key in the lock.

I screamed and kicked and hollered and convulsed in pain on the padded floor until I couldn't yell anymore. Oh God, how painful it was. I thought I was going to die. I would pace back and forth and scream. I ended up lying in a fetal position like a frightened, exhausted animal. I don't know if I was there the rest of the weekend or the one night. I just remember the excruciating pain. I must have gone unconscious at times because my next recollection is seeing two officers coming to the cell to let me out, remarking they thought I had gotten all the screaming out of my system. They brought me back to the same holding cell. I was warned that if I let out a peep, it would be back down the hall again. I merely asked to see the doctor. My request was denied. In the cell, I took the knee-high bobby-socks they had provided me with and soaked the socks in the lukewarm water in the steel sink in the cell. I wrapped the wet socks around my knees, and they helped to ease the joints a little. I couldn't lie still on the bed that night so I would put my blanket on the cold cement floor and try to sleep there. I could not lay still there either, so I would get back up and pace the cell trying to relieve the pain in my knee joints.

It was in the middle of the week before a doctor did come to my cell. I was still in withdrawal. The hallucinations had stopped and somehow I got through the worst part of going "cold turkey." By this time, withdrawal was mostly severe cramping in my joints along with hot and cold chills. Entering my cell, the short, aged doctor sat at the edge of my bed. He asked a lot of questions about my drug use. I informed him that I had been using heroin for the last year. When he asked how much I used, I told him as much as I could get. Since I was through the worst part, he informed me that I would not be given anything to relax the muscles nor would I be given anything—nothing! He suggested I refrain from ever using heroin again. I knew that I would never forget this ordeal for the rest of my life. I was sick for the next long while. My body craved heroin. I couldn't eat or sleep for days. I'd sweat and feel clammy and my joints ached non-stop. Three weeks from the time I was arrested were to pass before I started to feel normal again. I remember only one small act of kindness there. On Valentine's Day when I was lying on my bed, a kind deputy on night duty came by and shoved a piece of chocolate cake through the small opening in the door near the floor of my cell. I enjoyed the sweet taste, particularly since it was unusual to get anything extra in jail. I thanked the deputy for bringing the cake. I quickly ate it, licked my fingers and wished for more.

Art finally came to visit. He told me he was not able to raise our bail, and we'd both have to stay in until he could. He came to visit regularly and gave me messages from John. John was concerned on how I was handling it. I felt better and was relieved to have survived the worst part. I decided never to touch heroin again.

7

BEYOND PRISON WALLS

L ight crept in through the window high on the cell wall and filtered through the long hallway and into the lockup cell. Lockup was taking its toll on me. I not only craved heroin, I was also craving a cigarette. During the week, whenever a new inmate was booked and placed in the holding cell directly across from my cell, I pleaded for a few puffs from her cigarette before she butted it. Sometimes the young woman would roll her lit cigarette across the floor to me and I would take the last couple of puffs. The odd time I was lucky enough to get a whole one. While I still felt nauseated at the smell of anything, smoking a cigarette was a bliss.

Inmates are kept in lockup, or one-woman cells, until the staff decide the individual is safe to join the general population. In my case, I was too unpredictable with outbursts of screaming, having hallucinations, and attacking others. While there, I talked with a middle-aged, overweight woman named Victoria, who was in the cell at the end of the hallway. She was kept in lockup continually because she was so disruptive. She had been in the general population but got into a fight so she went back into isolation. She sang at the top of her lungs and yelled all the time, "Sergeant Slamma, let me out of here!" I heard her repeatedly calling the police. Whenever they did come, it was always in twos. Sergeant Slamma was a tall, slim, auburn haired and attractive woman. She was polite and soft spoken. However, she was stern with Victoria. She never used force on Victoria; she tried to negotiate order. I strongly felt Victoria belonged in a psychiatric ward. Somewhere in the aftermath of murdering her husband Tom, she lost her mind. She became criminally insane. She'd laugh. She'd cry. She'd yell at the police. She would beg for cigarettes. When I stood at my cell to talk to her, I could see torn up pieces of toilet paper she had hung on the door of her cell. She would do anything for attention. Victoria was going to be in lockup until she was sentenced. She knew she'd be going to the Women's Correctional Facility in Corona, probably for life, but she wanted to go because she knew she would get better treatment there.

The following week, the deputies decided that I could now come out of lockup. They felt it was safe to place me among the other inmates. They were assured there was not going to be any more screaming and kicking. I could still hear Victoria's hollering sometimes during the day or late into the night. It echoed throughout the monkey cages. Then there would be silence.

The area for the general population was enclosed by yellow painted steel bars. There were three monkey-cage-like sections in front of the long-windowed officers' station. One section to the left was filled with bunk beds. The middle section had long tables joined with stools cemented to the floor. The far section was filled with bunk beds. Off to one side in the back was a recreation room where the young women could sew, listen to music or sit on couches. There was no TV in there, only a small transistor radio. To the right of the far section was a visiting area. Inside this area were glass windows and stalls with telephones attached to the walls.

When I moved into the general population, I was in a fight the first night. A short, podgy red-headed young woman thought I had made too much noise screaming my lungs out in the holding cell. We started arguing and I told her to shut her mouth. I told her I was still miserable and didn't need her two cents worth. She leaped from her bottom bunk bed and pounced on me, and we went at it. I pulled her long hair as hard as I could. Others cheered her on. They were still all mad at me for making so much noise in lockup. They couldn't wait to see the woman beat the crap out of me. I yelled as loud as I could. A couple of the deputies came quickly from their station. They broke up the fight and I was taken back to lockup to cool off over night.

Two of the trustees came by the next morning handing out breakfast. Trustees were inmates who were at the jail for some time awaiting sentencing. A trustee was considered dependable and trustworthy by staff and given special privileges. They did janitorial duties and other duties such as serving food, handing out food trays to lockup inmates and other small tasks separating them from the general population. To me, it was a simple matter of hierarchy in the prison system. Generally, it is to make individuals appear superior to the others. They slid my tray under the opening of the cell door. They sprayed hair spray in my cell, called obscenities and threw little chunks of paper in. They warned me to cool it or things would get worse. I didn't say a word. I didn't eat the soggy cereal for fear of what they might have put in it. Who knows? If they had access to the janitorial room there could easily be Lysol sprayed in it.

After breakfast, Victoria and I could visit. Our cells were unlocked and we could wander back and forth within the small lockup area. The main gate to the holding cells was locked, but we could come and go inside. Victoria regularly came to sit on my bed. We talked. She'd begun to tell about shooting her husband, Tom. She'd laugh, especially when she got to the killing part again. I asked her why she did it, and she replied, "Because I couldn't take his abuse anymore. He drank and beat me. So when he was passed out one night, I took his rifle and blew him to pieces." Then, tears would form in her eyes and she would ponder what she did. She wished he didn't have to die the way he did and said she didn't mean to kill him. I told her it was over and there was nothing that could bring him back. She said she missed him but still didn't regret doing what she did.

She would then slap her knee and laugh and tell how she thought she outwitted the officers by bugging them always. I told her it would only make things worse. She replied, "It doesn't matter. I won't be here long." She added that she was now used to the padded cell, directly across from her cell. She closed her eyes and blinked and grinned as she slicked her short dark hair back with her chubby hand. She complained about the night she got so unruly she was placed in the padded cell, and left overnight. I remember her screaming. She said her hand still hurt from when she had it caught in the door as the officers slammed the steel door shut. She had blood dribbling all the way down her arm, but the officers kept walking away.

A few days later, I was placed back with the general population. The officers warned, "Mind your P's and Q's or it will be longer in lockup next time." The other woman was not reprimanded. From their observations, it appeared that I was the troublemaker.

For the next few meals, as I went down the serving line in the cafeteria section, food was plopped sloppily on my plate. A trustee had done it purposely to miss the plate and hopefully splatter food on me. I just kept pushing my tray along, not saying a word, keeping my eyes cast down. I didn't want any more trouble. From then on, I realized there is a certain "status quo" inside. If you're a rookie, you ease your way into the system. You learn to keep your mouth shut and talk only when the other women talk to you. Anything that is disruptive causes dissension among other inmates and is retaliated, eventually. I learned to keep to myself and mind my own business. Everybody belonged to her own little clique and if anyone upset the apple-cart they were treated badly. By remaining quiet and observing I learned to adjust to the system quickly.

I had to bunk beside a young Black woman who sang loudly at bedtime. She was a veteran there and everybody listened to her high pitched voice. It irked me and I wanted to tell her to shut up. In agony I listened. By others, she was well liked, and some said she sang like Dionne Warwick. Personally, I thought she couldn't carry a tune. I didn't care for her, because she was loud, used offensive language and acted like she owned the place. To others, she was a leader.

One morning while doing morning chores, my name was called over the loud-speaker. Quickly, I went to the window at the glass station. I was told I would be bailed out the same day. Happily I went through my locker. I willed all my personal belongings to the ones who were now good to me. One got my notepad and envelopes; others got the surplus of chocolate bars, soap and toothpaste. I changed into my "street" clothes—a pair of blue jeans and sweater, soft brown leather boots and a rabbit fur short jacket. I was let out the back through the R&R (receiving and releasing) door. I took the elevator to the main floor.

I was so glad to get out of jail. It took Art a month to raise our bail. When I got downstairs, John was standing in the front area. We acknowledged each other but there were no hugs or kisses. We just got into Art's Falcon and drove down the freeway. John was busy talking with Art. I sat in the back seat and gazed around, happy to be free. Art pulled up to a motel about ten miles from the Redwood City Jail. He handed John some money and we got out and took our suitcases from the trunk of Art's car. We checked into the motel. I showered and changed into my old clothes. It was good to feel like a human being again. I laid back on the soft mattress and watched TV. I felt a sense of identity again wearing my own clothes rather than the jail uniform of a short light blue tunic dress with long socks. Although John and I shared the same bed, I don't recall any intimacy.

After we had a decent meal in the restaurant next door, we planned our next move on how to get money. While we ate, I told John of the painful first three weeks in jail. I asked him how his withdrawal was. He shrugged and said he could handle pain but, of course, his main complaint was that Art hadn't bailed us out sooner. I had no desire to hustle money for drugs anymore. I wanted to live a normal life. After going through the court system, I hoped that we would not be facing time. I had never done time, and I was in a foreign country, I had no idea what a women's correctional facility was like nor did I ever want to be in one. I knew what county jail was like but had really no idea of what a correctional institution was like. John had several charges. There were many NSF cheques turned into the police by the many department stores. He didn't seem worried, though. He still wanted to get drugs and wanted to go back to dealing and being a middleman. I told him that I wanted to stay off the drugs. Although I still craved heroin, the memories were too fresh and vivid in my mind to think about fixing, ever.

Our money was running out, and our days at the motel were few. We could not borrow from Art again. On the night before our rent was due, John phoned Art and asked him to stop by on his way into work in San Francisco. In the morning, we caught a ride with Art. John asked him if we could borrow his car to get around the city so he could look for work. Art obliged. We had a full tank of gas, and John still had his cheque book. Immediately, we went to the stores again. We weren't sick anymore and looked clean and presentable. The clerks didn't suspect us. Easily, we were back into the money and this time John avoided the big department stores. During that day, we went to some discount stores, like the Drug Emporium and others, rather than the chain stores in the malls.

That evening we went to Daly City, scored and then returned Art's car back to the TV shop where he worked. Having no place to stay, Art offered to let us stay at his home. He told John he could come into San Francisco each morning with him and look for work. I hesitated, thinking of Sharon, but we had no choice. It was that or sleeping in the streets. We moved in and I finally met Sharon. Slightly overweight, she had long, light brown hair and a round face. Looking at the wedding picture on the mantle, she was pretty when she was young, but now she had too many bulges around the waist and her stomach protruded. She acted differently toward us than I had expected; she was polite, friendly and hospitable. I found this to be quite a switch from someone I thought despised us. I assumed that Art told her to be nice to us or else!

Within a week, John was working. He found a job in a paint store in San Francisco selling and mixing paints. It paid minimum wage. When he got comfortable in his job, he began to scam again. When the boss wasn't around, he helped himself to the paint. When he could, he carried a few gallons of paint and stashed them outside behind the garbage bins. After work, he'd get Art to park behind the store and he'd load up the extras. He said it was compensation for the low wages he had to work for. He sold the paint to whoever wanted it, at half price. Everything was a hustle and bustle in the city. It didn't matter what it was, it could be sold to a fence, and John knew where each one was.

Every morning John would leave with Art to drive to the City. Sharon and I were left with Artie, their blue eyed twelve-year-old son and Annette, John's five-year-old daughter who had been raised since she was a baby by Art and Sharon. The four of us got along okay. Annette's real mother was a Mexican woman named Lucy who abandoned Annette and fled from John when Annette was a baby. Because John and Lucy had separated, and he had a long history of incarceration, Art and Sharon took in Annette. As I got acquainted with Sharon, she wasn't the old grouch she was made out to be. I attended some of Artie's baseball games with her. He played in the big diamond near his school for his team, called the Angels. As well, Sharon made a good meal and afterwards we would eat wholeheartedly, munching on everything. She also made a tasty hamburger and noodle dish with a tossed green salad. Lightheaded with pot, John and I would do up the supper dishes.

Usually on Fridays, John would get Art to stop in Daly City on the way home from work. He'd pick up a spoon of smack. We'd borrow Art's car and drive back into the City and wouldn't come back until Sunday night, broke. Eventually, Sharon got fed up with our using.

John and I began to fight again. He hadn't beaten me since leaving Vancouver. One night before dark, after supper, I was washing dishes and he was drying. I snapped at him for no reason and he pounced on me. He hit me a few times, and I ran out of the kitchen and through the garage. As I ran through the garage, I picked up a sharp digging tool. I kept running out into the street and was out by a telephone pole when he stopped me. I was screaming at him at the top of my lungs, and neighbours were looking out at the ugly scene. When he yanked me down to the ground, I yelled at him, "If you come near me I'll stick this in your gut!" He grabbed the tool from my hand. He dragged me into the house and into our bedroom. He pulled my hair and punched me in the face and head until I was dizzy. He slugged me in both eyes and they began swelling up right away. I hurt everywhere. The pain was unbearable. This time I really felt it.

Art and Sharon stayed in the other room. They knew of John's temper but never saw him in action. Inside the tiny bedroom, he threw me on the bed. I yanked a small jack knife from the night stand. With it still closed, I started swinging it at him and threatened to use it. He grabbed it from me and opened it up and pointed it toward me. I knew then that I was fighting a losing battle. I just lay there with my legs bent up toward my chest and my arms shielding my face. I didn't want any more blows coming to my face. He slashed at my leg, opening a small cut. I yelled, "Okay, you win. Stop!" Whenever he knew he had complete control, he pulled off me. When he stood back, I went into the bathroom. Both eyes were closed right up. Nearby, Sharon and Art looked on but didn't make a peep. Art looked disgusted and Sharon was horrified. When things settled down, John joked about how

I should keep my mouth shut from now on, especially when we were doing dishes. The kids didn't say anything but now looked at me like I was a freak.

Following this incident and as sore as my body was, I thought of how to escape. I wanted nothing more than to get as far away from John as I could. I didn't care if I were facing court. I knew that once I was back in Canada, I would never have to see California again. The following days, John tried to be nice to me but I hated him for beating me. I despised him but still had to sleep in the same bed with him every night. I cringed as he lay beside me on the small single bed. When he tried to get passionate, I always made up the excuse that using drugs had robbed me of any sexual desires. I did not want him to touch me, ever!

Being about three thousand miles from home, I was stuck in Milpitas. I had no way of getting back to Canada, nor would I be safe in that country since John had done something very wrong there. I felt the people whose money he had ripped off would come after me if they couldn't find him. I suspected that all the money I couldn't even begin to count as we were leaving Vancouver was stolen from someone. So I had no choice but to stay with him now. Also, I had no money, no idea of how to get out of Milpitas and, furthermore, no place else to go so I decided to try to make the best of it. Besides, it would be just a matter of time before John had to go to court and hopefully would end up doing time. I wished for him to do lots and lots of time. I let the beating go by when he brought a spoon of dope home the following Friday. It was the only escape I had living in this hell.

Within a month, John's job ended. He was laid off. Perhaps the owner suspected the theft of paint. Art and John joked about his thievery. During this time, whenever John had extra money from the stolen goods, they brought a small supply of pot home. Sharon was good-spirited. She and Art argued a lot though. She was cranky until she had her goblet of white wine and her toke. Usually, the men got home around eight p.m. After John's job ended, our light-hearted evenings of pot and wine stopped. Sharon became miserable. Despite her mood swings, we stayed there another month. During that month, John went back to court and got his sentencing date. I appeared, too, and pleaded guilty and got a sentencing date. Sentencing for both of us was two weeks away. When our court dates came up, we didn't show up. We left Art's place and headed down to the Tenderloin District in San Francisco. We walked the streets and John pulled out his cheque book. We started hitting the stores again. We scored dope whenever he would write bad cheques. But there were many days we didn't use. We stayed in cockroach-infested rooms in the large dirty hotels downtown. It was disgusting.

John was determined to get back into business. In Daly City, through our faithful connection George, we met a Mexican named Johnny Rodriguez. He and John became friends and before long they were planning ways to make some fast money. Rodriguez, as he was called, had lots of connections. Together, he and John talked about setting up a deal to sell cocaine. It was something they had talked about and planned for some time. Rodriguez lived in San Francisco and had a wife named Vicki. They had two little kids.

One warm afternoon, we rode the bus to their place. John and Rodriguez did some more planning. Rodriguez was on the phone setting everything up. That night, John told me to wait at Vicki's place until they returned. They told us little. Vicki was nervous, but I wasn't concerned. They promised to bring back lots of money. They didn't tell us a whole lot about their plan, but we knew it was going to be in Redwood City, and the sale was going down early in the afternoon. There was no word from each of them until late in the evening. Rodriguez phoned to tell Vicki they had been busted. They had been set up. Nearby, narcs waited to rush them the minute they handed over the drugs for cash. We never did find out for certain who set them up, but it wasn't hard to figure out. We suspected the man John dealt with after we landed in San Francisco. John had met him in Vancouver and obtained his Seattle address. So when we passed through Seattle, John contacted him. Shortly after we landed in San Francisco and John purchased the green Cadillac, we began making runs up to Seattle to score large quantities of heroin through this same dealer. John planned to sell the heroin in the Bay area. We had relied on the connection while in Seattle, and John trusted him. It would have been a lot cheaper on gas to get somebody locally in San Francisco to buy from, but that kind of rational thinking did not play any part. John was only concerned on who he could score good, clean dope from for a good price. So we travelled a long ways to get the drugs.

Having gigantic habits we ended up using the ounce ourselves. It lasted about ten days, and filled a condom right to the top. In all, we made about three long trips back and forth between Seattle and San Francisco. During the runs, the connection in Seattle built our trust more by saying he was facing prison in due time for trafficking heroin, so we knew he definitely wasn't a narc. We never thought of him as a snitch. He was gradually building this trust and preparing to set John up for the big bust. Once busted on a drug charge, it was very common to make deals with the prosecutors for a lighter sentence. In a case where a big bust is involved the snitch usually walks on all his charges.

Another good lead to suspecting the connection is that he was the only other man who had been involved with John and Rodriguez as they planned the cocaine deal and, coincidentally, he was not at the location when the drugs and money were exchanged. Nor did anyone hear from him once John and Rodriguez were locked up. So it's very easy to figure out since he was nowhere around when the heat was on. There was gun fire in the small parking lot where the deal was going down. John was not wounded but Johnny got grazed in the arm. Both went to Redwood City Jail. This time John had no bail.

The next morning, I watched the little ones as Vicki went straight to the jail. At times I wanted to see John go to jail. But now I felt a sense of loyalty. I appreciated how he spent his money on me and took care of me since leaving Vancouver. I wasn't going to turn my back on him now. Still I resented him for his hostility over the last year. Vicki was so upset. She loved her husband dearly and was devastated. I thought of how I would support myself. I knew I couldn't live at Vicki's, but there was no place else to go.

John and Rodriguez were charged with illegal possession of cocaine for purpose of trafficking, resisting arrest, and selling to undercover police. Both were kept locked up with hefty bonds. John was facing two to five years and Rodriguez, too.

I left Vicki's the next day and wandered around the streets of San Francisco. I had nowhere to go and no idea of how I was going to live. I walked into another store and went to the appliance section. I pulled out a boxed iron and took off the price tag and opened the box up. I took it to the cashier and asked for a refund. I told her I lost the receipt. I was spotted again by security and taken back to jail. I didn't really care. I didn't know where I could stay or where my next meal was coming from. Getting arrested came as kind of a relief. I was sent back to Redwood City facing another charge of returning merchandise for a cash settlement. My bail was around two hundred dollars.

I was back in the same holding cell where I twisted and writhed and tossed and turned, going "cold turkey" just two months prior. Luckily, I didn't have a big habit to kick this time. I still had an ugly feeling being in this jail remembering the "blue baby" and other experiences. This time I was taken right to the side where the general population was. Most of the young women from before were still there and were friendly. I didn't have to go through too much withdrawal but still had the aches and sniffles for about a week. I adjusted with the general population. I was now considered a repeater.

Right away, Art came to visit us both but never offered to raise bail money. He was fed up but didn't say it. Our visits were pleasant, though. He said it was probably best for both of us. Now we'd have time to think about what we were doing and how turbulent the last few months had been. I shrugged him off, but agreed. I looked forward to Art's weekly visits. Sometimes, he'd leave about twenty dollars on the books. With that I would buy the necessities in jail. I'd order from the canteen a writing pad, envelopes, chocolate bars, toothpaste and shampoo. At every visit I asked how John was doing. Art said he was fine and missed me. I didn't really miss him.

When court came up, John was sentenced to two years at Vacaville Federal Prison. Shortly after that, I was sentenced, too. The Judge looked down from his platform and lectured briefly of how I was a menace to society. He said I deserved to be sent to where such incorrigibility as mine could be dealt with. The paraphernalia (bogus) charge, the warrant for Failing to Appear, and the returning merchandise charges warranted me an indefinite sentence at CRC (California

Rehabilitation Centre in Riverside near Corona, California).
I was sentenced until such time recovery from drugs was evident. No definite sentence was ever handed down to any of
the women sentenced to CRC. A parole board decided release dates once a person had spent time there. The board
reviewed each case. If the board was convinced the individual
was sure to abstain from drugs, a release date would be given,
usually after an inmate served six months. The average stay
at CRC was seven months. I looked blankly at the judge and
accepted my sentence. At least I would have a place to sleep
now and three square meals a day. I was apprehensive though.
I feared the unknown.

One evening as I was sitting on my bed in Redwood City
Jail, before being transferred, I was called to the officer's station. The deputy slid the phone beneath the small window.
It was John who was allowed a phone call before going to
Vacaville. Everything we said was probably monitored, as well
the deputy stood nearby and listened so we talked generalities on the phone. John never did explain how they were set
up. I wished him well and told him how much time I was
facing and where to write. We said goodbye and hung up.

On the day of the plane ride to southern California to
begin my long stretch of time, I was nervous. The other
women said it would be like living in a resort. They said the
food was great, and there were palm trees and a big swimming pool. I was also told it would be like a retreat and a
chance to take some courses. I feared what the "big house"
offered and wished I could be going back to Canada instead.

Two deputies escorted Sue Buzzy, a blonde, blue-eyed
pretty young inmate and me to the airport. We were handcuffed together before going to the airport. Walking through
the airport and boarding the plane, we kept a sweater over
our handcuffs. With little dignity left we still hoped no one

would notice that we were inmates. Walking briskly onto the plane, we were seated and took off on a pleasant journey through cloudless blue skies above San Francisco, headed south.

We landed at an airport a short distance from Los Angeles. After we got off the plane, the deputy took off our handcuffs as we were turned over to the police who were waiting at the airport. We were driven by the police escort to the California Rehabilitation Centre, near Riverside.

The police car pulled up to the gate. A high wire fence surrounded the huge yellow-coloured, two storey building that sat on the crest of the hill. Tall palm trees surrounded the building. It was a warm afternoon, and the sunshine was gorgeous. However, I dreaded having to be locked up, spending summer here and possibly winter too. I expected to be here no less than eight months. I judged this by listening to other inmates at Redwood City Jail who were repeaters, going through the system again.

A correctional officer met us at the gate and escorted us up the hill as the police car pulled away and sped down the country road. The officer was pleasant and treated us respectfully, not the attitude I had expected toward petty criminals and former drug-users. We came to another gate bolted with a big padlock. Unlocking it, the officer led us inside. We walked to a side entrance of the building. A few inmates were working in the Receiving & Releasing Unit. One was on camera taking the mug shots of inmates. Another handed us out necessities such as a toothbrush and a small tube of toothpaste. Everything was systematic, and the correctional officers led us through the procedures for new inmates. After the mug shot we were assigned a number, given a new pair of thongs, a list of the rules and regulations, and assigned a room number. Sue looked completely at ease as though she had been here before. I was nervous and a little frightened. I hoped that it wouldn't be as rough as it was when I first went to Redwood City Jail. Luckily, a few other inmates from Redwood City Jail who had arrived before us came to visit as soon as we were in the dorm. They somewhat initiated us by showing us the ropes, informing us of where this and that was, and introducing us to a few of the inmates. It was more of a welcome than anything else. We weren't looked on by other inmates as green horns.

Sue moved into her room down the hallway, and I settled into my room. The long hallway had a polished old wood surface and each small room had two, 2-tiered bunk beds cramped inside with one desk and chair. A small bathroom was off to the side. It was very crowded; there were four women to each room, but no one complained. The walls were a drab colour and the officers' cubicle was situated midway down the hallway. In front of the officers' station was a huge recreation room. Tables, chairs, couches and a TV filled the room. On one side of the room was a glass double-door exit leading onto a yard of plush, manicured lawn. To the far north was the famous HOLLYWOOD sign on the mountainside. Although CRC was about fifty miles away, the sign was still visible. I felt privileged to have a glimpse of Hollywood—too bad it had to be under such circumstances, I thought. A large oval swimming pool sat directly in front of the double-door exit. Although it might seem like we were at a summer resort, I still felt lonely and trapped. It didn't matter how nice it looked outside—the palm trees, the lush lawns, the swimming pool—it still had a high wire barbed fence and a sense of impending doom. I was deprived from the one thing I wanted most—Freedom!

8

ROCKY SLEPT HERE

After placing my new thongs, towel, facecloth, toothbrush and toothpaste on top of my bunk bed, I settled into a nearby chair. It was a hot June day and there wasn't a wisp of cloud in the clear blue skies. Subdued, I gazed out the window, scrutinizing the inmates circling in little groups outside my window. Some were sitting on the plush lawn, cross-legged. I felt alienated and shy of these strange women. To my astonishment they looked like ordinary women, dressed in casual summer clothing. Looking directly across the lawn I could see the annex that was the administrative part of the institution. Here, trained instructors came in to teach clerical courses and to offer Grade 12 equivalency upgrading.

I resigned myself to giving up my freedom for the next six to seven months. Contemplating my present existence with uncertainty, I disliked my uneasy feelings. Feeling weepy, I wished I were back in Canada. I started to cry. While I was blinking back the tears, a woman, probably in her early 20s, entered the room. She did not introduce herself and nor did I. Cockily she walked in and since I was weepy, she taunted,

"Poor little chickie." I ignored her comment and tried to look unruffled. With her back to me, I studied her for minute. She had boyish cropped hair and was short. She looked like a young man. She busied herself digging through the small dresser drawer beneath the opened window. With eyes that seemed to intimidate, she looked again at me and then went back to shuffling papers in the drawer. To her, I was just the new kid on the block who hadn't made a very good first impression; I was a sissy. I knew if I did not act strong, I would face the same intimidation I did during my earlier incarceration at Redwood City Jail. I remained quiet and observed. Above the pillow on her bed, taped to the wall was a hand-printed sign that read "ROCKY SLEPT HERE." I wondered who Rocky was. It was not long before a tall, pretty dark-haired Chicano woman in her early twenties came bounding into the room. I knew the pretty woman was Rocky. The women hugged and teased and pinched each other like a couple of playful young girls. Realizing I would be sleeping on the top bunk with a butch on the bottom, I really did not care. Nor did I care if Rocky slept in the bed. I just hoped the two lovebirds did their thing in privacy. Being in the presence of a butch and her companion was not surprising. I recalled a warning at Redwood City Jail that everybody took a partner once she was at CRC. Also, their behaviour did not surprise me because I had observed such lesbian teasing at Redwood City Jail. From my lockup cell, I watched a couple of the trustees, an attractive dark-haired Chicano woman and her petite, cute blond girlfriend, kiss and hug. They also touched each other's breasts while cleaning the cells and mopping the floors in the lockup area. They giggled and murmured passionately. There was no direct eye supervision behind the officers' station so it was a moment of privacy for any couple who wanted to feel each other up. I was embarrassed at first but soon disregarded the obvious sexuality. I had other things on my mind such as thinking about sentencing. When I observed this again at CRC, I vowed to myself no matter how lonely it got, I refused to turn to someone of the same sex. When Rocky and her butch left the room I climbed up on my bunk and lay down, thinking about home. I became more homesick. Strangely, what I missed the most were the rugged mountains back home.

In the dorm, a whistle sounded down the hallway to mark the day's events. Blown by the correctional officer, it signalled meal time, count time, bed time, work time, sleep time, group time, counselling time or whatever the weekly schedule posted in the dorm dictated. Everything was done in routine. Any infraction to the rules of the institution guaranteed a "115", an automatic 30 days added to the violator's time.

Later that first day, following the five o'clock head count, I joined the others and we went by twos to the cafeteria located down a flight of stairs in the administrative annex. In the big cafeteria were about fifty tables, twenty-five on each side. We all went into the cafeteria and then went single file through the long serving line. Each woman picked up her tray as other inmates standing behind the assembly-line steam tables served food. Inside large aluminum pots were steaming mashed potatoes. Smaller containers held various cooked vegetables. There were big grills to keep the meat portions warm and further down the line were the desserts. Little cartons of milk and desserts were placed on ice beside two large coffee urns. Passing along the line, I realized meals were everything that the women at Redwood City Jail had promised— so much better than jail food. The on-duty correctional officers joined the line but sat at different tables near the front of the cafeteria.

I survived my first week. Heck, I had worried it would be like those prison movies on TV. I expected big bully types, hookers, and lesbians waiting to pounce on the first new woman who came here. Not so, the women were ordinary, like you would see in a college dorm. Respectful-looking, not hard-core, most of them were pleasant and easy to talk to. My first encounter with the butch had been unpleasant; however, when we got to know each other we respected one another. During the first week she stole my new thongs and printed her name in black felt on them. I was not pleased but was hesitant to ask her about it. It would have caused friction between us and she would have just denied it anyhow. I was left with a used pair, which undoubtedly were hers. I wore them and could not get another pair until they were beyond wear. I was angry to see such thievery take place right under my nose, but this was a prison and honesty is not what got these women here.

The following week, all settled in, I found a message on my bed commanding me to report to the correctional officer at 9:00 the following morning. The correctional officer's name was Jackie. She also acted as a counsellor and support worker who listened to any drug-related or other problems coming from the women. She worked in her office at the end of the hallway Mondays to Fridays, nine-to-five. Before being assigned to the PK, I was assigned to mop-dusting the hallway. During such regular morning chores, I observed Jackie's daily entrance. I wondered why the women made such a fuss over her every time she came on the dorm. As the dyed-blond, disorganized and chatty woman almost sprinted to her office, "Good Morning, Jackie" sounded down the hallway. She was well liked and whenever she came on duty, the women working outside would escort her upstairs as others lingering in the hallway would join the procession. During such brisk walks, the women would politely fire questions at her, usually about their parole hearings or little things that Jackie had promised to look into. She was popular because she was the one who recommended what women got to see the parole officers. Jackie, always rushing, clicked her spiked high-heels down the hallway, clutching a big pile of files in her arm, acknowledged the women with a nod or "Good morning." She was jovial but businesslike and didn't mind the tugs and hollers. During our meeting at 9:00 that following morning, Jackie looked upon me from behind her desk. Her glasses had slid slightly down her nose. She appeared firm and calculating in her approach. Almost as though she had every word memorized from doing it so often, she began: "This is the routine," she explained, "weekly drug therapy group sessions, work involvement at CRC and further training to upgrade your present skills. First you will be assigned to a job. I'm going to assign you to the PK (personnel kitchen). This pays $16.00 a month. Do you have any questions?" She asked.

"No." I answered. I already was aware of the procedure from small talk with others. " I'm ready to do my time and get it over with," I added.

"What about your drug problem?" She asked.

"That too." I replied. "I'm here to take care of that too."

"Good," she said, "I expect that of you."

"When do I get out?" I asked curiously.

"When you are ready. I will need to see some changes in your attitude—rehabilitation from drugs and street crime."

"But my charges were so petty." I said defensively.

"I don't care. You're here and not out there." She lectured. "Right? So what does that tell you?" She continued. I knew she was a no-nonsense type and although she was friendly and approachable, she also would stamp out any nonsense behaviour.

I looked to the floor and nodded my head in a good-natured gesture.

"What do you want to do with yourself when you get out of here?" She asked. "We do offer training here as you probably know. Would you be interested in taking the clerical course?"

Pausing for a moment, I replied, "I would like to take it." The GED did not interest me then.

"I'll sign you up. You can join the others already in progress tomorrow at 1:00 p.m." She said decisively. "That will be it for today, I expect you to participate fully in your work, group and class. I'll see you in group Friday."

"Okay. Thanks." I replied timidly. She excused me from her office in order for me to go to R&R to get a white uniform and white, rubber-soled shoes. I headed to the ground floor, thinking about getting up at 4:30 a.m. and reporting to the PK in the twilight of dawn. Starting at 4:45 a.m. the job detail involved preparing and serving breakfast to the correctional officers before we had our own breakfast. After that we cleaned the huge kitchen, stacked the folding chairs, dust mopped then wet mopped the enormous black-and-white checkered marble dining room floor. Next we returned to the dorm for about an hour to rest before going back to prepare and serve lunch to staff. This would be followed by having our own lunch there and cleanup. When finally done, I had to go quickly to the other side to be in class by 1:00 p.m. Whew! It was a tight and rigid schedule. The notion of a full-time course and work was overwhelming, but I thought of how quickly time would pass and was certain I could handle it. During the meeting, Jackie also told me I would be moving to another room to join four other PK staff. Right away I transferred to the other side of the dorm. I was relieved I would not have to experience any bumping and grinding should Rocky come sneaking in after count time and crawl into the bottom bunk bed with her lover.

Up at 4:30 the next morning, I splashed cold water on my face, had a quick shower and combed my hair back into a ponytail. I put on a pair of silky white baggy pants, a top that was too large and new shoes that fit. I made my bed and joined the other sleepy women, now dressed too, as they headed to the secondary gate. In the emerging dawn, a tired-looking correctional officer on night duty scrutinized each ID and nodded for us to go through the gate. We crossed the yard to a large brick building, an old-fashioned two-storey structure with a big kitchen area on the main floor. In the large dining area were many tables and stacking chairs on an attractive black and white checkered marble floor. By the main entrance was a grand piano. The short and aged crabby kitchen manager warned us never to touch it, as it was there for appearance only.

On the second floor of the building, the infirmary housed the sick from the young men's institution. Sprawled at the bottom of the hill behind the women's institution, separated by a high barbed wire fence, the men's compound held about 800 drug-related offenders. Every morning, the young men made deliveries to our compound. Big tasty bakery rolls along with the special cuts of meat such as steaks were daily deliveries. The young men were mostly good-looking Chicanos who ogled the women during the deliveries. Everyone had to maintain their distance and were under close security by the male trustees during such deliveries. The men, attracted to certain women, managed to smuggle "kites" to them. Inside these folded-up little pieces of paper were scribbled notes introducing themselves to a new female inmate or answering a previous kite. These kites usually contained handsome Mexican designs. Notes were found underneath the sweet rolls and inside supplies, or they were handed to a woman when the trustees had their backs turned. It was always intriguing to scheme and get away with little things such as this. Usually some good-looking Chicanos poked their heads out the window whistling low wolf calls at us whenever we returned to the dorms midmorning. The women were thrilled and responded with hoots and hollers. The male officers in the hospital unit quietened the men quickly whenever this occurred and the windows were shut and locked. Whenever the crabby kitchen manager got wind of such outbursts, the women were scolded. Reprimanding us, she guaranteed she would do a write-up to go into our files for the parole board to read indicating that we were teasing the men. Everybody ignored her warnings and continued acknowledging the admiring looks and sounds coming from the second floor.

In the kitchen, we prepared bacon and eggs, boiled eggs, and made hashbrowns and toast for staff. For breakfast we could have dry cereal or boiled eggs with toast. It reminded me of the early days of residential school where staff ate fine foods while the rest of us ate lumpy cold and uncooked cereal with reconstituted powdered milk to wash it down. For lunch, we prepared soups, sandwiches and salads and served the staff elegantly. Here, we could drink the fresh brewed coffee that was definitely a treat and eat the same soup and sandwiches as we served staff. We were to conduct ourselves as though we were working in a restaurant. If we did not do as we were supposed to, another 30 days was added to our sentence. Most women worked diligently but complained about our early rising to "feed the pigs."

During leisure hours, sometimes the women would stand on the hill crest waving white scarves to the men down the hill. The men would respond waving white cloths as well. If caught, it meant a 115. Quite often the women were caught gesturing to the men. The officers were very stern about agitating or encouraging the men on. They were afraid of riots and cautioned the women that this type of behaviour enticed the men. Regardless, this activity continued. During the week, the men were on yard maintenance outside the fence by the main gate, pulling down or chopping tall weeds. It was a perfect opportunity for the men to flick their kites over the high wire fence and whoever it was addressed to received the note. It served a good purpose. The women got promises to meet their new heartthrob upon their releases from CRC. The notes carried romantic messages full of flattery that took the edge off the boredom and loneliness.

The clerical course was tedious. I was so weary by class time, I'd sometimes fall asleep in class. The instructor would come along and poke me on the shoulder to wake me up. One afternoon following class, I told her I had to be up at 4:30 every morning to go to work. She suggested I go to bed earlier. I continued with the course and time went by quickly. The routine at CRC was so humdrum. Friday afternoons were a relief as we did not have to work, instead we participated in group therapy. The most boring time was the weekends. There was nothing to do but write letters, watch TV, lie by the pool or swim. To someone on holidays in the far south, this would be ideal. But here it meant absolutely having nothing productive to do but wait for time to pass and think about doing time for the state. It felt like a waste of life ticking slowly by.

Regularly, John and I corresponded. Through our letters we remained committed to each other in a partners-in-crime type of loyalty. I now felt sorry for him, locked up in maximum security in Vacaville, while I was in a very laid-back institution. Of course, our crimes were much different. Letters from John came carrying promises of love but I still felt no love for him; I felt loyalty and remained devoted, expressing my undying love but never meaning it. Sometimes I felt guilty for lying to him but when I thought of how he beat the crap out of me, it was easy to continue fooling him. The only good thing he could do for me was to bring me home. When he had served his two years and returned me to Canada, I would leave him. Then, we'd be even. I'd done my part as the loyal common-law wife and waiting faithfully as he served out his time. Now that my mind was somewhat unscrambled, I began to realize the destructiveness of our relationship: how he used me for sex and I used him to get drugs. As I got healthier through the drug therapy sessions, I learned I was co-dependant and John was a mentally disturbed person who preyed on helpless victims to brutalize, sodomize, and torture. Yet, in my mind I knew he was my only ticket to get home. I needed to use him for this and we were to remain compatible through our letters until I set foot on Canadian soil. Besides, I thought, he deserved to be used one last time for the way he had treated me. This was my way of paying him back. His letters were boring. I hated to read the same thing repeatedly: of his undying love and how boring life was now for him, and so on. He whined. Sometimes I never even read the letters and just threw them in the garbage. There was hardly a day I did not receive a letter from him. I made myself a secret promise to remain in touch with him until he returned me safely home.

One day while I was at work in the PK, there was a catastrophe in the dorm. Someone, out of sheer boredom, held a lighter up to the water sprinkler suspended from the ceiling in one of the rooms. The flame eventually caused the sprinkler to go off. As a result each sprinkler in each room automatically squirted water everywhere. The mattresses in each room had to be removed and placed in the hallway to dry out. Luckily, the plastic covering protected the mattresses from permanent water damage. The correctional officers began investigating and were not at all amused. They never did find out who caused the sprinklers to go off. Surprisingly, we were not locked down in our rooms until the guilty person owned up. Perhaps the officers thought it would be a waste of time because the code of silence existed. Nobody squealed despite any disciplinary measures.

That afternoon, when I returned to my room, the mattress had been removed and was standing upright in the hallway. On top of my bunk there was a letter from Yvonne. I was so happy to receive her letter that I tore it open quickly. As I read the short letter from home, I learned that my Uncle James had died. Yvonne went further to explain that he was found lying near railroad tracks in Oroville, Washington barely clinging to life. He died shortly afterward in the hospital from severe internal injuries. The police report suggested that he was hit by a train and thrown several feet. A proper investigation was never done. To this day, no one really knows the cause of death. However, word does get out and it is believed a fight broke out which involved James outside a bar in Oroville that ultimately caused his death. I became very upset as I read the letter. What was more disheartening is that the officer, having already opened and screened the letter, did not even bother notifying the chaplain to deliver the news of a death in my immediate family. I hated this place more so than ever now. How cruel and inconsiderate I thought. I wanted to return home but already the funeral had taken place. I got the news too late. I was sent to see the nurse as I was crying uncontrollably. She provided a tranquillizer to calm my nerves. Many women expressed their condolences as I grieved for several days. I could make a col-

lect call to Yvonne and we talked of our sorrow over the long
distance.

The months slowly passed by. Life was the same, day after day, month after month. In our shared room, there were
two lesbians: Katie, a tall, good looking dark-haired woman
and another who was a petite, long-haired, perky brunette. I
never witnessed anything sexually compromising between any
of the women but observed many form tight relationships
with each other. "Tight" relationships at CRC meant homosexuality between females. Exhibiting sexual desire towards
one another often came in the way of holding hands, stealing kisses, rubbing down one another at the pool or any kind
of intimacy they could get away with. Often someone would
stand in the hallway outside the bedroom door to "Keep 6"
while the women had their privacy. If an officer on duty came
down the hallway the woman keeping watch would tap on
the door and the women would get out of their compromising positions. Some were actually caught under the covers in
others' beds going down on the other engaging in oral sex.
They got together in the showers. When caught an automatic
30 days was added to an already indefinite sentence. It was
quite the normal behaviour for most of the women at CRC.
Big buxom blondes discreetly took on sweet young women
as they came into the institution and together they did their
time, a comfort to each other. I was turned off by so much
female homosexuality but understood because I knew loneliness, too. Turning to writing poetry, mostly about boredom
of doing time, the conditions at CRC, alcohol and drugs or
whatever whim I felt that day was my way of handling things.
I became a model prisoner by completing the secretarial training and going to work faithfully. At the end of six months I
made an appointment to see Jackie. I asked when I could see
the parole board. She replied that she felt I had become reha-

bilitated and would begin paperwork toward my release. I was elated! I could look forward to a release date.

It was early in January, 1974. I was now 24 years old. The past several months were lonely although there were many other people around. It certainly hadn't been any fun being confined and celebrating my 24th birthday incarcerated, spending Christmas locked up, and watching the fireworks display from the small nearby city of Corona on the July 4th weekend from my room. When I think of it now, it was a lenient correctional facility compared to other institutions. There was no clanging of cell doors, no deputies in regal blue suits, no smells of urine, no maniac prisoners retelling their murderous exploits. Better yet, the food was edible. Still the most precious thing was denied and that was freedom. I didn't do hard time but I suffered the loss of being out of the country and the loneliness almost did me in at times. I ached for home, wherever it was, as long as it was back in Canada. I reflected on the past year as I awaited my parole hearing which was just two short weeks away.

On the day of the hearing, I was nervous. I didn't know what to expect. These strange people held my future in the palms of their hands. I had no idea of how much time to expect. I just knew that I had done way too much time for such petty crimes and definitely had been railroaded to CRC. When I had told others of the crimes I was in for, they laughed. Most of the women were serving time for possession of drugs and/or trafficking. Here I was doing almost a year (including county time) for being convicted of returning $20 items for cash settlements and possession of paraphernalia (which, to this day, I swear was put in the cell deliberately because I was a foreign resident and therefore a "menace to American Society"). Usually, my crimes would have warranted county time, no more than three months.

However, it was the best thing to have ever happened. I got off the drugs and now had some training to fall back on. I was not bitter. I just wanted to go before the board and ask for my freedom.

We sat rigidly around a table in an office near the personnel kitchen. The board, eight men, dressed in blue suits, looked at me pensively. Having been told where to sit, I looked at them and smiled politely as I sat uneasily in the chair right in front of them. They ruffled through the papers and commented on the time I had served at "their" institution. I waited patiently, allowing them to furtively glance through their files. They read monthly commendations by the grumpy old kitchen supervisor that my work was done exceptionally well. I had served the staff with integrity and good manners. From the clerical instructor was a photocopy of my certificate. Jackie had written a report showing I had participated willingly and energetically in the group sessions. She stated she observed rehabilitation and recommended a parole date. The parole board asked a series of questions, probing what my plans were if I got a release date. I responded that I had chosen to live in San Jose because I liked the city and could begin a new life there. I told them how I would find a job, attend regular Narcotics Anonymous meetings and refrain from ever doing anything illegal. The hearing was short. I got a release date, two weeks away. The board informed me that a parole officer would arrive at CRC to accompany me on the plane. From the airport, she would drive me to a halfway house in San Jose. I chose San Jose simply because it was the closest city near San Francisco that I was familiar with. Also, it was a new place to begin putting my life together. San Francisco held too many bad memories and it would mean returning to the scene of all former drug behaviour. Redwood City was definitely out and so was nearby Oakland. So the only place left was San Jose. To me it was perfect to parole to San Jose.

The conditions of parole were that I had to report every two weeks to the parole officer. Refraining from use of drugs, providing random urine samples and attending regular Narcotics Anonymous meetings were other conditions. I agreed. I was also told that my period of parole was indefinite, that I now had a "seven-year tail," which meant that for the next seven years if ever caught under the influence of drugs I would be immediately returned to CRC without any court appearance. I thought this to be a very tough condition and felt that it would be like I was still incarcerated. Seven years was a long time to be on watch. But I was delighted to have a release date. I couldn't wait to get back to the dorm and tell everyone I was getting out. When I left the small office, I hurried across the yard. I squealed out my release date as I passed down the hallway to my room. Time couldn't go fast enough now.

I continued to go to work each morning. When my release date arrived, in the middle of January, I could not get into my street clothes fast enough. I put on my faded blue jeans with a pullover top and slipped on my brown leather boots which had worn-down heels. Carrying my blue suede jacket, I walked down the hallway and bid the women in the dorm farewell as I headed toward R&R to pick up my personal effects. The small cardboard box containing my personal belongings was inspected for any contraband, propaganda literature or paraphernalia before I could leave. I had written a small collection of poems, but after leaving CRC I found the booklet had been confiscated. I was annoyed that they would keep my writings. This was the first time I attempted to rhyme words and I felt I had made a good effort. I understand now it was kept probably because some things I had written were considered untruths about the place. Finally the parole officer arrived at R&R. She introduced herself as Pat. She was an attractive middle-aged blonde lady. Right away I liked her and we hit it off well. She was informal and I sensed a friendship would grow between us. I got $200 at R&R and was handed a plane ticket by Pat. We were on our way. We left the main entrance gate and were driven by a male CRC officer to the airport. Again, my memory does not recall the plane trip to San Jose. I suspect I have a fear of flying—because I cannot recall the plane soaring through the skies, and this time I was squeaky clean of any mind-altering drugs. I do recall arriving at the halfway house in San Jose and Pat introducing me to the staff.

9

SLEEPY SAN JOSE

Although it was January, the air was humid. There was very little change in the weather from day to day. Except, of course, at night it cooled down and usually a light jacket was required.

As I was shown around the coed halfway house, I thought the older two-storey structure looked homey. I was introduced to staff and shown to my room upstairs. A mattress had been placed on the floor in the centre of the room where I would now sleep. I unpacked my few belongings but was somewhat withdrawn around strange people. There was a smaller cot on the far side of the room and I was informed that another woman would be sharing the bedroom. Downstairs on the main floor, there was a fireplace in the living room. On the light-coloured carpeting sat a few young people with their backs against the walls. I don't know why they didn't sit on the couches, as there were many. They probably just felt more comfortable.

I later learned the men and women were from various state correctional institutions. A condition of their parole was to remain drug-free. After supper that evening I went into the living-room and watched TV. Some people there were talking about going to a Narcotics Anonymous meeting shortly and asked if I wanted to join them. I declined. It was too soon and I felt uncertain about even staying at this place. I did not want to live in a house full of strangers. Always a loner, I wanted privacy. I wanted to get my own place and find a clerical job. I had no urge to use drugs, so I did not feel the need to rush out to a meeting. Besides, I'd had enough group therapy at CRC to do me indefinitely.

Early the next morning I had breakfast and informed the staff person on duty, who was the house parent, that I wanted to go downtown to start looking for work. She agreed and I left. As I strolled along Second Avenue I came to a small sign in the window that read: "San Jose Friendship Centre." I hesitated briefly and went inside. Calmly, I went to the receptionist desk at the entrance of the large but shabby office space. Old couches were placed along the wall with used clothing on some of them. The place looked really rundown. Everyone was quite busy at their desks, but I was pleased to see friendly Indian faces. Although the staff were of strange tribes such as Sioux and Apache, and I had only seen pictures of such tribes, coming into this place didn't make me feel uncomfortable. I liked to see Indian people again. It had been so long. It relieved some loneliness from being so far from home. Behind the receptionist's station were about six desks stationed in two rows of three with a wide aisle between the rows. At the far back was a small enclosed office space and at the rear were more offices up a short flight of stairs.

I asked the dark-haired young receptionist if she could help me. Explaining that I had just arrived in San Jose and was looking for my own place to stay, she suggested I talk to the Assistant Executive Director, Bea. She pointed to Bea's desk, the third desk on the right-hand side of the two rows. Bea smiled pleasantly as I approached her desk. A large-figured woman, she had dark hair with strands of grey, tied back tightly. Oval-faced and olive-skinned, she looked typically Indian to me. Immediately, she asked me if I would like to go downstairs and talk privately. We went downstairs into the basement that had a small kitchen, a few tables and some long benches against the far wall. As we sat, she asked me if I wanted some bannock. I said, "No thanks" but felt such hospitality—the ol' Indian way. We talked for several minutes and I explained my situation. I told her I needed to find a job and maybe share rent with someone until I got on my feet again. I learned she was an Okanogan Indian from the Colville Reserve in Washington and that we were distantly related. My grandmother was related to her elders who originated on the Okanagan Reserve where I lived in early childhood. Historically, "Okanagan Indian" was spelled "Okanogan" in reference to natives tribes across the US border. We were of the same tribe except for this change in spelling.

Instantly Bea and I bonded. She must have felt an urge to help a lost and unknown relative. When we went upstairs, she got on the phone and made some calls. She then gave me a phone number and told me to give a woman named Vicki a call. She said that Vicki was a student at San Jose University and needed a roommate. She also told me to fill out an application form and leave it with her. She said the Friendship Centre may soon be needing a receptionist as the woman who was there was soon leaving. I took the application form and the phone number and thanked Bea for being so helpful. I gave her the number of the halfway house I was at and told her I would fill out the application form and telephone Vicki right away. Leaving the Friendship Centre I felt that everyone there really went out of their way to help me. They were all so friendly and eager to be helpful in any way.

The next day I returned to the Friendship Centre and left my application form with the receptionist. I went to Bea's desk, and she was happy to see me again. I had contacted Vicki and would be able to move in with her in a short time. I still had the two hundred dollars from my departure at CRC and would use this to pay my portion of the first month's rent. As I was about to leave from Bea's desk she asked, "How'd you like to start Monday?"

I asked, "What do you mean?"

She replied, "Here. You can have the job at the front desk if you want it."

"So soon?" I probed. Bea announced the woman was leaving sooner than they anticipated. I was delighted. I could not believe that I now had a new place to stay and a job. I could not wait to begin work. I told Bea I didn't have any work clothes, so she suggested I use some of the money I had from leaving CRC. My rent would be a very small amount for the remainder of the month. On the weekend I went to the address that Vicki had given me. She was home that Saturday morning and was eager to help. I moved in and took a large bedroom in the four-room apartment in the six-plex. That weekend I also bought a few items of clothing for work. After moving in, I learned that Vicki was in her second year at the University of San Jose. I also learned that she was the San Francisco Indian Princess for that year. She was not the stereotypical pretty-faced princess. Instead, she was tall, had long hair and looked ordinary. Later, as I observed pictures of her, I noticed her beauty. Her publicity photo showed a traditionally dressed Indian princess, with long braids and white doeskin attire. She was nice and polite. It was easy to tell she was well brought up by parents who loved her. At first, I thought she was a "square" comparing her to the women from where I had just come from: an institution of streetwise young women. Sharing accommodation and starting a new job gave me a new outlook on things. Later, the following week I called my parole officer and gave her the new address. She was not too pleased that I had left the halfway house; however, she said she believed I could adjust on my own. After I assured her I would attend Narcotics Anonymous meetings regularly, she made an evening appointment for us to get together so she could also take a urine sample.

My job at the Centre involved opening mail, handling all telephone calls, transferring them to appropriate persons, filing, and typing letters for anyone who needed them done. I was nervous and awkward at first, trying to learn how to transfer calls but soon became confident in my new position. I adapted to office procedure quickly. A few days later, Pat came to our apartment in the evening around five-thirty. She approved of the apartment and was pleased to hear about the job. As I continually produced clean urine samples over the next several weeks, trust grew between us. She was more like a good friend and our visits became monthly. There were times we even went out to dinner together for a down-south Mexican supper of enchiladas, tortillas and chili beans. I really don't think she was allowed to be dining socially with her parolees, but in our case a mutual friendship had blossomed. It was probably her way of showing how pleased she was with the progress I had made, in a short time, of adapting to a new city.

At the office, I met a man named Tom Eaglestaff. He was the education counsellor for the Friendship Centre. He was a tall, full-blooded Sioux Indian. He was married and had a son named Cheyenne. His wife Ursula came to the office usually on payday. She was the controlling type, and

Tom followed her every whim. As I got to know the staff at a more personal level, I joined them after work for a few drinks at the "watering hole" just around the corner. It was a small pub that smelled of stale smoke and sometimes carried the foul odour of uncleaned toilets. But after a few drinks who noticed? Tear-jerking county music warbled from the juke box any time of the day, morning or night. The regulars sat slumped on bar stools or at tables. I was happy to be a part of the staff team that worked hard and socialized together.

Dutifully, I carried my work out during the day, but when 5:00 p.m. rolled around, the same small group of us went to the watering hole. Usually Simon, a support worker, Doreen, a job placement worker, and I went. Sometimes Tom would join us but leave early because he said Ursula got very upset if he was not home right after work. As time went on, and I mixed work with pleasure I began to feel a strong attraction toward Tom, though he was a married man. Whenever he joined us after work in the bar I would flirt with him and urge him to stay longer. Despite his insistence that he had to be home, the more he drank the less will power he practised. Later, one Friday night after going to the bar, I lured Tom back to my apartment. He parked his truck in the underground parking lot and came upstairs to continue drinking with me. He stayed the night and the next day. When I awoke the following Saturday morning, we were both lying on the mattress in the spare bedroom. When he opened his eyes, I hugged him gently. He looked around the strange surroundings and there was a twinkle in his sleepy eyes. He said he was going to be in a lot of shit when he went home. I replied, "Who cares? It's only Ursula." We made love passionately again, although we were quite hung-over. He then got up and got dressed and left. Following the incident, I appeared at work a little embarrassed to face him. Knowing he was married did not change things; I was more attracted to him. There was security in being involved with a married man. This way I would never have to make a commitment of any sort. It felt so good to be with someone this special.

The letters from John now came to my new address. He had been transferred to Soledad, another maximum security federal penitentiary, where it was located I had no idea. I never wanted to see him but knew in the letters I would have to lie and say I'd missed him and would be out to see him. Knowing John's volatile temper, I knew he would flip out and maybe end up doing more time if I ever told him I was involved with someone. Especially after all those months of lying and saying how much he meant to me, it would come as quite a blow. Also, I knew he would probably kill me once he got out because he was an extremely jealous man. In Vancouver, he'd beat me almost unconscious if he thought I had even looked at someone in the street or in the elevator whenever we went out of those ritzy high-rise luxury rooms. So I thought it best to keep this top secret but still wanted to continue my affair with Tom. While I had secretly hoped he would leave Ursula and be with me, I knew this was not possible.

One evening, late into the night, as we were sitting together at the table sipping beer at the pub around the corner, Ursula walked in. She came right over to us and slapped Tom so hard across the face, he tumbled off his chair and fell to the floor. She looked at me furiously and suspiciously. Quickly, I told her there was nothing going on. When Tom got back on his chair he insisted she calm down and sit. She positioned herself at our table and continued to vehemently put him down. She said she wanted him home where he belonged. I offered to buy her a beer and unexpectedly she accepted. When she had calmed down a little, she told Tom she wanted to talk to me alone. He left. Secretly, he knew where to meet me later and I looked forward to spending a short time with him at my apartment. Ursula and I left the bar and went to another night spot to talk. She addressed all her suspicions and said she knew I was having an affair with her husband. Of course, I used my buddy-buddy tactics by sucking up to her and befriending her. This diffused any distrust and convincingly I spoke of never having messed with her husband. Meanwhile, Tom went to another bar. Later that night when we got together at my place, he expressed his guilt over doing such a drastic thing to Ursula. We made love again. I was not to spend another evening with him. Our affair ended and he would not be as friendly toward me at work. I expected they would mend their relationship and I would be the one expelled.

Sometimes, I would see them at powwows in San Jose. Once I saw them at the fair grounds sitting in Tom's truck. He completely ignored me when I walked by. With Ursula beside him, they had their little baby in the car seat and looked like the perfect family. It became quite uncomfortable at work but I managed to carry on despite being unable to see him anymore.

I continued working at the Centre for about five months. During this time I finally made it to see John. One Saturday morning at about 8:00, I boarded a bus to travel quite a long distance toward Salinas and then to Soledad to visit him. On our first visit, he told me how good I looked. It fell upon empty ears. I was wearing a miniskirt and he had commented on how much better I looked since our departure in Redwood City. I didn't want to visit; I was merely fulfilling the obligation I felt toward him. So guilt tugged at me at times. I still believed more than anything else this was a big farce and the sooner I could get him out of my life, the better. I often wondered if he really knew how I felt. Regularly, once a month I caught the bus and travelled south to visit him. Our visits were informal and he went on about how he could not wait to get out. He whined about my being free and him not. I reminded him of the seriousness of his case. I despised going into Soledad prison. It was exactly like the prisons shown in TV movies. Around Soledad there were watch towers, high 14' fences, steel bars at the entrance to the building and officers in their pressed drab-looking musty-yellow uniforms. Inside the visiting room we sat, talking among a large room filled with other visitors. I could not wait for the two-hour visit to end. Strangely though, I always felt a sort of loneliness when I left and walked to the parking area where the bus was. Solemnly, I climbed aboard, waiting for others to get on and the driver to take all the visitors back into town. I know the sadness was caused by entering such a depressing place. Its atmosphere was not like CRC at all. This place was eerie. When I was inside it was like an impending cloud of doom lurked above.

One day, at the bar after work I took a couple of swigs of beer and got sick to my stomach. This was unusual and I went on home instead of staying with the others. Shortly after this, I began to notice I had been putting on some weight around my stomach. I never kept track of missing my period because menstruation had never been regular since I had started using drugs. There were months that I never had a period at all when I was on speed and heroin. So I dismissed counting the days since I had been so irregular previously. Shortly after that, at work I decided to make an appointment and go to a doctor. As I returned, Bea jokingly asked, "Did the rabbit die?" I smiled and shook my head. To my consternation, a few days later the results were back and I was pregnant. I had no idea who the father might be. While carousing the bars I had dated a few different men, had sex, but never used a condom or birth control pills. There were two men that I thought were possibilities but I was not sure. I did not know what to do now. I had settled into my job and was now at the Friendship Centre almost seven months. I hated the thought of having to go on maternity leave. I was not ready to have a baby in my life right now. The worst thing was not being sure who the father was. It never crossed my mind that it might be Tom.

10

A BOUNCING BABY GIRL

Soon after the doctor's diagnosis I gave two weeks' notice at the Friendship Centre. Entering my fifth month of pregnancy, I did not enjoy the daily heartburn and sudden weight gain. I was not prepared to have a baby nor did I feel responsible enough to bring a child into the world. I had just gotten out of the correctional facility and had been having the time of my life. There was partying, holding down a steady job but refraining from using drugs. I did not feel the need to attend Narcotics Anonymous meetings or maintain an honest relationship with my parole officer. What I did not realize through the regular drinking was that I was replacing the drug addiction with alcohol addiction. Luckily, the pregnancy restrained me from further alcohol abuse. The smell of booze was a turn-off, and I am thankful to this day that it was. I was totally ignorant of fetal alcohol syndrome. I now realize my younger sister Harriet was affected by it. However the perils of drinking and pregnancy were not well understood back then.

Leaving the Centre meant leaving behind the circle of friends I had made and a job I really liked. Instead, I now sat at home mulling over the situation that presented itself—unmarried and expecting a baby. With the uncertainty caused by the thought I would soon be a mother, I wished that I had someone there. Being so far from home, I became more lonely. I had no idea of how to raise a child and support it, let alone deliver one. The process frightened me. I had heard so much about childbirth and how painful it could be.

Once I left my job, I maintained no contact with my partying co-workers at the Centre. Bea was the only one who was really concerned about how I was doing. She called occasionally and had come to visit bringing Alice Millard, an elderly Apache woman whom I had grown to admire and respect at the Centre.

I settled into accepting that I was going to be a mother, and as I felt life growing inside I started to think like a mom-to-be. I decided to move from the six-plex and find a one-room apartment. There was a vacant apartment on the other side of town I had looked at and liked. It was small, had gold shag carpeting but would be big enough for the two of us. I rented it, and on the first of the following month, moved in. Situated at 377 Willow Avenue, it was on the west side of San Jose.

With motherhood approaching, I began to look in stores for baby items. I bought cute little sleepers and began a collection of baby things such as a cradle seat, bottles, a sterilizer and whatever else I could afford. The motherly instinct took over and I became very health conscious. I enrolled in prenatal care, attended exercise classes and watched my diet. I drank lots of milk and alone at my new apartment patiently awaited the birth of my baby. I was able to get a used couch and table and chairs from a surplus store called Levitz. I always remember the slogan, "You'll love it at Levitz." The couch had saggy cushions but served its purpose. Using the last pay from work and my holiday pay, I got everything that was needed. There were daily ads in the paper for various items of used furniture for thirty dollars. I got a nice oak dresser with a mirror, a bed, and the crib, all for less than a hundred dollars. I then went to the welfare office, feeling absolutely degraded, but I needed medical and social assistance as well. I hadn't thought about my eligibility to collect unemployment insurance. Definitely, getting the resources to pay my medical bills was the priority.

I took the bus and went to visit John at Soledad to break the news to him. I was about six months pregnant when I finally appeared in the visiting room in a maternity smock. I didn't have to tell him. Surprisingly, he just nodded his head as I confessed that being off drugs I now felt the normal needs of any woman. I lied, saying that loneliness for him led me to being unfaithful. He asked me who the father was and I replied, "I don't know." I also told him that I had been drinking heavily before getting pregnant and was not the way he had left me in Redwood City. I suspect he did not blow his stack with the news because there were guards all around the place. Instead, he acted supportive and said he understood. I asked him if he were embarrassed to have his fellow inmates see us together and the situation I was in. He shrugged it off and said he didn't have to explain "his ol' lady had been unfaithful." He said it was not any of their business.

I promised I would continue coming to visit until it got too uncomfortable to travel. He told me that he was being transferred again. This time to a minimum security camp that had no more bars and was out in the mountains somewhere. I was happy that he was finally getting near a release date. I promised to come to visit him when he was transferred. He told me to get a hold of his brother in Milpitas to make arrangements for monthly visits once he was transferred. I assured him I would. Since getting out of CRC I had been seeing Art on occasion. We went out to the bars a few times, drank and ended up at my apartment, later having sex. Looking back I'm ashamed of my behaviour. I was not a very good person upon my release from prison. I had no values and was out to pacify my selfish needs with no concern for whom I might hurt. I did not have any respect for men and was out to use them now. Perhaps my actions were caused because I had been so ill-treated by John prior to our incarceration. His abuse made me want to use others, though not consciously, of course. I agreed to let Art know of John's transfer and give him the details.

In about the seventh month of pregnancy Art and I finally made it to the camp where John was stationed. The ride was very uncomfortable. I forget the name of the place or the exact location. It was quite a long drive out of San Jose, up a steep mountain pass into the hills of California. When we arrived, John hugged me and was happy to see us. I did not want him touching me. Our visit was not supervised and Art left us alone to talk. We walked toward the edge of the grounds and admired the greenery below. It was like he was camping. The only hints that he was still in the penal system were the officers again in those dingy yellow uniforms inside the small office building. He told me how he could not wait to get back on the streets and asked if I would be there for him. He also asked me to masturbate him as we stood looking downward. I was repulsed and appalled at his vulgarity and said we would get caught for sure. So he kept his pants zipped up. I assured him I would be there for him when he got out in a few months. If he only knew what my thoughts were.

In my mind I had it all planned. He would return the baby and me to Canada and it would be *C'est la vie* or however that French saying goes. He still repulsed me! I felt degraded around him—like a prostitute because that is exactly how I was with him before. In exchange for drugs I allowed him to use my body to fulfil his perverted sexual fantasies.

The guilt and remorse tugged at me every time I saw him. I didn't need him for drugs any more so why did I feel such a loyalty toward him? I believe it was the control he still had over me because he had physically abused me so much I still felt that I was trapped and that he had authority over me.

He said the baby would be ours. He played around with some names and underneath my breath I thought, "Like hell. You'll have no claim to my baby." I was torn with guilt every time I left. I was wearing this mask of loyalty but underneath I really felt hatred toward this man and wanted revenge. It would be the last time I visited John. Art and I had a good time during the long drive home. He was like a real brother-in-law to me—caring, and attentive. He also let me know he was available sexually if I wanted. I declined, being so big now. Our sexual excursions had not been very meaningful. They had been the odd one night stand. He had confided how unhappy his marriage was. Of course, there I was, again, to the rescue.

Into the ninth month, late one night, while laying in front of the TV, I suddenly felt strong surges of pain. I rolled over on the floor trying to get comfortable. No position offered any comfort. The pain was really more discomfort than anything. I remember what I had for supper that evening. I did not know how to cook too well and made meatballs and rice. I made these little shrivelled up meatballs along with soggy instant rice.

When the pain got more forceful I got up off the floor and went out to use the neighbour's telephone. I called an old friend, Gloria Garcia, who had been, at one time, a sheriff but had worked at the Centre as a support worker. I don't know why I didn't call Bea, my closest friend. I suppose I felt safe with Gloria because of the field of work she was in. Immediately she came to my apartment and took me to her place. Carefully, I marked down each contraction. They were five minutes apart. From seven o'clock on until the Johnny Carson show at 11:30, I timed the contractions. It was comforting to have Gloria there, but after the Johnny Carson show I asked Gloria to drive me to the hospital. I knew it was going to be a long haul and I didn't want to keep her from going to work the next morning. She drove me to Santa Clara County Hospital.

I checked in and was taken to the maternity ward. In the early hours of the morning, the contractions became more severe. I stopped keeping count; instead I stared at the big clock on the wall. My muffled whimpers developed into screams of pain. All night I yelled as the pain got stronger. Once, a young nurse with long, natural curly red hair tied back in a ponytail came to my bedside. She told me sternly that there were other woman expecting and that I was not the only one going through childbirth, nor would I be the last. She flatly told me to shut up, that I was disturbing and causing fear in the other women. I did not hesitate to tell her to Fuck Off.

This was my baby and I would damn well scream all I wanted. I begged to see a doctor to get something for the pain. I never once saw a doctor or got anything to lessen the pain. I was in labour for twenty-one hours. At times I felt like I was going to pass out from so much pain. The only times the nurse came were to shush me up. I wanted to yank her red hair out by the roots and claw her face for being so unkind. I was kept in the same room the entire time until a few minutes before delivery. The room I was in had about eight beds, all filled with mothers in labour. Never do I ever recall any of the women telling me to be quiet. Those Mexican women are gracious and understanding.

On November 11, 1975, at 4:42 p.m. I gave birth to a beautiful baby girl weighing 8 lbs. 10 oz. I named her Michelle. I was delighted but exhausted. By the time I got out of the delivery room I barely had a voice. Little raspy sounds were all that could come out. It was such a relief to be out of so much agonizing pain. But it was all worth it. Just before I gave birth the doctor said he was going to have to do an incision because there was not enough room for the baby's head to come out. What he didn't tell me was that he was not going to be doing any freezing. I felt the blade of his scalpel making the incision. I remember the feeling of the knife tearing my already ripped skin. I screamed one last time before almost blacking out. He said that he froze the area but I told him, "No, you didn't." I still have ill-feelings toward how incompetent the doctor and nurses were at that hospital. Of course, what can you expect from a state-run hospital that attends to social welfare recipients? To them, I was probably just another welfare case—a number to send to Medicare—a second-class person, and a foreign one at that.

From the moment I lay eyes on my baby I forgot everything: the ugly red-haired nurse, the incompetent doctor, my discomfort. Instead, there was this beautiful little baby. When they brought her at feeding times, I examined every little inch of her body, stroking the fine light-brown hairs of her perfectly rounded head. She was the most beautiful thing I had ever laid eyes on. And she was all mine!

Shortly after Michelle was born, one evening many friends from the Centre came to visit. Gloria, Bea, Bea's daughter Joey, Doreen, and a lady from the health department came. As they crowded around my bed, congratulations came from everywhere. I was so pleased to see them all; they felt like family to me. I could barely talk but acknowledged everyone with whispers of appreciation for their coming. We all shared in the excitement. Leaving, Bea looked at me and joyfully said, "Just think, Mary, you are never going to be alone again." I have never forgotten what she said. She must have understood the alienation and loneliness I felt living so far from any family or home.

Within a few days, I officially named my baby Michelle Babette Marie Lawrence. I chose Babette because John wanted that name. Again, in loyalty to him, I honoured his request and gave her the middle name he wanted. I put his name on her birth certificate as the father and to this day regret it. I have meant to change it so many times but never have. Somehow it's a reminder to me that he was there for me, even though he was cruel there was a kind, caring side to him.

After four days in the hospital I went home. Proudly, I carried my baby and left with Bea. She felt I shouldn't be alone with the baby, probably because of post-partum depression. She suggested I come to stay with her family for a few days. I agreed and while there, fussed over Michelle the whole time, making her bottles, bathing her and rubbing baby lotion all over her after bath time. We slept on the hide-a-bed in the living room, and I got annoyed because Bea and her family were fussing too much over her. I wanted her all to myself. Feeling sensitive and emotional, I wanted to be at home. I asked Bea to take us home and was happy to leave their place, although they were so supportive and loving and kind. I just wanted some time to spend with my baby.

At the apartment the first thing I noticed on the stove was the dried-up meatballs and bacteria growing over the rice. I quickly washed the dishes and scrupulously cleaned the apartment. Things were going well. I was not lonely anymore. Busy each day, I cared for Michelle. My days were filled with joy. I regretted feeling my apprehension about motherhood before her birth. Everything now came naturally. I became a doting mom and she became my most prized possession. Whenever we went to the store for groceries or took the bus anywhere, I proudly showed her off in her cradle seat. Whenever we went back to the hospital for her regular checkups, the nurses marvelled at how healthy and beautiful she was. Of course, I agreed.

Letters still came regularly from John. His parole date was coming up soon and he asked if he could use my address, requesting I write a letter to the parole board. I agreed. I sent him pictures of Michelle and this time I had meaningful things to write about. I'm sure he found all the baby talk boring.

I felt the urge to have the odd beer again. I would go across the street and get a six pack from the grocery store while Michelle was having her afternoon nap. In the evening with everything done, I enjoyed sipping from a cold can of Slitz malt liquor. Sometimes, I'd have Art over. He would marvel at Michelle too. After drinking beer we would end up in bed making mad passionate love. Knowing John would be home soon, we decided to cool our affair. We agreed there would be no more intimacy. I asked him if he felt guilty doing this to his brother and his reply was simply, "Why should I?" They were close as brothers but when it came to women, Art was a big flirt. It didn't matter to him that John and I were still together. He had a completely different regard for John and made it quite clear that he would take advantage of a good situation if John was stupid enough to land himself in prison. Although Art always rescued John, I suspected there was some animosity between them. Art joked and said somebody had to look after me—and better yet, it could be kept in the family. Those were his family values. To me, it showed disrespect for John. So while I felt tremendous guilt, subconsciously I kept wanting to punish John for the beatings that I had lost count of.

When Michelle was about three months old, John was released. He had served pretty close to the full two years. I was apprehensive about him coming to live with us, and yet I knew this would be the only way to get back to Canada. When he arrived I opened the door and greeted him, pretending to be excited that he was finally home. He fawned over Michelle and admiringly claimed her as his own. He was pleased that I had used his name and promised to be a good father to her.

Within a short while, John was back at it again—the violence that I thought was never going to crop up stared me in the face. One afternoon we were drinking beer and had enough to get a buzz on. We started arguing about my behaviour while he was locked up and before I knew it— WHAM! I got a severe blow across the face. He slugged me really hard, and right away I told him he had to leave. He did go and I was so angry. I never wanted to see him again. Later that evening he returned, and when I would not let him in, he kicked the door until it came off the hinges. I couldn't phone for help because I had no phone, so I just sat inside and waited for the expected. When he burst through the door, he beat on me again. I decided then he would never hit me again. I didn't need him for a drug supply anymore, so how dare he enter my apartment and beat me up? I'd had it with him! He never meant anything to me and what gave him the right to beat on me after all the visits and letters and loyalty I had shown toward him. I was furious! I was also fearful he would hurt Michelle. It was time to make some hasty decisions.

After his blow up, things were quiet around our apartment. He was, as usual, remorseful that he beat me and the usual pattern before was to pacify me with new clothes, money, etc. This time he did not have any money to buy me anything. The money he got from leaving the prison camp was now almost gone. I continued to report to Pat but lied about my situation. I did not dare tell her that John was living with me. I would be in serious trouble if she knew I was associating with a prior crime partner.

I cannot recall having sex with John upon his release. There is a block there. We must have done it because two years is a long time for anyone to go without sex unless he was gay in prison. As I think of it now, I don't recall ever climbing into bed with him. I know we slept together but there is a complete blank. I remember everyone I was intimate with, except him.

11

HOMEWARD BOUND

Within the month, John had returned to using heroin again and of course, I went along with him. I had completely forgotten about my parole stipulations. Knowing that we would be leaving San Jose soon, I succumbed to his control once more. I felt badly that I was not being the doting mother that I had been all along. John was bringing home small amounts of Mexican Brown but I do not recall being overly anxious to doing drugs again. Besides, we only used the odd time so I was not addicted in the least. The cold-turkey spells at Redwood City remained etched in my mind, too vivid to ever leave, but they didn't stop me from shooting up.

John's parole officer had stopped by our apartment while we were out and left a note on the door. He reminded John that he was still on parole and wanted to see him immediately. John took the note and tore it into shreds. He defiantly declared that we would be leaving the next morning. When I asked where, he replied, "Canada." He had borrowed Art's Falcon for the last few days. I asked him how we were going to travel and he said, "We'll take my brother's car." Anxious to leave San Jose, I packed our clothes, leaving plenty behind. I knew it was time to flee. We would both be producing dirty urine tests if we continued to stay in San Jose, and the way it looked, we were heading right back to where we started two years earlier. I couldn't wait to leave. I didn't give a second thought to leaving an apartment full of furniture behind. I knew I could rebuild somewhere else. All that was on my mind was getting back to Canada.

We took Michelle's crib mattress and spread it across the back seat of the Falcon. It fit nicely. Quickly packing our belongings into the trunk, we pulled out of the apartment parking lot and headed out to the freeway. John had a little bit of heroin on him but I do not recall using any. We drove north. As we drove, I thought about the long relationship I had maintained with Pat and felt badly about jumping my parole. Getting back to Canada was most important and overruled any further feelings of trepidation. As we drove, John became very annoyed with Michelle's crying. She was in the back seat, and whenever I attended to her to give her a bottle, I would reach behind from my bucket seat. She became restless lying on the mattress all the time.

For three days straight, John drove. When he got too tired we pulled over to a rest stop and he'd close his eyes and take a power nap. We were both snapping at each other and with Michelle fussing, he had little patience. I counted the hours when I would be free of him.

On the third night as we travelled the highways I dozed slightly. We were now going north east and were heading toward Idaho. John had decided to visit his sister Claudette in Kettle Falls, Washington. Suddenly, in pitch-black darkness outside, I opened my eyes wide. I don't know what could have awoke me. I looked ahead and we were heading straight for a guard rail. My sense of impending danger caused me to yell at John. He had fallen asleep at the wheel. When he straightened out the steering, I could see down a steep canyon alongside us. Had he not turned when he did, the car would have definitely gone over the embankment. We would have crashed and dropped several hundred feet below. I'm still amazed at how we didn't crash. I urged John to pull over at the next rest stop and when he eventually did, we both got large containers of coffee. I never shut my eyes again to doze off. I kept talking to him to make sure he did not fall asleep again at the wheel. Michelle slept peacefully in the back seat. I was pretty shaken up. I still question what premonition woke me at the moment before disaster.

Travelling and almost reaching our destination had pretty well exhausted our reserve of money. We left with barely any gas money but made it as far as the small farming community of Kettle Falls. John's mom was there also. She turned up wherever we went. In Vancouver, she had an apartment nearby and John always had to be near her. Then she went to live in Florida after John gave her lots of money. Apparently, she handled all his business affairs, such as laundering his money in different places. She lived pretty high-class. When we first moved into the west end apartments she appeared from out of nowhere once John was making big bucks.

Kettle Falls turned out to be an okay visit until John's mom said she wanted to talk to me outside on the front lawn. There she attacked me by pushing and shoving and throwing punches, aiming for my face. She told me I was nothing but a junkie and had messed her son's life up badly. I ducked from getting hit and we rolled around on the grass. It wasn't much of a fight, and I thought she looked ridiculous—an old woman in her fifties pouncing on me. John and his sister stayed in the house. He later stuck up for his mom saying he couldn't blame her for not liking me. Imagine that! Ooh! How I hated him, more than ever now. That evening they all huddled in the kitchen visiting. Claudette and her husband had given up their master bedroom for us, so that's where I took Michelle for the whole evening. I'm pretty sure they had a couple of kids although I don't recall meeting them. Upstairs, still fuming over John's lack of concern and his mom's erratic behaviour, I called Yvonne collect and asked her to send me bus fare. I think she sent around $50.00 to the Western Union in the tiny town of Kettle Falls. The next morning we used the money, instead, to put gas in the car. We now had enough for milk, cigarettes, gas and a little for food. John must have had much more stashed away because he wasn't concerned about money. He announced he was planning to go to Edmonton. We left that morning as soon as we picked up the money and continued our journey.

As we neared the Canadian border, John became nervous. We had California licence plates on the car and he worried about there being an alert at the border on his parole violation. He cautioned me to look attentive and to leave the talking to him. It was late in the afternoon and we looked grubby. When we drove up to the window, the custom officer peered in asking our purpose of going into Canada. John said we were on holidays and were going to Canada for a few days. Luckily, we got through. I believe when the officer saw Michelle in the back seat he assumed we were ordinary, although scruffy-looking parents. As we drove into Canada I wanted to throw my arms up in glee. John warned me to stay calm and not look back or act conspicuous. He didn't have any drugs on him but had a syringe hidden somewhere in the car.

That old Falcon made it all the way to Vernon! We never had any car problems. The only problem was the door on the passenger side had come off slightly from its hinges from being slammed shut too many times. It was hard to close and had to be slammed to catch properly. This was a small problem, though. John was fortunate to have a brother who would lend him anything. Except that Art could easily have reported the car stolen since we didn't let anyone know we were leaving San Jose. John could have been picked up on car theft but he hadn't been. John knew he could almost get away with anything with Art.

As we headed north toward Vernon, I couldn't wait. While I was living at the first apartment in San Jose, I had written Marge the odd time. I knew her address in Vernon and told John I wanted to see her first. When we arrived at Marge's apartment block, I asked John what he wanted to do. He said his mom was headed for Edmonton, and he was going to meet her there. I'm sure that he borrowed extra money from her while they made their plans in Kettle Falls. I know how she wanted him away from me, so it doesn't surprise me at all that she would give him gas money and make arrangements to meet him in a week or so. It was ironic! All along I was planning a way of getting rid of him once I got home and he had it all planned. He was getting rid of me first. He didn't say he was coming back to get me, so I knew it was the end of the line for both of us. It was a secret we both had kept. His loyalty was there all along too; he must have felt he owed me this much for the hell he put me through. I'm sure he did not feel at all guilty that I got railroaded through the penal system and ended up doing seven months for my small crime. So our feelings were actually quite mutual. He didn't need me nor did I need him anymore.

Marge lived at the Valleyview Apartments just off the highway on the crest of the hill, as you enter Vernon from the south. It was not far from the Vernon Jubilee Hospital. It was early in the spring but had been so hot when we left San Jose that we were already wearing summer clothes. I had a halter top on and Michelle had only her Pamper on. It was a little cooler in Vernon. As I stood by the intercom, Marge's voice came over. She was happy to hear my voice. Right away she said, "Come on up." I went to the car and gathered up our few belongings and took Michelle from the back seat. That crib mattress had served its purpose well. Standing briefly by the driver's side, I said to John, "Well, this is it. Have a good trip to Edmonton." He just nodded his head and didn't say anything. I turned and headed toward the glass door entrance to the modern apartment building. John peeled off and sped away. There was no last farewell; he was on his way to Edmonton. I felt absolutely nothing upon his departure. No sentimental feelings whatsoever! I felt relieved to finally be rid of him permanently. It was three years since my nightmare began and now I could begin my life again with my little Michelle.

Marge already knew I had a baby girl and was anxious to see her. I had not even sent her photos. I took the elevator to her apartment carrying Michelle and our bag of clothing. Upstairs, Marge welcomed us into her home. She had a little boy named Derek. Her oldest son Daryl was being raised by his grandmother on the Reserve. Marge was proud of her new little niece. She offered to help us in any way she could. Since it had been over three years since I last saw her, there was much catching up to do. Marge had never met John but certainly knew his history, and she was very relieved that I had finally got completely away from him.

The following week I went to Social Services and applied for assistance. I was able to rent a suite on the third floor of Valleyview Apartments as soon as I obtained the cheque. It was unfurnished, but in time I got a table and bed from a lady who was moving out. She sold everything to me quite cheaply. In fact, she pretty well gave it all away.

A couple of weeks later, as I was visiting Marge, her intercom buzzed. When she answered she looked at me and said, "Someone wants to talk to you." I looked outside the window and down below was the green Falcon. I told John over the intercom that I did not want to see him. I told him we should now go our separate ways. He talked me into letting him come up, and he stayed for a few days. During that time we went to the bars for an evening out. He met a Frenchman named Marcel and they hit it off, getting drunk together. When John and I got back to the apartment, we got into it again. I know we were arguing, but I don't remember getting hit. The next day I told him it was definitely over. He didn't say where he was going but left without any hassle. In my mind I was finished with him and hoped never to see that lanky, poker-faced man again.

12

DRINKING WON'T KILL ME

Marge and I began to drink together every weekend. She could always come up with a twenty-dollar bill and we'd order a case of beer, have a few drinks and go to the bars downtown. Before I arrived, she was already a regular at the bars every Friday night. Secure in the knowledge that John was out of my life completely, I was ready to party. We always found a baby-sitter in the building and although we never could afford to pay them, we still managed to go out. Usually, after a night out we picked up our kids and went to Uncle Freddie's house. He was an old man with money and we all adopted him as our uncle. He was our bootlegger, except that we didn't have to buy from him. He'd take care of the little ones while Marge and I drank into oblivion. Usually, in the bars I would snag someone who looked like he had a few bucks and con him out of his money. I would sit and be a companion for the evening. When the money was all spent, I would quietly sneak off. Sometimes I would offer to score pot for whomever I was sitting with, and when I got the twenty-dollar bill, I was gone. Vernon is not a very big town, so it did not take long before I had to stop doing the hustle I had known so well from living in Vancouver. My drinking got worse. I was not as good a mother as I had been in San Jose. I neglected Michelle and left her with a baby-sitter much of the time. I wanted to make up for lost time. I had missed the pub environment in San Jose and now jumped in with both feet. It seemed there was always money to buy booze but never any money to buy milk.

As the drinking scene developed, I found that I was becoming again plagued with the depression I had experienced so often while living in Vancouver. What would begin as a night of rowdiness would later end up with my stopping by the hospital on the walk home and checking myself into the psych ward to talk with any nurse who was on shift. After a couple of hours of pouring out my sadness, I would leave and head back to the apartment which was just a few blocks away. I'd promise the baby-sitter to pay whatever I owed the following week and snuggle into bed beside Michelle. Guilt tugged at me daily. Drinking and promiscuity became a daily pattern of life.

I went to our family doctor and obtained a prescription of antidepressants. I informed Dr. Williams I had been on such medication in Vancouver regularly. Still unable to cope with the return of depression, I asked Dr. Williams to give me a referral to the Mental Health Unit to get professional counselling. It did not take long before I was sitting in the psychiatrist's chair undergoing medical hypnosis. There, I came to the realization that there was a very saddened, abandoned little girl. Losing her mother at the early age of eight, I had never learned to cope with such a loss. Therefore, I turned to drugs and alcohol to numb the deep pain. Each week I visited the psychiatrist and we embarked on an in-depth journey into the dark annals of my past.

Upon each visit I received more prescribed pills to combat the feelings of depression. I'd swallow a few pills and go drinking every chance I could get. Neither I nor the psychiatrist ever made the connection that, maybe, the drinking was a cause of my depression. Rather than getting more pills, I should have looked at the drinking problem instead. Perhaps I should have been directed toward a treatment centre rather than given another prescription of antidepressants. Soon, I was elevated to taking Thorazine, which is only prescribed for schizophrenia. It made me so clumsy and drowsy I ended up living in a vacuum. I would take the pills all week and every weekend get drunk. Sometimes I flipped out in the bars, but I never realized how fatal mixing alcohol with potent pills was. I would pick fights with somebody who looked at me the wrong way, arguing incessantly. I felt like I was going over the edge. I became dependent on pills, and when I grew tolerant to a prescribed pill, I'd have Dr. Williams try me on something else.

As the depression got worse, I told Marge I couldn't take it anymore and was going to take my own life. She called the police and they took me to the police station. In the two years that I had been away in California I held a secret within that I had never told to anyone other than John. I finally confessed to Marge that, while living in Vancouver, I was busted for possession of heroin in New Westminster and had gone south to avoid prosecution. I told her my conscience couldn't take my guilt anymore, causing a lot of the depression. As a good sister, she informed the police of this when they came to attend to the suicide call. As it turned out, I faced the courts. I had also violated my parole in California. Luckily, through Legal Aid I got a really good lawyer named John Orr, who was able to get me one year probation and clear me of the "seven year tail" and the parole violation in California. So it came as quite a relief. I did have to spend a few days in jail, but Marge looked after Michelle, and I was able to clear up the wreckage of my past. I suppose the parole officials in California were glad to see that I was no longer a resident there. Therefore, they did not have any reason to have me extradited. Besides, possession of drug paraphernalia does not warrant extradition! I now had a good lawyer and could easily place a civil suit on the state for wrongfully imprisoning me.

Our careless lifestyle of boozing continued. I kept seeing the psychiatrist, and he kept me on pills. The therapy didn't help because I would just go out and drink on the weekends to drown the sorrows. It was a vicious cycle.

Late one night, well after midnight, as Michelle slept and I watched TV, someone rang the buzzer. When I asked who it was, a strange voice came over the intercom. I didn't recognize the voice and asked again, "Who is it?"

"Open the door, let me in. It's Marcel," came the reply. I vaguely remembered Marcel and wondered why he wanted to see me. I had seen him in the bars the odd time after John left but we were never really acquainted. I thought he probably had something important to tell me concerning John as they became such buddy-buddies in the bar .

I replied, "Sure, come on up" and pressed the button on the intercom. Relaxed, I opened the door when I heard a light tapping. In the doorway stood John. I gaped at him, not expecting such a figure to be hovering in the doorway. He smelled as if he had just come from a barn, like cow shit. He obviously hadn't bathed in some time and he exuded a strong body odour. Suddenly I became paralyzed with fear waiting for his next move. Quickly, stepping back, I asked why he disguised his voice.

"Because you wouldn't have let me in if I said it was me." He responded cockily. Looking me square in the eyes he turned very serious and said, "I've come back for one reason—to kill you!" Startled, I moved backward as he came closer. On the floor at the entrance to the bedroom was Michelle's Fisher Price toy. It was a big plastic ball with the merry-go-round inside it. He snatched it up and held it in his hand, threatening to use it over my head. Panic-stricken, I almost wet my pants. As frightened as I was, I tried to look calm and not to provoke him in anyway.

"Why?" I asked.

"You screwed around on me when I was in jail and now you are whoring around this town," He said, in his best controlling voice. I told him that it was over between us and what I did now should not concern him anymore. In malicious pleasure with a cold-hearted merciless glaze in his eyes, he sneered, "Don't worry, I'm not going to hurt your baby, just you." I had backed away as far as the balcony window. He then dropped the toy on the floor and pounced on me knocking me to the floor. Before I could shield my face, I felt a closed fist come down on my forehead. He held me down and was getting ready for the next blow when the instinct for survival kicked in. I remembered a tactic I used in Vancouver that had worked then. But this time I didn't know what would work. Neither of us was on drugs now, and his reaction was unpredictable. But I was fighting for my life and I would try anything that worked. I knew he meant business. I remembered from before how he would stop beating me if I showed no fear. For some reason it always worked.

Before the next blow I calmly said, "John, why don't you let me up and I'll get us a cup of coffee and we can talk about everything." He looked down at me with crazed eyes and I said with such sincerity, "Let's try to work this out." He got up, and I staggered toward the kitchen. I felt my forehead, and it felt like the bone was jutting out. There was a big lump in the middle of my forehead, exactly the same place as it was when he hit me in the bedroom at Sharon and Art's place. As I went to the small kitchen my instinct for survival kicked in again. I opened the cupboard and turned to him and said, "I have to go down to Marge's and get us some coffee. Is it okay? I'm all out." He had calmed down a little but was watching every move I made. He told me to make it back fast. As I left the apartment I felt like I was falling apart. I was weak-kneed and dizzy from the severe blow.

I rushed to Marge's apartment, and when she let me in, I phoned the manager. I asked him to call the police and to get that crazy man out of my apartment. I shrieked, "He's going to kill me. And my baby is in there!" The manager was hesitant. He said he didn't like to get involved. When I told him that if anything happened to my baby he would be responsible, he agreed to go up. A short while later he came down to Marge's apartment and told me I had no reason to be alarmed. He reported that he had asked the man to leave. He said he didn't know why I was frightened because when he went into the apartment the man was sitting calmly in the bedroom beside my baby, looking harmless. I pointed to the bump on my forehead and told the manager the man was very dangerous.

I returned to my apartment only when I was certain John was out of the building. John returned the next day and rang my sister's buzzer again. I was still frightened, so I had spent the night at her place. When I saw him outside, I went to the intercom and told him to leave. He apologized for what he did. I told him everything between us was over and had been for a long, long time. I announced he would never interfere in my life again, truly meaning it. Marge was aghast that I was involved with such an animal. I explained how he tricked me, and she cautioned me to be very leery of what he might try next as he was now stalking me. I told her I would never open my door to anyone unless I could see the whites of his eyes. It was a good lesson but a hard lesson. It would not be until seven years later that John would haunt me again.

Living in the fast lane of drinking was taking its toll. It was creating more havoc in my life than pleasure. I now began doing the one year probation and seriously had to consider my drinking because it could affect my probation. But there was something missing. I wanted the love and security of a meaningful relationship and was searching to find Mr. Right. Looking in bars and picking up various men did not have any more appeal. I was tired of the one-night stands, the promiscuity, and waking up not remembering too much of what I had done the night before. Inside, there was a yearning to be a respectful person. I did not want to live my life around the drinking scene anymore. I wanted to settle down and take proper care of Michelle. She meant everything to me and yet I was throwing it all away. I decided that the next time I picked someone up in the bar, it would be someone who I could have a relationship with.

Again, Marge and I went to the National Hotel on a Friday night. Sitting in the middle of the room was a stocky but nice looking man, in his thirties, with short-cropped brown hair. He was wearing a white T-shirt with blue jeans. I was immediately taken by him but hadn't had enough booze in me to get up the false courage to give him the eye. I leaned over to Marge and told her to go over. I said, "See that good-looking guy over there. Go ask him to come over. I'm too shy." Of course, Marge, never one to be shy, got up and walked over.

She returned to tell me the guy would be over soon. I drank my beer quickly to get up the courage to talk smoothly when he did come over. A short while later the man walked over and joined our table. He introduced himself as Bruce. Soon we were talking freely as though we had been lifelong acquaintances. When the evening ended, I invited him up to my apartment for drinks. We talked and drank until the early hours of the morning. I informed him I was tired of one-night stands and wanted a meaningful relationship. Bruce came regularly following that evening and a relationship began. Within the month, he moved in.

He was everything I was looking for—a good drinking buddy, someone who wanted to spend more than one night with me and, just plain and simple, he was special. As the weeks turned into months our relationship grew. We fell in love and I got to meet his wonderful elderly parents, Verna and Bert Wragg. Immediately, I felt accepted by them. I knew Bruce and I were going to last.

I met his two young kids Greg and Lora-Lee who were being raised by their mom and had spent weekends at the Wraggs. They were nice kids and anytime that they could spend time with their dad, they would come to our apartment. We went camping during the summer and did all the normal things families do. Except there was one problem: Bruce and I continued drinking heavily and now began fighting. Our arguments escalated into physical fights. We always started on a happy note. He had quite a little nest egg from his last job on the highways and within a year we had drunk up every cent. We were living off my welfare cheques to pay the rent and used his savings to drink at every opportune moment. Our relationship was compatible when we weren't drinking except that boredom always set in and we would drink, time after time.

After seeing how our relationship was deteriorating we decided to move out of town—the old geographic move—away from our drinking environment. I gave notice at the apartment and we spent a couple of weeks out at Bruce's folks' place before making the big move to Red Deer. Michelle was now about three and toddling around, as cute as ever. We thought that by moving away, we could get jobs and have a better life for the three of us.

We piled all the furniture into the garage at Bruce's folks' place and later rented a big U-Haul. On the day we left, I was apprehensive about a new life in a town I had never been to. What I didn't realize was that we would be taking our drinking pattern and problems with us. Bruce didn't want to leave his two kids, but he also wanted to work too. So it was a sad farewell and we were off. I was anxious to find work when we got settled.

Arriving at night in Red Deer, Alberta, we checked into a motel and got some rest. The next day we looked up some of Bruce's relatives and visited them. We found a basement apartment that was in bad need of renovations but rented it just the same. We made an agreement with the landlord that if he wouldn't charge us rent for the first month, we would renovate. Bruce's mom had given us $2,000.00 to begin our new life in Red Deer. We didn't have to pay the first month's rent, so we had some savings to get set up. The landlord bought carpet. We bought paint and began. It was frustrating work, but it kept us busy for the whole month. We laid the bright orange carpet and painted the yellow kitchen walls a nicer colour. We'd work all week and drink all weekend. Bruce would hit the liquor store and pick up a bottle and we'd get into it. We'd take Michelle to the baby-sitter, go to the bar, get drunk, pick up Michelle and come home and fight. I began calling the police whenever it got physical. There were so many times the police were called. I never pressed charges but would leave when the police arrived, taking Michelle in the middle of the night to a seedy hotel room downtown. I could not afford to pay for the hotel and there were no Women's Shelters in Red Deer at that time, so I ended up phoning the Salvation Army. Their organization would foot the bill for a few days' stay in a hotel until the air had cooled, and I'd go home again. This became a weekly ritual in our early months in Red Deer.

We finally found work. Bruce got a job on the oil rigs. I got a job in housekeeping at the regional hospital until the smell of disinfectant in the early morning was too much to take. It hinted to me that I might be pregnant but I hadn't gone to the doctor to find out. Soon I quit working at the hospital.

Before leaving Vernon, I had stopped taking birth control pills. I wanted a baby but would not tell Bruce I was secretly planning pregnancy. Although we fought violently and drank heavily, I yearned for another baby. I thought I would trick Bruce into getting me pregnant because he wasn't planning to have any more kids. I thought a baby would bring security to our relationship. Finally, I went to the doctor and it was confirmed. Luckily Bruce hadn't punched me in the stomach when we were going at it. When I told him I was almost three months pregnant, he was not pleased. First, he suspected that he wasn't the father. Often we would split up in Vernon and he'd leave for a couple of weeks and I'd carry on, sometimes seeing other men. But it was always back to Bruce. I knew we loved each other. We had gotten engaged while in Vernon and I had taken off the engagement ring so many times it was almost like the ring itself was a jinx.

When Bruce and I were together, I didn't feel depressed and stopped taking all the antidepressants and seeing the psychiatrist. I felt secure with him, though we had major drinking problems. We both liked drinking but hated what it was doing to our relationship. In Red Deer, Michelle got pushed aside and denied the proper attention she needed as a little girl. To fit into our lifestyle, often she joined us playing nearby during our evening of drinking. Sometimes she'd dance in front of us, joyfully entertaining as I sipped on a Caesar and Bruce drank his favourite, Scotch on the rocks.

Because we were fighting too much, I left Bruce and moved into an apartment. Our relationship was so topsy-turvey. Eventually, Bruce moved out of the basement apartment and moved in with us. We tried to make a decent life for ourselves. He still worked occasionally on the rigs but we ended up living off my welfare cheques.

That year, on June 8, 1980, I gave birth to a beautiful, healthy baby girl at the Red Deer General Hospital. We named her Jaclyn. From the moment Bruce laid eyes on her, he knew she was his; I knew all along. Looking at her tiny turned up toes confirmed she was his baby. She also had his nose. She looked more like the Wragg side of the family than my side of family. When we brought her home, Michelle marvelled at her. She was a little jealous, but it didn't take long for her to get used to her little baby sister.

When Jaclyn was about four months old, I decided to leave Bruce permanently. I couldn't take the abuse anymore or the drinking and its destruction in our lives. Following another fight, I packed up the girls' clothes, hopped a train and headed back to BC. It was the hardest thing to do because I still loved Bruce but knew we'd never make it. He absolutely loved Jaclyn and the pain was insurmountable when I separated him from his baby. But I had no choice. We couldn't live like two animals in a cage anymore. Neither of us were going to stop drinking, and it was impossible to live together.

It was a sombre trip back to BC. The train ride was long and when we arrived in Salmon Arm, I called Yvonne. She came to pick us up right away. We stayed with her for a short time, before I decided to settle in Westbank. Just behind Main Street I rented the upstairs of a dilapidated duplex a couple of blocks from where Yvonne and her family lived. For Yvonne, Westbank probably held a warm hometown feeling. For me, it was just a place to start all over again. It was dusty and the streets needed sweeping. There were many orchards surrounding the town and Main Street was also the highway through town. There was really nothing there such as you'd find in the big cities, however, who wanted to live in big cities anymore? Not me.

A couple of months passed, and I never heard from Bruce. I missed him terribly but knew this was the only thing to do. Eventually he returned to Vernon and stayed at his folks' place. We made contact again, and he came to Westbank. Bruce missed the girls, and we tried to patch things up. He was still the same Bruce, mean when he had too much to drink, so we ended up going at it again.

Following another fight, it was over. I wish now that we had sought out professional help to curb our drinking because I think we would still be together to this day if we had. We had an amicable separation. I agreed never to keep Jaclyn from him, and without any legal documents, we agreed to joint custody which, to this day, has remained intact. Our relationship changed once we no longer lived together. We became the best of friends and on weekends or holidays he has always taken Jaclyn. From this, she has become a well-adjusted young woman.

Soon after moving to Westbank I got a receptionist job at the Friendship Centre in Kelowna. I started there in 1981 and things got better. Michelle was now in grade one and Jaclyn was a year old. While at the Centre, I bought my first new car. It was a 1981 Pontiac Acadian. I found out about a house that was available, and because I was a single parent with two children, I qualified under Section 40 Native Housing. I had been working well over a year at the Centre so when this opportunity presented itself, I applied. I also held down a weekend job as a homemaker. Holding down two jobs made my application look even better.

In August of 1982 we moved from our old, dilapidated duplex into the new home. It was beautiful! Michelle had just finished grade one and Jaclyn had just turned two in June. We hardly had any furniture, so I went out and got a used fridge and stove. We brought the few pieces of furniture from the other place, such as an old couch and used mattress. It wasn't long before I was out purchasing new living room furniture. We got nicely settled. Drinking was not so heavy now; only on weekends I would "tie one on". It seemed that the move from Red Deer was a good move.

As I worked at the Centre I got to know my co-workers on a personal level. Before long we were socializing at the bars on weekends. I worked all week and carried out the responsibilities of motherhood. Then, fate reared its ugly head again. I began to drink in excess. Faithfully but hung-over, I would still show up for work Monday mornings. This continued for three years.

Around this time, which would have been approximately seven years since I last had seen John standing outside the apartment in Vernon, I received a phone call. Not recognizing his strong French accent, I asked again, "Who is this?"

"It's John. Remember me? You should!" came the unrecognizable voice. Suddenly, as I stood by the telephone, my knees buckled, and I almost fell. I froze in the moment. It all became very clear; it was the man I never wanted to see or hear from again. I visualized him holding Michelle's toy, ready to crash it down on my skull. The fear was still alive in me. I trembled as I searched for quick answers to persuade him never to contact me again.

Pretending to be calm, I asked, "How did you get my phone number?" His reply was, "You know me, Mary Lou, I never forget. Your sister gave it to me. When I was passing through Vernon looking for you, I looked her up." I almost wet my pants at this point. I had told Marge never to give out any information, especially to him. He then informed me he was calling from Vancouver. He had just been released from doing seven years in a federal prison in Montreal, and he now wanted to see me. Quickly I asked what he had done time for.

His nonchalant response was, "I killed someone."

Shivers went up and down my spine. My mind searched for a quick end to the phone call. When he asked how I was doing and what I was now doing I informed him that I was getting married soon—to a cop—and that I was now living with this man. Somehow, telling him this gave me some security. The old defense mechanism kicked in. I never knew a policeman on any personal level, but my gut reaction was to inform him that I was now well protected. I added how happy I was, looking forward to married life. With this, our conversation came to an abrupt end. To this day, I have not heard from him and hope that I never will again. By now he would be almost sixty years old and probably doing life somewhere in the California penal system. I don't care to investigate his whereabouts but do sometimes wonder if he is still alive.

When speaking with Marge several months later, I asked her why she would ever divulge my telephone number when she knew how he had beat me. Her reply came candidly. She simply said she felt sorry for him as he had come a long way searching for me. She also added that he left a message. Marge recanted his exact words: "Tell Mary Lou she doesn't have to be afraid anymore." Marge said he then limped away. So whatever he did wrong in Vancouver to get all that money, he now had paid the price for. I know this is exactly what he was referring to when talking to Marge. I felt just as much responsible because I was with him and helped spend all those fifty and hundreds dollar bills on heroin.

In 1983, shortly after this incident, I met someone whom I immediately fell in love with. I was swept off my feet by this young man. There was quite an age difference, as I was 13 years his senior. It was not more than two weeks after meeting him that he moved in. When I was two days away from turning 34, we got married. He was only 22. I married him because he genuinely cared for my girls. He treated them with utmost love, and Jaclyn not only had her dad in Vernon, she now had a wonderful step-dad too. Michelle looked up to my husband too, and the wedding was the most beautiful time in my life, other than when I gave birth to my daughters. We were married in front of his parents' trailer on the small Duck Lake Reserve in Winfield. As we drove to the park to take our wedding pictures, we stopped at the downtown pub, of all places, to have a few celebration drinks. I am dismayed to now see how drinking played such a major role in everything I did. What couple in their right minds would think of going to a bar on their wedding day?—especially before taking the wedding pictures. But we did. However, at the time, our marriage seemed like it was blessed from Heaven. Everything was perfect. I had the most gorgeous, young man as my husband. Not only did he love my girls, he fulfilled my every need. I felt a joy I had never felt before. I felt truly blessed.

It wasn't long before our love nest turned into a hornet's nest. Where we once shared devotion and love now was the same baggage as I had in previous relationships. The drinking and the fighting continued but in a different setting. It now looked like a divorce was on the horizon. We were married only four months and I had to get a restraining order. My husband grabbed me by the hair and with one blow he caused a hairline fracture of my nose. He then threw me down on the cement in front of a night club. It wouldn't have surprised me if he broke my nose again since it had already been broken by John. I knew that our marriage wasn't going to last. Another time, at a friend's house, he took a butcher's knife to stab me. Luckily, our friend Jim was there and stood between us and stopped our fighting before there were any fatal wounds. The police arrived and as we stood outside, I took the liberty to slap him across the face so hard my hand stung. I did it only because there were two big cops standing on each side of me. It wasn't long before we separated permanently and he took up with living common-law with another woman. Later, I often heard they battled it out too. I was very jealous of her because I still loved him even though I knew it would never work for us.

Due to getting caught on the wrong side of Friendship Centre politics in the Native movement, I decided to quit my job. It meant leaving behind a lot of good friends. I had one friend I could call my best, Marina Hunt; a vivacious Blackfoot Indian from the Blood Reserve.

Unemployed and living off UIC I managed to still maintain our home under the subsidized government assistance program. The mortgage payments were based on 25% of my net income. What a relief to have such a government subsidy; otherwise I would have lost our home a long time ago. Meanwhile I continued to drink heavily. It was inevitable divorce was next, and it was hard to cope with such an event.

A photo of me sitting on the steps of Sancta Maria House in Toronto after being released from Clarke Institute.

Tom Billy.

Michelle and I at our apartment in San Jose. Michelle is about 3 months old.

Bruce and I at our apartment in Red Deer.

Our wedding, September 8, 1984 with Michelle (age 9) and Jaclyn (age 4).

The last 'John' I was involved with. The photo is taken just prior to me going into the hospital.

Christmas 1994. Aunt Yvonne, Michelle and Jaclyn. (left to right)

Mary, 1996.

13

STANDING AT THE CROSSROADS

Living alone, I was intoxicated by my new freedom. I was relieved I no longer had to be abused by men any longer. I missed my husband terribly and hurt over our separation but still liked my new freedom. I decorated our new home with hanging plants, placed a few shrubs out in the front and back yard and repainted the living room. I began looking for work. The odd job came up in office work. I was never at one place very long. Perhaps the underlying factor why I never stayed is that the office jobs paid so little. It was almost cheaper to be on welfare—I didn't have to buy gas for my car or work clothes or pay a baby-sitter.

When Michelle was ten years old and in grade five and Jaclyn was five and in kindergarten, I met someone else. Another man named John and, of all places, he came from California. He was tall, dark and handsome with bedroom-blue eyes. I was swept off my feet after having one look at him in the bar one sultry summer night. I knew we were meant for each other. I lured him over to my table in the bar and we immediately hit it off. He must have sniffed me out as an easy one to manipulate. He was destitute and needed a place to stay. By talking to me in the bar, he found out everything he needed to know about me. He learned that I had a car, a monthly (small) income and a home. I must have appeared responsible. His intent was to find a place to stay, use my car to get around and live off my welfare assistance. As naive as I was, I saw him as a rugged, sexy, good-looking man. He told me he used street drugs but that didn't make any difference to me. It had been years since I used street drugs so I knew I would never be tempted to go back to using heroin. Besides, there wasn't any in our town. Only the big cities had drugs, or so I thought!

Before long, John was moved in and we began a relationship that was chaos right from the beginning. I still ached from the marriage that had failed. John's family had moved here from Santa Barbara. He didn't have a visa but his mom had landed immigrant status. John was looking for an easy way of life and I offered such a convenience.

We began making trips to different medical clinics. He told me to ask the doctor for pain medication, making sure the pills had codeine. Like a dummy, I went along with everything. Soon I was visiting different doctors up and down the Okanagan Valley complaining about severe chronic back pain requesting the strongest pain medication available. Some doctors didn't believe me but others did. When I could obtain a prescription, I would leave their office and we headed straight to the pharmacy. Using my native status medical card to pay for the prescription drugs, I obtained the bottle of painkillers. We would go home and immediately John would bring out a syringe. We would crunch up the pills in a spoon, use a piece of cotton as a filter and inject the diluted painkillers into our veins. The rush of codeine was a high I now enjoyed.

I was back on drugs again and didn't really give it any thought. Soon the codeine wasn't enough of a high. I then persuaded the doctors to give me Dilaudid. John explained the effects of this drug to me. This is the pain pill that is used for terminally-ill cancer patients. Crushed up and injected, it gives off the same effect as heroin. The only difference is that Dilaudid is a synthetic narcotic while heroin is derived from opium. I got the same feeling as I had in using heroin. Whenever we got these pills we'd pull over off the highway into some park or secluded spot and cook up right in the car. Instead of drinking heavily, I switched addictions. Almost overnight I became a "pill head" junkie. John would direct me to which doctors I could hit on, and with a con story I could get the pills. We always kept enough Dilaudid for ourselves and sold the rest of the prescription. I would get a bottle of thirty pills and at the time, in the mid-1980s they sold for $40.00 a pill. Had we sold the thirty pills we would have profited $1,200.00 but never once did we sell more than a few pills. The pills were so hard to get that we really used them sparingly amongst ourselves and a few druggie friends who lived in Rutland, east of Kelowna.

In the meantime, when we couldn't get Dilaudid we would scavenge the backyards of all the houses in Kelowna looking for dried up poppy plants. The bulbs, when dry and out of season, produced seeds which retained an opiate. We would go around to different houses and ask the owners if we could pick the bulbs of their poppy plants. We used the excuse that we were making poppy bread and needed the seeds. When we gathered these dried up bulbs and brought them home, we'd split the tops off and boil the bulbs. It produced a tea-like mixture and after straining it we drank the liquid. It produced a repulsive taste but after the taste came a big buzz. We got a warm, glowing feeling inside our bodies.

We would scratch our noses, our faces, backs and all over our bodies because the opiate had the same kind of reaction as heroin or synthetic heroin would. The only problem I found in drinking this "tea" was that it created insomnia. The drug produced a long coming-down period. At one point I remember not sleeping for three nights in a row.

I began to hallucinate and called emergency to see if I could get something to bring me down. The nurse I spoke to at the hospital refused my coming in. I was told to see a drug counsellor. That night, I remember going from my bedroom to the living room couch, trying to sleep. Every time I closed my eyes I saw visions of big ugly faces on the living room wall. They were exactly like the same ugly faces I had seen in the apartment in Vancouver in the early days of my drug usage, years ago. John was not affected the way I was. He didn't hallucinate and could sleep and carry on. He couldn't figure out why I was so messed up. Finally, on the fourth day I went to our family doctor and got a prescription of tranquillizers. I went up to a neighbour's house, drank a couple of beer, swallowed a few pills and came home to sleep. The pills kicked in and I was out for that day and almost all the next day. As usual, John took my car and went about his business. It was still summer holidays and Jaclyn was at her dad's for the summer.

Being at the age of 10, Michelle was fully aware of what was happening. Jaclyn, being only five years old, really didn't understand drugs. To her, it was just Mom and John "acting different." Michelle had found different pills around the house and sometimes had seen syringes. Naturally she was devastated by all of this. She was always angry with me and at times cussed me because I was always taking off and leaving her at home to care for Jaclyn. The drugs had taken such control that I was unfit as a mother. I hated myself for getting up every day and doing the doctor routine but knew we had to have some kind of drug to use. The odd time John picked up a case of beer but it didn't have the same appeal anymore. Drugs had taken over completely. John was miserable to live with when he wasn't high. He was moody and snapped at all of us over the least little thing. Once he had his injection, he became the most loveable and enjoyable person to be around. I found him romantic during these interludes.

We used drugs the whole summer. In the fall, when the girls went back to school we would leave early in the morning. Michelle, 11-years old, went into grade six and Jaclyn, now six, went into grade one. Right after they got on the bus, we headed out to scam the doctors. It was a vicious cycle but when we obtained the drugs we were worry free. With hardly any money to feed the kids, we always managed to get our drugs. Once, we had gathered beet leaves during one of our poppy raids and filled the fridge with these. John said they were very nutritious when boiled. There was nothing else in the fridge except the leaves. Jaclyn still remembers living on tomato soup and Kraft dinners that year.

As Christmas neared, John and I were still badly hooked on prescription pills. I recall one afternoon around four-thirty calling home and talking with Michelle. I told her I was in Penticton at the mall looking for Christmas gifts for her and Jaclyn. She asked when I would be home and I replied, "Soon." John did not want to keep using the same pharmacies, so we began filling our prescription out of town. That day, I hated myself even more. I had just lied to my own daughter—at Christmas time. The guilt tugged at me daily but the desire for drugs was stronger. It turned out we did get Christmas gifts for the girls, using my Woolco credit card. I had abused my card so badly it was well over $1,000.00

now. I had worked hard to get a credit card and now abused the privilege of having one.

Shortly after New Year's day in 1986, John invited his sister, her husband and son to visit. They came and as we were sitting in the living room visiting and drinking Orange Crush, I began to feel nauseated. I went to the washroom and started throwing up. Looking into the toilet bowl I was surprised to see my vomit was black. I'd throw up, finish, splash on some cold water and return to the couch to drink more pop. I became very dehydrated. Each time I took a big gulp I would have to go to the bathroom and throw up again. Finally, I told John, "I think I had better go to the hospital and get checked out." His family left and we drove into town. We left the girls alone and they played in the bedroom. I actually drove into town although I felt really weak and on the verge of wanting to throw up at any moment.

When we arrived at Emergency, I walked through the double doors, and suddenly my knees buckled and I fell to the floor. John helped me up and right away a nurse brought a wheelchair. I was put in a bed directly across from the Emergency station. Soon the nurse was taking my blood, checking my pulse and taking my temperature. I managed not to throw up in Emergency. John was asked to leave and I was wheeled up to the Intensive Care Unit. I had no idea of what was wrong except that the vomiting had begun again and this time it was non-stop. Along with the vomiting, I felt excruciating pain coming from my stomach. As it became unbearable, I begged for anything to kill the pain but our family doctor, having now been contacted, ordered the nurses not to give me any pain medication. He informed them that I had abused prescription drugs.

For the next day and a half I was in and out of consciousness. I remember only two things: the endless flow of blood that came spurting from my mouth at different intervals and the severe pain. I began bleeding rectally as well and the only things the nurses could do was to clean me up and change my sheets each time I filled them with diarrhea mixed with blood. I didn't think I would make it. I suffered a massive esophageal hemorrhage which put me close to dying. During those two days I vaguely remember John coming. Once, I opened my eyes and he was sitting in a chair beside my bed. He told me he could give me something to stop the pain. When I asked what he meant, he pulled up his pant leg and showed me a syringe full of Dilaudid tucked inside his sock. I told him that was the damn stuff that got me where I was. I turned away from him and kept fighting for my life. The hemorrhaging continued. I remember two new doctors coming to my bedside.

One began telling me I had a ruptured stomach and if the bleeding didn't stop, they would be taking me down to the operating room to do an open-abdomen type of surgery to sew up the tear. They informed me they would try to clamp up my stomach to stop the bleeding. I was hardly aware of their conversation. I just wanted the bleeding and the pain to stop. Once, they took me to X-rays but because I was screaming so much the technicians couldn't do their work. Finally, the doctor gave permission for them to give me a shot of morphine. The pain was still excruciating but the shot helped some. I lay still and they X-rayed and returned me to ICU. Then, a miraculous thing happened—and to this day I am puzzled—but don't question such mysteries: I stopped hemorrhaging. The nurses began blood transfusions right away. I can remember counting up to seven empty blood bags being removed. On or about the fourth day in Intensive Care, the same two doctors returned to my bedside. This time, because I was more conscious of what was happening, they delivered the most stern lecture I had ever heard. One doctor warned me that if I ever took another drink or drug it would be my last. The other doctor told me that if I drank again I wouldn't see forty. I was 36 at the time and I remember thinking about what each had said and wondered which doctor was right. I wondered if I would see 40. Still in so much denial, I tried to figure out if I could still drink because obviously drugs were no longer a choice.

Eventually I was transferred to Detox. I had a very sore stomach and didn't know if it would flare up again. I just knew that I could never go through such pain again. In the meantime, John came to visit me while I was in Detox. I asked him how the girls were, and he told me that the welfare had come and taken them away. He said he was out for the day, and when he got home, they were gone. I became enraged. I told him off and said that he was irresponsible and useless, and I blamed him for my ordeal in the hospital. I told him that if I hadn't got involved with him I would have never gone back on drugs. I walked to the lobby with him and told him that when I got out of the hospital, I wanted him to move out and our relationship to end.

Then, I went to the nurses' station and called the Ministry of Social Services. I asked where my kids were and got referred to a caseworker named Peggy. She informed me that the welfare people were informed of my drug abuse by an informant in our neighbourhood, and she knew the real reason I was in the hospital. I couldn't lie. At first I told Peggy it was for one of those "women's operations", but I knew my game-playing and conning was over. I told her the truth and asked where my girls were taken to. She told me that they had been placed in foster care at the Valeys' home, south of Westbank. She told me they were fine and that I now had to look at getting some professional help before I could ever have them back. I was devastated! I had almost lost my life and now had lost my girls, perhaps permanently. I was so angry with Peggy I began to tell her off. She hung up and I went back to my room feeling utterly defeated. I sat on my bed for a long time and tried to sort out the mess I was in. A nurse came to my bed and asked me if I would like to talk to someone from a 12-step recovery program. I wondered what good this would do but in my desperation I agreed. I went out to the small smoking room and lit up a cigarette. John had brought me some tobacco and I rolled a cigarette.

As I was sitting in the small room puffing away on the cigarette a stranger approached me. She was kind-looking, tall, and elderly. In a distinct Scottish accent, she introduced herself as Morag. She asked if she could join me and we could talk. I said yes and she explained that she was a recovering alcoholic and had abstained from abusing prescription drugs as well. I looked at her and studied her for a long while. Somehow the light came on. She told me she had been clean and off pills for seven years. In my despair I felt a surge of hope. It sounded like she was relaying my own experience as she retold of her addictive experiences. I listened although it was hard to concentrate on what she was really saying. Her appearance and actions spoke rather than what she actually said. She gave me hope. I thought that I was at the end of my rope, losing my girls and my health. I saw that she could get off drugs and alcohol and somehow that triggered something in me that I might have a chance. When she left I immediately called the alcohol and drug clinic and asked to speak with a counsellor. I made an appointment for follow up as soon as I was released from the hospital. It wouldn't be until several years later Michelle told me that she was the one who called the welfare people telling them I was in the hospital and John had left them home alone. She told whomever she talked to at the welfare office I was hooked on drugs. So, right away the worker had come and removed them from the house. After she told me this, I thanked her for turning me in.

Returning from the hospital to an empty house was eerie. I walked through the bedrooms and touched the girls' clothes and a few things lying around. I cried. I hurt so deeply. I didn't think there was any physical pain that could equal the emotional pain I was feeling. The house was so empty. It looked so filthy too. It looked like a drug-house. Filthy garbage piled up, dirty ashtrays everywhere, dishes in the sink, and the carpet unvacuumed for a long time. I shuffled through the house and cleaned up a little. I got on the phone and found out where there was a meeting place for recovering alcoholics. I got the address and planned to go the next day. I didn't think a visit with the girls right now was best for us. When John called I told him to pick up his belongings and leave permanently. He agreed except that he said it would take him awhile to take his box of clothes away. When I told him I would leave them down at the Fire Hall beside the police station, he came and picked everything up. He was out of my life now and the most important thing to do was to get my girls back and get into a treatment centre.

The next day at noon I caught a bus and went to the address I had written on a piece of paper. I found a noon meeting and went slowly up the stairs. I was so full of fear. Inside, I found a seat and sat nervously. When the meeting opened I heard, "My name is _____ and I am an alcoholic." Somehow I felt relief. I didn't talk at the meeting; I just listened. When the meeting was over, I left right away. It was a big step. That was all I could do that day but it sure felt better. When I got home I called the Alcohol and Drug clinic and made an appointment for counselling as well. I wanted to get some direction. I needed help badly.

I went to meetings faithfully. I got to visit with Jaclyn and Michelle a few times and began working with a counsellor on getting into a treatment centre. My girls were doing okay but were like little lost orphans. I hated being separated from them but knew this was the only way to go now. Bruce never took Jaclyn away and I wonder why he didn't. Perhaps, he felt that I had to work out this problem and he didn't want to interfere. I am grateful that he didn't take Jaclyn; otherwise it would have caused more problems. The girls didn't like staying at the foster home, but they understood that their mom was very sick and needed to get help. During our visits I explained to them that I would be going away for a while so that I could come back and be a better mother.

14

TURNING POINT

Within a month of leaving the hospital, I was given a date that I would be able to go to the treatment centre. Usually there is a two-month waiting period but my counsellor, named Pat, was very good at rushing things. She spoke with the social worker, and I was reassured that upon my release from Aura I could get the girls back.

On a Saturday morning in February, 1986, I left to go to Aura House in Vancouver. I climbed aboard a Greyhound bus that regularly stopped at the small cafe on top of the hill on the outskirts of Westbank. Pat had informed me that there would be another lady on the bus that would also be going to Aura. She had suggested I phone Brenda (which I did before leaving) and arrange to sit together on the bus. She felt it would alleviate some of the anxiety that we both would probably be feeling. As I made my way down the aisle I looked for what Brenda described she would be wearing. She said she would have on a multi-coloured winter coat with shades of purple in it. Sure enough, toward the middle section of the bus there she sat, reserved. As I approached the seat she was sitting in she said, "Mary?"

And I said, "Brenda?" We greeted each other as I joined her. Although we spoke briefly by telephone earlier I still felt she was a stranger but thought that in time we would get to know one another. During our bus ride we were both quiet. We carried on a light, rather strained but congenial conversation. I didn't know what lay ahead and I'm sure she was apprehensive about going to a treatment centre as well.

Our bus ride took about eight hours, and we arrived in Vancouver around eight that evening. As soon as we got off the bus we went to use the telephone. I called Aura House and the person who answered politely told us to get a cab and come on up. Both of us were nervous. I don't know if we helped or hindered one other by coming together. We caught a cab and rode to the treatment centre. When we paid the driver we got out, unloaded our belongings, climbed the many stairs and rang the doorbell.

Opening the door was a small, kind-looking elderly woman. She asked us to come in and introduced herself as Becky. She told us she was not a counsellor. She said she was the housemother who gave the girls tender love and care. Right away I liked this affectionate, fragile woman. She showed us into a bedroom directly across from the staff office on the main floor. We unloaded our belongings and proceeded to get checked in. Brenda went in first. We were handed our list of regulations and were told the counsellors would be in on Monday morning. In the meantime we were to just relax and enjoy the weekend. We both were rather apprehensive. It was a relief to share the same bedroom with someone I knew. As it turned out, Brenda and I became very good friends. We confided in each other and were supportive to each other in our fight to gain a new freedom.

I had no idea what Aura House would be like. The following Monday morning I met with a counsellor named Mim. At first I felt uncomfortable. I didn't take to her right away. To me, she looked like someone who should be working as a professional—in a law firm or a bank. She was dressed fashionably, looking high-class and reserved. Boy, was I wrong when I got to know her a little more. She was the most down-to-earth counsellor I have ever met. Later, I trusted her with my heart and soul.

During our first meeting, Mim informed me I would be keeping a daily journal and would be doing a lot of writing. She handed me some lined paper and a pencil. I thought this would be great because I loved to write. I thought this would be an opportune time to hone my writing abilities. When I asked her what I was to write about, she replied, "Anything. Anything and everything that comes to your mind." I didn't think anymore about it. Little did I know what kind of writing was intended. After some further conversation, our visit ended. It was more of an orientation than anything. I was eager to begin journal writing. Then, before leaving she instilled something in me which I have not forgotten: she told me in order to stay sober I must become honest—no more conning, no more lying and no more cheating. Somehow that, too, struck a cord.

I went back to my bedroom and propped myself up on the bed with the pillows all puffed up, ready to begin writing. Just as I began to write a few lines, I felt a surge of fear swell inside me. It wasn't the words I put on paper as I hadn't really written anything yet. It was as if my life began to unfold before me. Just like the way it is described when we die—our life flashes before us. Suddenly I began to recall certain unpleasant episodes of my past that greatly affected me. I had a stark revelation that I would be now faced with revealing every twisted and dark cranny of my past. I would now have to write about them on the pages of the tablet that lay on my lap. I knew that from now on I would have to be totally and rigorously honest if coming here was going to work. I realized that remaining clean and sober depended on such an act. The hairs on my arms stood straight up. Fear engulfed me. I became terrified from this revelation. Mim's lecture on honesty came back to me. This wouldn't be leisure writing . . . it would be a painstaking inventory of my life, accounting for everything that came to my mind. From here on my conscience would do the talking and I had to be prepared to do the writing. Secrets I had planned to take to the grave would have to be told as well. I didn't think I could go through with it. It wasn't that I had done really bad things in my life.

It was the fear of reliving frightening experiences and also dealing with very painful things of the past. I also had to bring out all the skeletons from my closet and this frightened me. But I was willing to go to any length to stay off drugs and alcohol, so I was prepared to do anything that was required. Still engulfed with fear, I began to write. I jotted things down as they came to mind. I wrote about the shame of being an alcoholic, the guilt I carried in doing what I did to my kids, the failure I had become in losing my girls, the isolation, the loneliness and the fear that faced me now. I wanted to run. My emotions were too overwhelming. Writing about certain episodes I was filled with embarrassment, anger, then pain, then remorse but worst of all . . . guilt.

In the journals I wrote, I found myself telling the naked truth about every thought that crossed my mind, every action that I had done while drinking and taking drugs, the con-games, the promiscuity, everything. I bared my soul to Mim in each journal. I hadn't gone to confession since early teenage years. Now, it was as if I had returned to the Catholic faith and was finally confessing everything. But I wanted to. I put my pad away and decided that I had written enough for the time being. Each time I wrote I experienced an unknown but paralyzing fear. It was a fear that I can't explain. I also felt weak, helpless and so fragile. I now understand this paralyzing fear is very common in newly recovering alcoholics. It's like being a little child afraid of the bogey-man. In reality it is just a fear of the unknown. It stems from the insanity of alcohol and drug abuse. Only now I had come face to face with all my fears.

We all had certain light chores we were assigned and which we rotated with the other women weekly. Each woman had a turn cleaning toilets. I think, aside from maintaining cleanliness, cleaning the toilets was also intended to be a lesson in humility. And it was a very humbling experience, kneeling on my hands and knees, especially during the women's time of the month. When you have twelve women sharing the same bathroom, hygiene is essential. When someone on her period walked into the room, I could smell a faint odour of blood. It was not pleasant. So when I cleaned the bathroom this odour was very strong coming from the waste basket, too. Perhaps, now having such a weak stomach, I was more sensitive to smell. I found through this experience, the smell of blood was truly an awakening because it was not so long ago that I reeked of my own blood while I nearly lost my life. So the lesson of humility and gratitude were profound. Just kneeling on my hands and knees made me realize that alcohol and drugs had brought me to the bottom in my life but only because I had hit such a low point in my life could it now get better. The self-willed destructiveness of my earlier life could no longer exist. Somehow, down on the floor smelling the blood was the beginning of my spiritual awakening.

Every day was filled with activity. We had a morning meditation of reading spiritual literature, exercise which involved a long nature walk, yoga twice a week and classes in the afternoon to enlighten us on addictions. Every day at one o'clock we gathered in a circle downstairs on the carpeted floor. Everyone dreaded Wednesdays because it involved group the entire day. Emotionally draining and very painful, we took turns exposing our innermost weaknesses. We acknowledged in front of others our grosser handicaps, such as being a prostitute, liar, cheat, thief, and worse, a mother who neglected and abandoned her children. The psychology behind this was to get to the bottom of why we drank or took drugs. Bottles and pills were only symbols. Of course, we were never forced to confess; it was our choice. However, honesty was the underlying factor here.

With things that were too intimate to share in the group we shared confidentially with our counsellor. This was a tearing down time but following these intimate confessions became a time of restoration. We were able to let go of pain that caused excessive drinking or drug abuse. It was a time of rebirth. We always had home-made pizza following the Wednesday sessions. Sometimes, letting go of a big chunk of truth about our past left a big void inside. I always felt hungry after a day of intense work on letting go of the "unnecessary baggage" I had been carrying in my adult life. While the alcohol once fuelled the pain, I felt a big emptiness from letting go of certain people, places or things which related to alcohol. So, a big serving of pizza and yogurt dessert sure made the intensive day worthwhile. To this day, chilled yogurt mixed with whipped cream, sliced bananas and miniature marshmallows is my favourite dessert.

We investigated how alcohol and drugs affected every area of our personal lives. Once a week we met with our counsellor to discuss our innermost feelings about anything that was happening in group, anything haunting us from our past or just everyday occurrences or simply to expand on what we had just discussed in group.

On one day in particular, we went around the room and each girl spoke briefly of how she was feeling that day. When it came my turn I announced how annoyed I had been that the welfare snatched up my kids. I complained that the hot water had been shut off at my home, and it would cost me $150.00 to reconnect it when I got back. I also complained about the unpaid household bills and notices Yvonne was mailing me. Mim then interjected. Her piercing brown eyes rested upon me as I sat with drooping shoulders in a defenceless manner. She looked at me for a long while and asked, "What really got you here, Mary?"

I replied, "I just had a bad relapse from going back on drugs."

She responded, "What about your drinking?"

I responded, "I wasn't drinking that much before I came here. I was more into drugs."

Mim hesitated. Everyone in the group remained silent, all staring at me. Mim looked at me with seriousness, her eyes still upon me as though she were looking into the depths of my soul. She continued, "What about your heat getting shut off? What about the unpaid bills you are complaining about? What about your house going into foreclosure? What about losing your kids?"

I pondered on what she had just asked. It was almost like I got hit over the head with a 2x4, but instead of getting knocked out the light came on. Suddenly it was like someone took blinders off me that I had been wearing for the last twenty years. I fully realized that it was not only the drugs that got me here but it was the gradual and long duration of drinking too which led to my present futility. I had only recently switched addictions. Now, I was faced with realizing and admitting that I had a dual addiction. I had lost the girls because the welfare people had gotten reports of my drinking but hadn't acted on the reports until I ended up in the hospital. In the last few months I had been unable to make my full mortgage payments regularly because the money I got went to drinking in the bars and later toward buying pills from the street when I couldn't obtain prescriptions of codeine and Dilaudid pills. I began to see how my life had consisted of mismanaging of money as well as failing to take proper care of my girls. Mim looked at me pensively but nonjudgemental. She could see that I was now fully aware of why I was sitting in the group. I was somewhat offended that Mim would point out the entire shambles of my personal life before a room full of strangers but I became aware that exact moment.

Yes, I realized that alcohol had played a major role in my life. The abuse of the prescription drugs caused me to land in the hospital but it was a case of the combination of both that led up to such deterioration of my stomach that it was unable to withstand any more torture. I sat back and for a long moment was silent. I finally understood a little about the progressive illness of the disease of alcoholism. I realized I just took a very important step in recovery . . . admitting that I was powerless over alcohol and that my life had become unmanageable. This day was a big breakthrough. It was definitely my turning point. Now the work had just begun. I was so grateful that Mim helped me to see my biggest weakness which for so many years had gotten me into so much trouble—my ego!

As I continued writing, I found my conscience taking over completely. I'd start writing about a certain incident in my life and it would trigger off another incident and on and on it went. I realized that I was deeply hurt by my mother when she abandoned me at the young age of eight. This was always well known, but as I relayed the events I was actually able to feel the pain and anguish and anger and relive it as though it just happened. Writing about this part left me feeling like a wounded animal, lost in the woods. When Mim and I met the following week I asked her if we could discuss the part about my mom. In front of Mim were the smudged lines of my writing. I had cried while retelling of certain losses. Mim had me talk about how I felt when I saw my mom leave as she headed into town to get drunk again. As I recapped these incidents from my childhood I became angry. I wanted to scream at mom. I blamed her for making me feel lost and helpless. I felt angry for the times she left us to fend for ourselves so she could get a swig of wine. Mim let me get it all off my chest. When our hour was up, she suggested I write a letter to my mom. I said, "She's been dead for years."

Mim replied, "Yes, but I want you to write a letter to her as though she were to read it." I didn't understand.

When I returned to writing in my journal that night I began, "Dear Mom," and wrote everything that came into my mind. In the letter I told her how enraged I was at her and how her drinking caused me a life of misery. I blamed her for fulfilling her own selfish wants at the expense of our family having to become wards of the welfare and having to separate at such an early age. I blamed her for everything . . . my spiral turn downward which left me a hopeless alcohol and drug addict. When I was finished, I was horrified at her. I went to the top of the page and changed "Dear Mom" to "Hazel." I was so angry! I stomped into the staff office and placed the letter in Mim's basket.

When Mim and I met again she had the letter in front of her. She had read it and was pleased that I was now beginning to really feel the years of pent-up anger that had been locked inside for so many years. She explained that taking the drink and the drugs over the years was survival to keep me from feeling such deep-rooted anger and pain. The alcohol and drugs only numbed the pain and pushed the hurt feelings deeper. I agreed. Then, I asked her what I should do with such an angry letter. I felt guilty, after all she was my mother and my teachings have always been to respect the deceased. Mim comforted me and encouraged me to continue to be honest about how I really feel. She said the letter could now go in the garbage. In reality, she said the letter was only a fake letter. Its intent was to stir up the feelings I was harbouring. Mim said I could now work on accepting such unfortunate experiences and hopefully in time I will come to a place where I can forgive. She also reminded me that my mother had a disease called alcoholism and she was not as fortunate as me to find a recovery home. I thanked her for helping me through the most difficult and painful part of my past. Leaving her office I took the letter and ripped it into shreds. I felt an emptiness in my stomach and went to the kitchen and made a great big peanut butter sandwich. It tasted good and I felt so much better.

Each day was difficult. As I wrote I began to see how my young adult life was spent cultivating a drinking and drug habit which led to behaviour that I was not proud of. I was ashamed at how I had to live to support my drug habit. I was guilt-ridden that I resorted to exchanging my body and selling my soul to support my heroin habit while living with John. I realized so many things through group therapy and the confidential writings and further talks with Mim. Toward the end of my eight-week stay, I had covered my entire life up to age 36, to the day of entering Aura House. I went through my life with a fine-tooth comb, sorting out the wreckage of my past. I was also able to see the accomplishments of my life as well.

Certain positive things in foster homes had shown that I was a capable person, who, if given the opportunity could adjust and live in society productively. I was able to come to terms with cruel and unusual treatment I underwent at boarding schools, realizing the schools played a major part in my life at the time. If unable to go to Cranbrook and Kamloops at that time, perhaps I would have been denied a proper education. I am still working on forgiveness, though—toward the Catholic Church representatives and the government as well. Forgiving institutions has been the most difficult. To me, the institutions represent the complete control over my life since childhood. They represent the cause of my downfall because where I can see where the destruction began when we were taken as little children from our Reserve and placed in prison-type institutions which imposed rigid control by the government and Catholic leaders.

The roots of my heritage and culture were severed at this point and with all the pain and suffering I have underwent since then, I feel, the controllers at the institutions are responsible. It is hard to see it any other way and only time and more intensive work will heal this pain. But I feel I have come a long way since those drinking days. I think in time I can come to a resting place completely with a certain foster home and Kamloops and Cranbrook as well. There was a time I could not even talk about such incidents. Now I write about them at every opportune moment. Restitution and healing takes time. In doing my inventory I could see that I hurt my girls terribly. My atonement to them is on a daily basis. Each day that I am sober and cook their meals and provide proper care and attention I feel is making restitution for the harm I have caused. Today, we do not open the fridge and see a bunch of beet leaves. In our freezer there usually are pork chops, roast or other cuts of meat. I keep lots of fresh fruit in the fridge and we eat out occasionally. I love my girls, and they are most precious to me. I nearly lost them. It almost kills me to think of how I have hurt them, but I cannot take back the past. It no longer belongs to me. Although I turned my back on the Catholic religion since the age of 15, I have never lost God. I discovered through sobriety a loving God I like to call my Higher Power. I sometimes get angry and run on my own self will and think I don't need His help, but soon I get back on track and remember that it is by His grace that I am alive and well today.

Michelle, being the oldest, was severely affected by my addictive behaviour. She saw me drink from the tender age of two up to the age of eleven. So I understand that her anger will be there for a long time. I know only too well that it takes a long time to forgive completely. I can say sorry until I am blue in the face for denying her proper love and attention but it won't do any good. I have to show her through my actions. By maintaining sobriety one day at a time, to me it's saying, "I love you. I am sorry for what I put you through and hope in your heart you can truly forgive." With Jaclyn, she was pretty young when I sobered up so the scars are not too visible—but they are there.

Just before leaving treatment, I met with Mim again. Through the writings there were certain revelations she wanted to discuss. In her small office, she pointed out a particular thing that concerned her—my history had shown a certain pattern in choosing the men in my life. Throughout each involvement she said it showed a definite profile. I picked men who abused me—mentally and physically. I got involved with John in Vancouver, got beaten and tortured over and over, but kept going back to him. I realized I chose him to supply my drugs but underneath it all I had chosen this particular man to pound on me because I felt I deserved it. I was not proud of my actions of how I had obtained drugs on the streets or had sold them. So living with John was a good way to inflict punishment on myself. Each punch to my body, each blow to my face, each time I was ridiculed reinforced the low self-esteem I felt. My relationship with Bruce blossomed into love. Here again, I chose someone who would mentally and physically abuse me. I felt that I was a failure as a mother and as a provider. But most important, because I am an alcoholic, I thought I was a failure. With every long term relationship, Mim pointed out a definite pattern. If these men were not abusive at first, I groomed them to dump on me. Mim cautioned about the men I chose in the future as my recovery depended on it. It had never occurred to me. I was so caught up in blaming these bad men I failed to see my part in it. I didn't have to choose men who were violent and abusive but low self-esteem led me into their arms.

With the two "Toms" there was no physical abuse; however, there was something else. I was able to experience true love with Tom Billy; but he was really the vehicle I needed to be introduced into the fast lane of street drug usage. With Tom Eaglestaff in San Jose, I wanted to be loved and wanted and needed. By messing with a married man, I had the freedom of not making any sort of commitment. It was safe. And I was insecure. I was running from myself. With my husband whom I dearly loved and married, again I found another partner whom could inflict pain and abuse. I felt I was undeserving of anything better and warranted such treatment.

Before leaving Mim's office I assured her I would refrain from choosing unhealthy and addictive men to be involved with. Before, when these relationships failed I believed fate had dealt me another dirty blow. I didn't realize that subconsciously I picked out these partners. I thanked Mim for pointing this out and allowing me to share my innermost feelings. Most importantly, she did not judge me. Already I was feeling good about myself. I could forgive myself for past wrong doings. All these stark revelations were a teaching. Each experience had a cause and effect. I bounded up the stairs to my room feeling like I was floating on air. There was no more fear. I had faced all the bogey-men in my closet. I felt my slate was now clean and that I would always be accountable for any actions in the future. What I had really feared was that I would not be able to undergo what was involved in staying off alcohol and drugs.

At one point I phoned my uncle Jeff in Surrey. We talked a short while and I told Jeff there was something I needed to talk to him about. He told me to go ahead and say whatever I had to say. I told him how badly I had felt over the years of causing him grief and disturbance while I lived in Vancouver. I told him I felt bad for calling him at the time of arrest in New Westminster on possession of heroin. I showed absolutely no consideration in phoning him and asking him to come and pick me up after being released on my own recognizance from the New Westminster lock up. When he did come and had driven me back to the apartment in the West End, I hit him up for $20.00 to buy a cap of heroin. He was disgusted as he dropped me off in front of my apartment, and refused to lend any money. As he was returning to Surrey, he was involved in an accident on the Port Mann bridge. I didn't realize it until years later that it was his young son's birthday and he was rushing home. I am sure my actions that day caused him great distress and preoccupied his mind. He must have seen me as a hopeless drug addict. It must have upset him to see a close relative at such a low point in life. On the phone, I explained how bad I felt for causing him unnecessary aggravation and that now, I was finally doing something about my problems. I listened for his reply. Uncle Jeff understood and said he was glad that I was doing something good for myself. I felt some relief in that I had mustered up the courage to make such a phone call.

Mim had earlier explained that it would take a long time to make amends to the ones I hurt. Talking with Jeff and Bonnie on a more positive note was my beginning. Later, at home I sat the girls on the bed in my bedroom and made amends to them. I promised them I would try to stay sober a day at a time and make things better for them. Of course, they were happy to see a sober mom and who's more forgiving than your own kids? The deeper scars are there, but it takes time to heal and I can accept that.

Brenda and I had the same dates of departure from Aura House. We had our graduation ceremony, got our pin and made our sentimental rounds to tell to all the girls whom we had come to deeply respect how much we would miss them. Before packing I sat in the living room and wrote in my journal one last time. I thanked Mim again from the bottom of my heart for being there at a time I needed it most. I was so grateful that she showed me the path of destruction I had created and the tools to use in preventing any further destructive behaviour. I thanked her for showing how dishonesty leads back to the old addictive thinking and behaviour. I thanked her for her trust and confidence, promising her that, yes, I would get a counsellor upon my return to Westbank and go regularly to 12-step meetings, maintain a follow-up by having a sponsor and using the people in the program for support, friendship and camaraderie.

The next day, Brenda and I anxiously awaited the cab driver to take us to the bus depot. Leaving, we waved good-bye to everyone and walked down the flight of stairs. My bags felt much lighter than when I first climbed those steep steps. Everything looked brighter. The day was beautiful! I looked at the blue sky above, enjoyed the warm and sunny day. My mind had never felt clearer. Brenda got in the back-seat and I got in the front. We were both joyous in going home but were very sentimental about leaving the counsel-lors and the women. We had bonded closely with everyone.

Driving across Cambie Street bridge I looked back at Brenda with tears in my eyes. Hers were watery too. We hardly spoke and were both deep in thought. I had tears of joy and sadness. I was coming home to my girls whom I had missed terribly. I was anxious to begin reparations to put my family back together. It was sad to be leaving so many beautiful peo-ple who had helped me so much. I had never felt such a free-dom!

I even wanted to hug the cab driver. He just drove quickly, dropped us at the bus depot and departed for his next fare. Brenda and I boarded the bus and came home. We got off in Kelowna and she went home. I went inside the depot and called Yvonne. She said she would be in to pick me up right away. I could not wait to tell her of this new found freedom I had just discovered. I sat in the restaurant, anxiously smok-ing and drinking coffee, waiting her arrival from Westbank.

15

TRUDGING THE ROAD

During the first year, I faithfully continued on the road to spiritual, emotional and physical recovery. Immediately upon returning home, I phoned Morag and asked her to be my sponsor. Our kinship from the hospital had sparked a devout friendship which, to this day, is intact. I found large meetings were frightening at first, and I became even more fearful of people than I had ever imagined. Booze and drugs had provided false courage, but now I could no longer hide behind such a mask. It was very difficult in the first year. Fears still plagued me. Whenever this happened, I called Morag, and we talked about the bogey-man syndrome. Mostly my fears occurred whenever I faced a challenge, such as a new job or training of any sort. In time, I became more stable. As I remained alcohol and drug free, my most enlightening relationship developed. In finding sobriety, I found God. Early in the program I also experienced being "on the pink cloud." This has best been described by others in recovery as a profound alteration of the mind and soul where everything feels so peaceful, sort of like being all warm and fuzzy inside. It is a rebirth, however, and the pink cloud does not last forever. Its span is short but the experience is etched in my memory vividly.

As reality set in, I underwent difficult times. Earlier in my life, given the same trials I would have changed cities, hit the bottle, tried a new drug, or got into another bad relationship. Now I would recall how badly I felt going into treatment and would realize a drink or a drug would only make things worse. The best drinking or drug-taking day did not compare to what I found now. A profound spirituality grew inside me. I began to feel I could now get through anything with the help of God, the people in the 12-step program and my sponsor. After a rough day I would thank God for giving me new and hard lessons. I felt like a baby just learning to walk. I'd fall down, get up, stumble along and finally take a few steps. At times I hated and loved this new life.

I did not work the first few months after returning from the treatment centre. This time was devoted entirely to working on, my worst enemy—myself. Gradually I learned to not be so hard on myself and to try forgiveness. It was a wonderful feeling to wake up in the morning without the nausea that followed a night of drinking. It felt good not to crave an injection of a drug into my veins. All I wanted was to be a good mother who provided for her children but knew this would take time—a lot of time.

I did not have a lot of training beyond the clerical course at CRC. As I approached two years' sobriety, I enrolled at the local college to take the five-month legal secretarial course. In September, 1989, I began the rigorous legal training which included legal office procedure, conveyance, litigation, corporate law, wills and estates. Being out of school twenty years, I found the transition was difficult. I was competing with young, energetic high school graduates who whizzed through exercises with such intelligence and aptitude. Struggling along, I managed to complete the course but did not grasp the concepts of legal office procedure and conveyancing. I was devastated. But unlike previous failures, I did not give up. I enrolled the following September to redo the two courses and on the 8th day of February, 1990, I achieved a B and C+ in them. When I received the certificate, I framed it in oak and proudly placed it on the kitchen wall. The certificate was a testament to who I was and what I could achieve. Unfortunately it did not lead to employment. I tried to get jobs in law firms but was not considered because I was inexperienced. However, this did not stop me. I continued applying for available positions. The lawyers wanted polished, refined and experienced women who could carry on where their last secretary left off. Perhaps, if I had relocated to a large city I could get a job easier. Meanwhile, I continued working at odd jobs in the clerical field.

The ordinary office procedures became so routine that I began looking at new challenges. In August 1991, I took a trip to En'owkin Centre, a First Nations' Training Center located in Penticton, about 40 kilometres south of Westbank. I enrolled in the fall semester and selected several creative writing courses in the Fine Arts program. Members of the Steering Committee of the Okanagan Indian Educational Resource Society for the School of Writing included high profile writers such as Margaret Atwood, Maria Campbell, Thomas King, Joy Harjo and Jeannette Armstrong. At the time I attended, Lee Maracle, editor, writer, and graduate of the National Theatre School of Canada was in-house resident writer. She attended and participated in our poetry classes. It was an honour to be with such a fine writer as her.

In September, 1991, I commenced studies at the School of Writing. The courses offered were transferable to the University of Victoria toward a Bachelor of Fine Arts degree. The following fall, I returned to complete the second term, taking eight Fine Arts courses. Everything was going along so well. At times, I felt so inspired after a writing class that I couldn't wait to get home to complete a poem. As I drove, with left hand on the wheel, my right hand would be scribbling on a steno pad the ideas that came to mind. Many poems were derived during such drives.

While attending school, I had been diligently sending a manuscript of poetry out to various publishing houses. I received many rejection letters along with some very encouraging words. In December 1992, my manuscript was published by Highway Books in Cobalt, Ontario. What a wonderful Christmas present to receive a first publishing contract to sign! It was exhilarating! I had actually reached a long term goal. I was overcome with emotion. Ten years of collected poetry had finally met the press. *In Spirit and Song* also contained a short story titled "Torn Roots" which unravelled the ultimate cultural shock as I left the Reserve to begin grade three at Cranbrook Indian Residential School. Upon getting published I now felt a strong desire to continue my writing career. Working in a law firm was no longer a leading force—writing was the ultimate goal!

In May, 1993, I graduated from the School of Writing with honours, and was now prepared to enter third year at the University of Victoria. Who says life doesn't begin at 40 - something? On Graduation Day we stood together as a few received awards and bursaries. It is my desire to one day complete the Fine Arts program and achieve a Bachelor of Fine Arts. At present, it would be difficult to uproot my family and move away. Perhaps when my daughters have finished their schooling I will have the opportunity. Until such time, I am happy to help them reach their dreams.

Following the School of Writing, I looked forward to a brighter and financially secure future. It had always been a long term goal to operate my own secretarial business which would include publishing creative writing. I wanted to provide desktop publishing and other services such as editing and critiquing. I applied for a commercial loan from a lending institution which assists small businesses. I borrowed $15,000.00 to set up a secretarial service. Receiving the money and purchasing all necessary equipment, I began the business on the 10th day of January, 1994. This opening date had extra special meaning as this was the anniversary of my eighth year of sobriety.

Running a business is a struggle financially. Just because the doors are open doesn't mean that customers are going to rapidly seek out one's services. By the third month, I had used up the entire loan payment and was facing bankruptcy.

It takes time to build a business and I feel a positive attitude is what makes it or breaks it. There are up days and there are down days. No week is the same. Some days I'm in the back room shedding tears on the brink of bankruptcy. Other days, I'm elated by the increase in clientele. If I'm not doing better next year, I will be returning to an eight-to-five job again, but having a business is the driving force. My stressor level is very low and I can't handle the kind of stress that comes with an eight-to-five job any longer. Operating a business allows me to work very flexible hours. I believe success lies in making a total commitment to whatever is undertaken. It is my passion to work hard and build a future in this business. Barely surviving the first year financially, I commenced into the next year with optimism.

My next trial came when I met a man I thought that, finally, I could begin a mature relationship with. He began as a client. At first, he usually dressed in blue jeans but looked professional and business-like whenever he came to do business. Later, he often wore grey sweat pants, white golf shirt, and a baseball cap tucking his light golden brown hair underneath. Whenever talking to him, I loved looking into his sincere, penetrating soft blue eyes. His intent look showed how interested he was in whatever the conversation held.

During the year, we became good friends and one afternoon we stopped working and talked. When he confessed that he was diagnosed with manic depressive illness, it surprised me at first. We then bonded and began to discuss his illness more often than working on his business plan. Don needed assistance in putting together a set of proforma financial statements to convince a small financial institution to lend him money to manage and operate a golf driving range in the Lakeview Heights area on the westside, a short distance from the city of Kelowna.

I thought he was sweet and secretly wanted to date him, but thought he was a little young for me. I won't disclose my age here, as I feel that's the only secret women keep best—I just felt in chronological years (thirty-something) he was too young, although he was sure my type. Oh well, I decided, it didn't hurt to have fun with him and enjoy his company. I think the feelings of fondness were mutual. Eventually we completed the business application and it was submitted to the Business Development Centre for board approval. We had worked endlessly on the financial package, but to our dismay, unfortunately, the business loan application was turned down. Don was very disappointed, but remained optimistic about securing operating funds elsewhere and still continue pursuing his goal. After this Don's condition was to deteriorate to the point where he was in danger to himself and those around him.

16

I'M HOME

While writing this, I had been sending samples of my work out to various publishing houses. I received a call from Caitlin Press in Prince George, requesting the complete manuscript. I was overjoyed! I felt so honoured because it has been my wish to share with others the trials and triumphs of my life, especially the battle over alcohol and drug addiction. I feel strongly that by sharing my experiences I can help others to understand themselves and to overcome problems caused by abandonment and addiction. However, I would like to round off my book by telling what has happened to those significant people in my life.

My Grandma unfortunately lost her life to cancer on April 21, 1990. She eventually had to be placed in a nursing home and resided there until passing on. As I visited her in the hospital prior to her being transferred to the home, there were great moments of healing for both of us. I brought her candy bars. Somehow it became symbolic of the times when I was a little girl and she handed me a piece of Jersey Milk when I did something particularly pleasing to her. Once, for example, I found a ring she cherished. It was sterling silver and had a face of an Indian warrior. Perhaps this ring was given to her by Grandpa. One day as she was throwing the dish water out, the ring slipped off. When I recovered it in the dirt, she was so pleased. There were other things that were significant during our visits too. Although she was unable to speak English any longer, her beautiful facial expressions and the sincerity in her eyes showed me she loved me, had always and only wanted the best for us. There was no need to forgive her for allowing the welfare worker and Indian agent to send us away. She wanted us to get a good education. She had no idea what conditions were like at the residential schools, except that we always returned home with short-cropped hair and perhaps a little less talkative. If she knew that our identities were being shredded, she would have never allowed them to take us. I am happy Grandma is no longer ravished by cancer and her passing moment was peaceful. She will always be the strongest role model in my life. She taught me the value of cultivating land, of being spiritual, and of respecting Mother Earth. She taught me survival by showing how to harvest food and can preserves for the approaching cold winter. She offered nurturing and closeness, the Indian way. These things have built my character. By being strict with us, she taught me how to choose the right path. Although I went down the wrong path for many years, her teachings brought me back in the right direction.

During the spring of 1993, I located my long, lost friend, Noreen. I felt that our friendship was left up in the air since I last spoke with her at the Sancta Maria House in Toronto. Over the years, I felt a loss because she had been my best friend. We had a joyous reunion recapping the highlights of our life over the past twenty-five years. I gave her a section of this story that involved her, and she was touched that I had written about our special friendship. She is now living in Vernon, has two children and is an avid Jehovah Witness. Upon leaving, she lent me a Bible of her faith. It has special meaning as it belongs to her oldest son, Joshua. One day, when we meet again I will return it. We have talked on the telephone once since our reunion and promised we would keep in touch, have coffee and visit more often. She never did stay with her hippie boyfriend, Kevin. Instead, she took up with a devoted Jehovah Witness family in Toronto and adopted their faith.

It seems that fate has a way of taking care of matters. Toward the end of June, 1994, I got confirmation about my natural father. It always seemed like a fairytale story when Yvonne told me I had this dad who died when I was two in a fiery car accident. When I attended a fashion show in Penticton in which Michelle was modelling, the master of ceremonies caught my attention when he introduced himself as Meyer Louie. During the break everyone clustered around outside the building. I approached the dark-haired, well-spoken young man. I complimented him on his pep talk of the importance of education during his speech. He graciously acknowledged the compliments. Then, I asked him who his parents were because the name "Meyer" had struck a cord with me. He informed me that his dad was Meyer Prince. I gasped for breath. This was the name of my father, I was always told. I could not believe I was standing face to face with a half-brother I never knew. This was such a coincidence. We exchanged the information we were given about our dad. Meyer also told me he was a student at the university in Spokane, Washington. He was home for a visit in Penticton when he was invited as a guest speaker and master of ceremonies for the fashion show. Upon departing, we exchanged phone numbers and Meyer returned to the US. Several months later I received photos, the write-up in the newspaper of our dad's death and everything Yvonne had told me was correct. I found out I'm half Jewish. So many questions were answered in my mind as I glanced at the pictures of my dad's headstone and where the car went off the road. I can now put this to rest. Originally, he owned the now very large department store in Oroville named Prince's. Brother Meyer called me before Christmas this year and said he had been in touch with our relatives at Prince's and had a message. There are an aunt and uncle who want to meet me. I suppose one day if I'm down at the border crossing, I will stop in and locate them. It took a long time to find out who my natural father really was and now there is no longer the curiosity. This is where I would like to leave it.

As for Yvonne, we maintain a very close relationship. She is still my favourite aunt and continues to be here for me, always. Recently she was diagnosed with sugar diabetes but luckily she will not have to inject insulin. She is under excellent medical care with her family doctor. She has dropped about thirty pounds but is still the beautiful aunt who once wore her reddish hair, piled up on her head in a bouffant hairdo. She lives on the Westbank Indian Reserve in a nice new home. Yvonne took care of Grandma right up to the time that she had to go into the nursing home. She struggled with feelings of guilt for having to take her to such a place, but could no longer provide the constant medical attention Grandma needed. She has worked through this and is doing well helping to raise her beautiful granddaughter, Chelsy, or better known as Yvonne nicknamed her "Peanut."

As for the long and arduous journey through prescription drug addiction, I felt a need to come to terms here. Although I have been diagnosed with a long list of psychotic illnesses, including manic depressive illness and borderline schizophrenia, I never quite accepted these. Sometime during the summer of 1994, I went to my family doctor due to severe bouts of depression. I asked him to refer me to a therapist or psychiatrist to be treated for mood fluctuations in which I would be tearful, irritable, angry and suicidal. As it turned out, the therapist wanted to do an assessment before treatment. Shortly after our visit, the therapist referred me to a psychiatrist. Based on both assessments in July 1994, there was no evidence to support a diagnosis of schizophrenia or manic depressive illness. The psychiatrist decided that I certainly suffer from unstable moods, rage attacks, and various other psychological difficulties. However, these primarily reflect a personality style that has strong dependent and borderline traits of depression caused by the day-to-day stressors.

I do not agree with the assessment that my previous psychiatric problems were "complicated by alcohol and drugs." I believe the underlying early problem was alcoholism, undiagnosed and therefore untreated. This was complicated by the run-a-muck of prescription drugs that only added to deeper-rooted emotional trauma. Instead of being handed another prescription of a mood-altering narcotic, I should have been directed to a treatment facility. However, I am not bitter at the medical profession. I'm just thankful that today I am not neurotic or psychotic. Had I not had these experiences, I would not have found the 12-step program that has set me free, totally.

My introduction to the 12-step program is the foundation upon which I have built the best life I have ever known. God as I understand Him is the Guiding Light beneath this exhilarating ride to liberation—mentally, emotionally, spiritually.

I always felt the need to try to locate Timmy, the little boy dunked in cold water. I often wondered what happened to him. I wanted to hear that he had overcome the unpleasant things that happened to him at the Stones. I have called a few names in the phone book with his last name but was unable to make contact. I just hope he didn't end up in a mental institution somewhere to be forgotten. I hope he got the psychiatric treatment he so much needed and deserved for the sexual abuse he suffered as a young child. I suspect that one day, we will meet again. I cannot forget those bright blue eyes staring at me from across the supper table, his impish smile and the strange look in his eyes as he sat on the edge of his bed after being dunked. I still feel a strong urge to know he is all right.

As for the Stones, I have no desire to contact or visit them, ever. According to my sister, Harriet, who keeps in touch with them, they are planning to buy a farm north of Vernon to spend out their retirement years. I have to come to terms here and am now moving on.

I have maintained contact with my brothers Bill and Ben over the years. There is a closer relationship with Bill. With Ben, it's more like a telephone call once a year from his home somewhere up north to announce a new birth in his family or a Christmas wish. I don't think I could ever consider Bill anything other than my "favourite little brother." Both have families and are doing well. We don't spend holidays or much time together but we all have each other's phone numbers. Harriet is now living on the Coast with her family. She and her family moved to Vancouver to be nearer the medical care her daughter Crystal needs.

Then, there's Marge, my very special sister. She still lives in Vernon. We visit now and then but are not as close as when we lived in the apartments at Valleyview. I miss her and know we would spend a lot more time together if she were not always drinking. Spending too much time around anyone who drinks alcohol causes my thinking to become negative. I prefer to be around sober and positive people. I still love her dearly and have accepted her the way she is.

There is one family I think about periodically and that is the LeDucs. After they moved out of province, no one in Vernon has seen or heard from them. I would like to see Lil again to thank her for giving me a home and such motherly love. I will never forget her warm, contagious laughter. I am sure her family is doing well.

Regarding relationships, I'm pleased that I have been able to abstain from getting involved in addictive relationships with the opposite sex for the past ten years. Although it gets very lonely at times, I prefer to be alone until I meet the right person. Perhaps it may never happen. Either way I can accept it. It's so peaceful living painfree.

Once, recently while I visited Marge, she suggested I go back to Kamloops and Cranbrook Indian Residential Schools. She said I talk about them so much that I should go there to put the past to rest. I realized just how much I was dwelling on those schools. So, I decided to make the pilgrimage to both places at different times this year. The experience to Cranbrook was profound!

I called Yvonne and asked her if she would like to take a trip to the Kootenays to revisit an old school she was quite familiar with. She agreed willingly and we began our journey on a Saturday morning in March, 1996. While driving, we discussed some of my experiences there at age eight. Yvonne knew pretty well how much this school affected me. She had listened often as I talked about the bad food, the forsaken feelings, the religious overfeed, and the mean-spirited Catholic nuns who instilled harsh discipline. Heck, everybody has their horror stories but mine could not find their place to the grave. So, Yvonne, always being supportive, was eager to make the journey and help me close this chapter of my life. We travelled about seven hours through the Kootenays heading east and dipping a little southward. Tired from the long journey, we entered the town of Cranbrook around eight that evening. We drove through the town looking at different large buildings expecting to see the old school still standing. I could only recall a big building in a large cleared area.

Unable to locate it, we pulled into a motel and checked in for the night. There, we asked the motel owners about the school. The woman said she heard of it and that it had been closed down for quite sometime. Her husband piped in to say he heard quite the horror stories about this place. When Yvonne told them that I attended and now wanted to revisit they looked sympathetic and wished us luck. They gave us a map of Cranbrook and directed us on how to find the school in the morning. During the early hours of the morning, unable to sleep longer, I arose at 5:10 a.m. and began reading spiritual literature I brought along and then began scribbling notes into my journal. I needed to go to this place open-minded and make this pilgrimage peacefully with forgiveness in my heart. I asked the Great Spirit to help me. Unexpectedly, sitting by the bedside, I burst into tears. Pent-up emotions engulfed me, and I became flooded with sadness. Yvonne awoke and quickly came to comfort me. I sobbed uncontrollably. I asked, "What is happening to me?"

Yvonne replied, "You're grieving. Go ahead and let it all out." I cried nonstop for several minutes. It became a wailing sound like a hurt animal makes when wounded. Yvonne stroked my head and passed me tissues as I soaked many. When it felt like I couldn't cry any more, we talked. I told her it felt like I was there just when we arrived in the middle of the night in this strange town. I experienced fear again. It must have been exactly how I felt as that little child not knowing where I was going or why. Yvonne helped me get everything out—there was much anger spilling over toward the Indian agent and the government and worst of all, the nuns. I blamed everybody again just like I did over the years before going into the treatment centre. Yvonne said it was okay to feel all the different emotions as this is where I must really let it out. After getting somewhat composed, I wanted to go to the school more than ever now.

I took out the map, studied it and said, "Yvonne, let's go. I'm ready now."

Driving through the town, I commented how the streets looked so dirty. The town badly needed its streets swept and repaired. That's all I could see. Yvonne commented on the beautiful slope of the snow-covered mountains directly in front of us as we headed north through town. Here were the Rockies in full view. It was magnificent! All I could see was how grim this town looked. Yvonne said I couldn't see anything beautiful because my experience of the place was bad. She was optimistic that after going to the school I would probably see this town differently. This made sense. As we drove, we talked more about the school. I was anxious to see it again. We followed the map directions and drove through a wooded area down a windy paved road, crossed a small bridge across a small but swift river and there it was! I always visualized this building as a two-storey red brick structure with a big manicured lawn out front.

The building was actually quite different in appearance. It was a large old grey stone building, behind an iron gate that was once painted white, with a paved driveway that once had a circular flower bed in front of the entrance. It was three storeys instead of two and had a big wooden door instead of double doors. Many emotions crept in as we walked up the path that led to the front doors. My steps along the way were slow as I remembered how I felt standing at the long driveway looking up to the big school building. It was so clear to me this day. Fear gripped me. I felt uneasy and tormented. I wanted to run but kept walking slowly alongside Yvonne. I felt hurt! I felt wounded! Although it was a short walk, I remembered it as a long walkway through my childhood eyes. Peeking inside we could see concrete beams throughout with brick walls, a short staircase leading to the second floor with flooring all worn and linoleum completely deteriorated with floorboards now showing through. Thoughts and emotions flooded my body as I approached the large door. Then I felt the strongest emotion of all - RAGE!

I visualized Sister Lois standing over me with her fat tummy bulging underneath her black habit as she held the strap in her right hand. I could see her round, fat face puffing up and getting ready to swing the strap upon me. I wanted to stomp on her shiny black shoes and run and hide. I remembered cleaning the parlour room after the guests left on Sundays. I remembered feelings of loneliness as I emptied the waste paper baskets and polished the wood furniture. I could remember the smell of the polish on the linoleum floors. It had a septic smell and looked like white lard until the girls came along with big polishers and smoothed it out perfectly and gave it the shine you could slip and slide on in stocking feet. The walls had been torn down and now all that was left inside were 2x4 beams and bare space throughout. I turned the knob on the front door but it was locked. I wanted to go inside and walk throughout the structure. I wanted to go to every room that held me in captivity—especially the dorm. There, I could go to the rear of this dungeon where I sat on my bed looking through the crossword puzzle book and to where I thought of Hugh stashed away on the other side of the building. All of a sudden I began to mourn the loss of Hugh, pint-sized and alone. I never felt such a loss in all my life. The emotions were overwhelming. I understood it was because I was too young to experience the emotions at eight, so now as an adult I could finally grieve. All I could feel was how terribly lost he must have felt. At least, I had Marge.

But what comfort did Hugh have? He had no one to tug at, to talk to, to comfort him. I felt angry with the nuns and priests for separating us. Yvonne helped me understand why I was engulfed with sadness. She comforted me and said that I was helpless and Hugh should never, or any of us, have gone through such an ordeal. I could now nurture the hurt feelings and loss for Hugh at the exact place the bond became severed. No wonder I never felt a tremendous loss or emotion at his funeral. We had not been close since 1958. I now understood why I felt rage as I walked up the walkway 37 years later. I wanted answers. Why did those government people do this to our family? What gave them the right to keep Marge and I away from visiting Hugh the whole year? It was now a time to resolve this pain.

By returning here, I wanted closure and this is exactly what I got. I could feel the loss of Hugh now, in childhood and in later years as a grown-up. I could say goodbye properly and try to put things into perspective now. It was at this school that I learned to stuff my feelings that I carried for the rest of my life—I learned how to survive—to shut out the pain of losses. In school, I acted out by playing with light switches until I'd get caught and get the strap. It was to get attention—although it was negative attention it didn't matter as long as it was some form of attention. I now understood why I left my bed at night and slid down underneath all the beds to make my way to Marge's bed so we could whisper and giggle together. I pondered on times when the other girls giggled while I'd be pushing myself along underneath their beds to chat and giggle with different ones. They'd say, "Mary Lou, go back to bed. Sister is coming!" I'd say, "No way" and keep on going until the lights would be turned on and the dorm flooded with fluorescent lights. Sister Lois would be standing tall and erect in the doorway with her often repeated words: "Mary Lou, get over here!" Standing in front of her to get the ritualistic strap one more time left me feeling powerless. Obediently afterward, I'd go crawl into bed. This explained why, three years later, I changed my name from Mary Lou to Mary. I dropped "Mary Lou" because it reminded me of the nuns in both schools. Especially it reminded me of Sister Lois's voice. It was one way I could now have control over things.

Walking to the side of the building, Yvonne and I went to a window that revealed an empty room. These rooms all looked so small to me now. This room was probably the scullery that contained all the nonperishable foods. Across from the hallway up from the scullery was the recreation room. This is the room I really wanted to go into. I needed to go in and out of this secluded room freely to not feel trapped as I did as a child. There was a chain on the side entrance door, so there was no way of entering this now "Condemned - unsafe" building. Having observed earlier the brick walls inside explained why my recollections of the hallways were so dark. It would be difficult to plaster wall paper on gigantic solid brick. No wonder it felt cold and dreary walking down that narrow hallway into the rec room. I understand now, too, why I kept playing with the light switches, besides getting attention it was also because I didn't like darkness which frightened me. Now, it all made sense. The next thing I needed to do was to see the chapel where we were persecuted religiously, hours at a time, morning after morning, Sunday after Sunday. How ironic though, as I try to recall one visit to the chapel I still draw a blank—no memory at all.

Yet, those Latin prayers that followed along with Mass are still etched in my mind. I got something out of it after all, I learned Latin! So are the many prayers we had to memorize: The Act of Contrition, The Act of Faith, The Act of Hope, the Lord's Prayer, and so on. The only memory I have is having an orange on the breakfast tray and a bowl of Rice Krispies after Sunday Mass. There was the chapel—adjoined to the building at the rear—with its tall, pointed steeple. I tried to justify the Catholic teachings and why I still dislike teachings of my Grandma's faith. I realized it was probably because the whole process was forced. The entire ritual was too rigid: having to get up very early and to dress in scrubbed clean bobby socks, pressed tunics, starched blouses, everything so medicinally clean. I was used to playing in dirt and wearing dirty clothes at Grandma's house. Besides the mind-numbing routine, and need to endure long periods sitting in pews, the kneeling and standing while in the chapel made me resentful. This is where I learned how to block out anything unpleasant.

Standing and looking upward at the steeple, I stared at the cross and thought of how God must have loved me to block out so much trauma. Yvonne and I turned to leave. I'd seen and experienced enough for one day. Looking over the field behind the building, we noticed a graveyard with faded wooded crosses. A sadness engulfed us both. I could not understand why a spot such as this could become a sacred burial ground for native people. I felt this was adding insult to injury. The burial ground had replaced the field that we played in. The fence that kept us inside was gone. Thick weeds and tall grass grew over the grave sites. I felt some chills go throughout my body. Although it was a windy, cold day for spring, I still wanted to walk between the old crosses and pay my respects to the deceased. It seemed appropriate, after all some of these crosses may have belonged to some fellow companions of the school. Instead, Yvonne suggested we leave.

There was a sign at the entrance that read: "NO TRESPASSING. TRESPASSERS WILL BE PROSECUTED TO THE FULL EXTENT OF THE LAW UNDER THE INDIAN ACT." When we were getting back into my car, I said to Yvonne, "It's ironic to have a sign like that." I thought, "How dare the government still try to control us after all that has happened in residential schools?" I detected harboured resentment still there. When I called St. Mary's Band office the following week, the woman who answered the phone explained that the sign was erected by members of their band and was not enforced by the government. I apologized for trespassing but explained our mission. I asked her when the school was closed and she said for many years. The woman also explained this site would be used as a golf course and the school rebuilt as a motel in 1997. I felt the building should be demolished. As we drove away, I reminisced about our nature walks along the roadside, singing at the top of our lungs, holding hands we walked back to the school. These were pleasant thoughts.

Driving further on as we headed home, a feeling of death became strong for Yvonne and me. We discussed our feelings and the irony is that someone did die—a child died on that spot. I left the tormented childhood of Mary on that same property. I left as an adult this time—stronger and more understanding, now able to put together the many pieces of the puzzle. I became whole. Although Cranbrook was a very unpleasant experience at the time, I had mended now. Nobody could control my mind, body or soul ever again. They belonged to me. I felt sad because I grieved that lost child. When Yvonne said she felt as though she had just attended a funeral, I said, "You did."

Today, it still makes me sad to think of what went on at Cranbrook and I shed tears at times because the healing is ongoing and grieving takes a long, long time. It is getting better though. I believe one day I will come full circle with this. I actually did write this part of the story without shedding tears. Today, I forgive the nuns as they never raised children so how would they possibly show patience, love and understanding to 200 children of a different culture? I feel the government is responsible for placing those missionary nuns and priests in situations that were beyond their control and which ultimately led them to abuse their control and power. Incidentally, I did go to Kamloops several weeks after the Cranbrook visit, but there was nowhere near the emotion as the initial shock of going back to Cranbrook.

Today, I continue to heal and rebuild the rubble of my life. To go on, one has to repair the damage from the past. In this fashion, I feel I have begun the slow process of restoration. I was around the age of eight when dramatic changes began. As I close here, I am approaching the tenth anniversary of living clean and sober. To me, it feels like a cycle has completed of an eventful journey that began painfully and ended peacefully. I look forward to the adventures life has ahead. No longer do I have to hide in West End apartments at the hands of a ruthless captor, mindless, and in the pits of despair. No longer do I have to live in fear or desperation. I would like to say that today I am living painfree and everything is rosy. Not so, life has its curves and every so often, just like everybody else, a swift ball comes this way. But the difference now is that I don't stand in the way and get hit. I get out of the way and work through difficulties.

I still have periods of depression, but they aren't as morbid as before. Usually in a couple of days the mood swings in a lighter direction. I have learned tools to use when darkness sets in. It is usually a visit to my dear friend, Morag who is now in a bad situation. She suffered a massive stroke in 1994 and is confined to a wheel chair. She also had a severe heart attack. But despite this, her spirits are always in tune to God. She tells me she is so tired. I try to visit as often as I can. It is even difficult for her to talk on the telephone as she had another stroke shortly after the first one. She has been paralyzed on her right side and is now in a rest home.

Each time I take a step toward the restoration of the past and present, it gets better. I have absolutely no control over the future, but am thankful I now have good friends, a strong support system and a loving God who leads me through difficult times. He has granted me the peace I have searched for all my life. Recovery is here for anyone who wants to change. Healing comes in many forms. Sometimes we cannot go ahead until we have gone back. It is my hope that my story will help others as it has helped me in sharing it. I believe our Heavenly Father never lets us down when we sincerely search to discover the simple truths.

EPILOGUE

I have devised this account of my life with the intent of understanding certain circumstances and form some conclusions in my mind.

Because of the intense sentiment of some of my personal experiences, I had some difficulty awakening the past, Yet, the most important tool I have always used to cope with affliction is through writing. I use this as a coping device to understand why certain unpleasant things happen. Self-discovery takes place and I find that my situations are not unique and others have pain, too. By sharing with others it helps to relieve some of the internal conflicts that surface periodically.

Each individual gave me something in return. The institutional teachers taught me compliance, discipline, obedience and respect which have carried over into my adult life. The foster parents gave me stability at a time when I needed it most. It gave me a sense of security. I also learned how to share by living in large families.

Although there were some loveless environments, I still bonded with other foster children and found solace.

Consequently, I am alive today. I managed to survive. Each individual has been an influence and has helped to build my character into what I am today... a survivor.